M.O.
CRIMES OF
PRACTICE

The Official CWA Anthology

Edited by Martin Edwards

CHIVERS

British Library Cataloguing in Publication Data available

This Large Print edition published by BBC Audiobooks Ltd, Bath, 2009.
Published by arrangement with Comma Press.

U.K. Hardcover ISBN 978 1 408 44180 0
U.K. Softcover ISBN 978 1 408 44181 7

'One Last Pick-Up' by Sarah Hilary was first published as 'The Ravages of Tim' on the Every Day Fiction website in October 2007. 'Just Coming, After I've Killed Myself' first appeared as 'Je me tue et j'arrive' in *Du Cyan plein les mains,* published by Editions La Courte Echelle, 2006. Reprinted by permission.

Printed and bound in Great Britain by
CPI Antony Rowe, Chippenham and Eastbourne

CONTENTS

INTRODUCTION

Modus operandi—there are not too many Latin terms that feature heavily in crime investigation, but this one (or, rather, its abbreviation m.o.) is an exception to the rule. And properly so, for understanding the culprit's *modus operandi* is central to any detective's work.

Think of the work that went into uncovering the crimes of Fred West, Dr Harold Shipman, and Steve Wright, the Suffolk murderer, among countless others— these were killers who, typically, worked to a particular method that served their purposes for longer than it is comfortable for any of us to contemplate. The m.o. *matters*, to the criminal, to the detective—and to the victim.

It matters equally to crime writers of all kinds and all backgrounds. Whether one is writing a dark novel about the brutalising effect of murder on contemporary society, a history-mystery that casts light on the way people lived in days gone by, or a puzzle story that hinges on a particular twist of fate, consideration of m.o. is at the heart of the author's task.

This anthology, brought to you by the

Crime Writers' Association, gathers together a wide range of takes on the theme of m.o. There are traditional mysteries and examples of cutting edge modern crime. Although the contributors are predominantly British, there are stories here by authors based as far afield as New Zealand, Germany, Las Vegas and Quebec.

You will find stories written by stellar names and also by those whom you are unlikely to have encountered before. Ann Cleeves won the CWA Duncan Lawrie Dagger for the best crime novel of 2006; Bob Barnard is a winner of the CWA Cartier Diamond Dagger for sustained achievement in the field, as well as the CWA Short Story Award in 2006 for 'Sins of Scarlet', which appeared in the previous anthology in this series, *I.D.* The contributors are united, above all, by their passion for fiction, and for the short story form.

Certainly, a good deal of time and effort has been devoted to this project behind the scenes over the past eighteen months. I would particularly like to thank Philip Gooden and his colleagues on the CWA Committee for their unstinting co-operation. The authors who supplied stories—including those writers whose submissions did not, unfortunately, make the final cut—have been patient and supportive and I am very grateful to them. Once again, our greatest debt is to you, the reader, whose love of the short story helps keep projects such as this alive.

Martin Edwards
March 2008

VIVISECTION

Bernie Crosthwaite

They shuffle into the room, half a dozen of them. They reek of cheap deodorant and alcohol . . . and sex. White coats flap open to reveal their scruffy clothes. My gaze fixes on a boy with spiky blonde hair, laughing with a girl in a short skirt and flip-flops whose knees are already turning blue. Serves her right.

I'm just about to make a start when another one lurches in, chewing gum, talking on his mobile phone, and wearing—I can hardly believe my eyes—a *hat*.

The ripple of chatter swells into a wave. Such appalling manners.

'Pay attention. I'm about to begin.'

A serious-looking young lady in glasses turns to me expectantly, but the rest take no notice whatsoever. A surge of bile rises in my throat. I pointedly walk to the door, left gaping open by the latecomer, and shut it firmly. My action serves two purposes: the temperature in the room drops once more, and there is silence. At last.

I return to my position behind the metal table. I know that deep down, despite the rudeness, they are in awe of my powers.

'I trust you have switched off your mobile

phones?' I take care not to look directly at the gentleman with the knitted headgear. 'Last time, someone forgot. The ring tone was so loud my knife slipped and . . .' I hold up my bandaged finger so they can see the damage, then carefully pull on a pair of disposable gloves.

In fact, it didn't happen quite like that—I don't even remember how I got the cut, only that there was a lot of blood—but it gets their attention and I'm gratified to see them all check their phones, reluctantly cutting themselves off from their lifeline. Young people seem to think that their electronic devices are a kind of umbilical cord and that without them they will die.

When the flutter of activity has settled down I peer over my half-moon glasses, looking straight at the boy this time. 'You—the one with the woolly hat—take it off.'

'But it's cold in here,' he whines.

'What do you expect? This is a mortuary, not an overheated seminar room. Can you imagine the smell if we had full central heating?'

'Whatever.' He pulls the hat off with a flourish, revealing his premature baldness. 'Happy now?'

I note the telltale nodules of fat around his eyes. High cholesterol. He'll be dead of a heart attack before he's fifty. 'Ecstatic.'

Titters of laughter flare up, die away. They

won't be laughing soon.

The time has come.

'Like you, I have never seen this specimen before. Normally I read the notes first.' I indicate a manila folder lying on the bench behind me. 'But I'm under great pressure at the moment—so much to deal with.' I grind my teeth, a habit I've got into lately. 'So together, our job will be to find the cause of death.'

There is complete hush as I peel back the sheet. The cadaver lies supine, quiet and obedient. That's something I admire about the dead, their beautiful quiescence. Most of the corpses I use for demonstrations, after several days in a chilled drawer, have a musty metallic smell, like thawing meat. But this one is fresh and has an odour of the sea—ozone and tissue salts in their last frantic throes of activity. Its recent demise suggests this might be an urgent police matter. Perhaps I should have read the notes after all . . .

I detect movement to my left, something twitching or flickering just out of vision. I jerk my head round but there's nothing. It must be that damn tic in my left eyelid that has plagued me for a couple of weeks now. Tiredness, that's all it is. I haven't been sleeping well.

'Right. What do we have here?' I cast a professional glance over the specimen. 'Female. Late thirties, I'd say. Any initial observations?'

3

No one answers. I'm an expert at silences. Some are thick with embarrassment from sheer lack of knowledge. Others are syrupy and lazy, the speciality of the *can't be bothered* merchants. This one twangs with hostility, a reaction no doubt to my firm handling of Mr Woolly Hat. I suspect they have the answers, but they are going to make me extract them by force, like pulling teeth.

'Come on. Come on. That's the easiest question you'll get all afternoon. If you can't answer that, it's going to be a very long session indeed.'

I can hear the drip from a tap, the distant buzz of a fly. I note that the bare feet of the girl in the mini skirt have turned a mottled mauve that perfectly matches the lividity of the skin six hours after death. She sees me staring, which must be what prompts her to speak up.

'She dyed her hair?'

I wait until the muffled laughter has run its course.

'*She dyed her hair . . .*' I glance down. I really should have cleaned my spectacles— they are smeared with dust and fingerprints. Squinting, I see that the woman's hair, now dulled by death, had once been a theatrical shade of red. A long strand of it has caught across her neck like a wound. I look away. Julia was a redhead too. Did she dye her hair? That's a question I cannot answer. 'This is the School of Forensic Medicine,' I say sharply.

4

'You'll find Beauty Therapy at the Further Education College down the road.'

The corners of the girl's mouth turn down like those of a petulant five year-old. She mutters something I don't catch. There are low mutters, shuffling of feet.

'Can we see any external signs of the cause of death? Is there evidence of disease? Any open wounds, operation scars, swellings, needle marks?'

They stare at me open-mouthed. I can see I'm rolling a ball uphill with this lot. Perhaps their silence is the ignorant kind after all. I've credited them with far too much intelligence. I won't make that mistake again.

'No external signs, then.'

Woolly Hat raises his hand. 'But what about the—?'

'Please don't interrupt.' I'm beginning to find him as irritating as that fly buzzing somewhere in the room. 'So how do we proceed?'

No response. *Quelle surprise.*

'I intend to start at the top.' I move to the end of the table and stand behind the head.

My instruments are laid out neatly on a trolley beside me. With an electric shaver I remove a circular area of the woman's hair, like a monk's tonsure. 'Now I'm going to use a saw in order to trepan the skull. Some pathologists use an electric one with oscillating safety blades, but I prefer the old-fashioned

5

manual kind.' I pick up the fine-toothed instrument and begin to score through the skull cap. Once I've cut all the way round, I use a cranium chisel to lift off the bowl-shaped section of bone.

'Now watch how I sever the nerves and the blood vessels so that I can remove the brain.'

I enjoy the mesmerised looks on their faces as I lift the organ out. No shuffling of feet now, no laughter, barely any breathing.

'Look at it. Just a wrinkled pile of jelly. Yet hidden within is the most sophisticated circuitry in the universe.' I strike a pose. I always relish this bit. *'Is this a dagger which I see before me, the handle towards my hand? Come let me clutch thee: I have thee not, and yet I see thee still . . . Art thou a dagger of the mind, a false creation, proceeding from the heat-oppressed brain?'*

I have been known to get a round of applause at this point, but there is dead silence.

'No doubt you all recognise the quote?'

It seems not.

'It's from *Macbeth*. By William Shakespeare,' I add drily.

'Personally I prefer *Rumble in the Bronx*,' mumbles Woolly Hat.

'What's that? Speak up.'

'You know, the Jackie Chan film?'

'Jackie Chan? I've never heard of her.'

The boy with the blonde spikes covers his

6

mouth. Is he going to be sick?

'You.' I glower at him, holding out the brain. 'Take it.'

'What for?'

I nod towards the scales that hang above the dissecting table. 'We weigh every organ and record the weight. Put some gloves on and get on with it.'

Grimacing, he tips the mass of jelly into the steel pan while I address the other members of the group. 'A woman's brain is slightly smaller than a man's. No less effective, of course. In fact, in many ways, more devious and cunning. Take Lady Macbeth.'

I retrieve the brain from the cream-faced poltroon, and selecting a knife with a twelve-inch blade, dissect the organ in half.

'Any abnormalities?'

They stare dumbly.

'I'll tell you then. The answer is no.'

Woolly Hat is craving attention again, his hand flapping like a flag in the wind. 'But there are tiny—'

'Be quiet! I was rather hoping for a tumour, perhaps an astro-cytoma grade 4. A swift and silent killer that may have explained this specimen's untimely end. But no such luck. So what do we do next?'

A spotty youth raises a tentative hand. 'Cut her open?'

'I assume you mean *make an incision*?'

The boy's skin flares up as if his whole face

is covered with acne rosacea. 'I suppose so.'

'Splendid. But what kind of incision?'

He shrugs his puny shoulders. Bad diet. Too much refined carbohydrate. A candidate for diabetes if ever I saw one.

'We have three choices. We can use a T-shaped or a Y-shaped cut. These give easy access to the body cavity. But who wants to take the easy way? I favour the single straight cut, right down the middle. Like so . . .'

The knife slices through the chilly flesh, which in a refrigerated specimen has the consistency of soft leather. But a fresh corpse retains its springy muscle tone, and because the bones are not yet dry and brittle, they can be surprisingly resistant.

'*Unseamed him from the nave to the chaps.* That's how Shakespeare describes Macbeth's favourite method of despatch. We go in the other direction, starting at the neck, taking a brief detour round the tough tissue of the navel and ending up at the pubis . . . There we are. Done.' I wave the knife two-handedly like a claymore. '*With his brandished steel that smoked with bloody execution.*'

I contemplate them over my spectacles, but I have failed to make a dent in the lumpen demeanour of the group. Surely some of them must have studied the Scottish play at school? Or even—radical thought—seen it performed in the theatre?

Apparently not.

8

'Of course, Macbeth was a violent man, a killer. I'm a mere pathologist. Generally speaking, I only unseam those who are already dead.'

Someone—I can't see who—mutters, 'That's a matter of opinion.'

I ignore the impertinence and plough on. 'It's an interesting fact that the real Macbeth, a tenth century Scottish king, was an exemplary ruler, not a tyrant at all.' Despite the cold, my face feels clammy. 'Another interesting fact: I met my wife at a performance of the Scottish play. We got talking during the interval. I was enthusiastic about the production. Julia wasn't so sure—too violent, she said. In the final scene she had to cover her eyes when they brandished Macbeth's severed head, dripping with blood. Excellent stuff.' I wipe my sleeve across my damp brow. Maybe I've caught something, probably from one of the students. Walking germ carriers, most of them.

'Now where was I?' The body has been slit open to reveal the bright yellow subcutaneous fat, the salmon-coloured muscle. 'Now I need my bone cutters . . .' I turn to the trolley. My hand falls on an instrument. I pick it up. A pair of forceps. Damn.

'Some pathologists prefer scissors to cut the ribs,' I tell them, to cover my undignified scramble amongst the steel blades. 'But I favour a good pair of bone cutters.' I hold them aloft in triumph.

There is a satisfying crack as the first rib snaps. Without glancing up from my work I say, 'I've known students faint at this point. I think it's the noise.' I let a few heavy seconds pass. But there is no telltale thud as a body hits the floor. 'Splendid,' I say, though in truth, I'm rather disappointed.

'Now I can remove the chest plate and expose the internal organs . . . And there they are. Packed in like a box of chocolates, the assorted kind, all shapes and sizes. The arrangement never fails to amaze me, such an excellent use of space.' I wipe my forehead again. 'Talking of chocolate, a word to the wise. I prefer dark chocolate. If funds allow, go for the best, with a minimum of 70% cocoa butter. But no end of term presents of that hideous milky stuff, or, god help us, *white* chocolate.'

I'm breathing faster than normal. It's surprisingly hard work, dealing with a dead body. 'My wife was very fond of white chocolate.' There's a buzzing in my brain as if that damned fly has got inside. I shake my head violently to dislodge the infernal noise. 'So plain chocolate every time. Understood?'

Fortunately I've given up expecting a response.

'Let's get on. What am I holding now?'

'Lungs?' The serious-looking female, the one with the unflattering glasses.

'Good heavens, someone spoke. And a

10

correct answer to boot. The lungs indeed. Think of them as a couple of flabby balloons inflated by the heart. Tireless workers, the lungs. The heart gets all the headlines, but where would it be without these backroom boys?'

Just as I'm chalking the weight of the lungs on the board I hear the thud I've been waiting for. Who is it? I turn round. The girl in the skimpy skirt? No. She's shivering with cold, but upright. Blondie? No, he's still standing too. The girl with the glasses? That attention-seeking baldie? No, both present and correct.

Ah, now I see. It's Spotty. His colleagues cluster round him, unbuttoning his shirt, placing a rolled-up white coat under his head.

'Leave him alone! Let him lie there until he wakes up. He won't come to any harm, not unless someone steps on him.'

They stare at me with what seems like one unified malevolent eye.

Feeling almost jolly I continue the post-mortem. I even start to hum. I'm on a roll now.

'The lungs are a little distended, but there's no sign of disease. She obviously wasn't a smoker.'

'And the pinhead haemorrhages?' Woolly Hat doesn't even bother to raise his hand this time.

'Did I ask for a comment? Moving on to the heart.' Although I'm sweating profusely I begin to shiver with cold. My fingers feel stiff

11

and clumsy as they wield the knife to slice through the connecting blood vessels. But finally I lift out the heart and hold it in the palm of one hand.

'Notice that the Valentine cards get it all wrong. It's basically nothing more than a bicycle pump. It's the colour of uncooked liver and shaped like a builder's backside. And as you can see, it's a heavy, floppy blood-congested lump of flesh that might well ache—angina is the usual culprit—but can never be described as *broken*.'

Angina . . . perhaps that's what's wrong with me. That heaviness in my chest like someone standing on it, the tiredness, the shortness of breath, the restless nights.

'Nothing sentimental about it. Can't bear sentimentality. My wife took me to the ballet on my birthday a fortnight ago. Never again. Sickly saccharine stuff. She gave me a rather splendid present though—a large bottle of what they used to call Kensington Gore, the artificial blood they use in the theatre, now known rather more prosaically as Pro Blood. A leaving present, she said. After all those years together . . . *Out, out, brief candle . . .*'

Someone coughs.

Where am I? Of course—the mortuary, the cadaver on the dissecting table, the woman with dyed red hair. Straight hair. Julia's had a natural and untameable kink, sprouting tendrils of copper wire when the light was

12

behind her.

'Time's getting on. Who can tell me what this is? You—the boy with the blonde spikes.'

'The oesophagus?' he asks sullenly.

I sigh deeply. 'Where were you during basic anatomy? No doubt doing unspeakable things with your girlfriend in some grubby squat?'

He doesn't deny it.

'No, it is not the oesophagus. It is the trachea. This is the oesophagus. Now for the abdominal organs.'

As each body part is removed I check it for disease, weigh it, record the weight. First the liver, then the stomach and the kidneys. And the pesky little thing known as the gall bladder, which can cause no end of trouble.

'Now we come to the uterus. The womb. From whence we all came. This remarkable organ resists putrefaction longer than any other. Women, it would appear, are more durable than men.' I tip the surprisingly small pear-shaped organ into the bucket under the table with all the rest. I doubt this woman had any children. Nor did Julia. And now she never will.

My glasses are misty with sweat. 'So, cause of death. I'm tending towards sudden unexplained heart failure. Any other theories?'

True to form, Woolly Hat's arm snakes up like a cobra rising from its basket.

'Could the ligature mark around her neck have anything to do with it?'

Ligature mark?

I squint at the corpse, barely able to see through the smeared lenses. Surely it's a strand of red hair? I touch it. A groove in the flesh. Damn him.

'I was wondering when someone would notice that. What does it suggest?'

'Death by hanging?' offers Miss Flip-Flop.

'Suicide,' says the studious girl.

I nod approvingly. Suicide, of course. No signs of disease or trauma elsewhere. An excellent theory.

'Or murder made to look like suicide,' says Woolly Hat.

I take up the challenge. 'Let's examine the hyoid bone, shall we?' I point to a spot under the chin. 'It's so fragile it breaks during strangulation, but not when the body has been hanged. Take a close look.'

The bald one comes round to my side of the table. He leans over the corpse and prods the bone.

'Is it broken?'

'No,' he admits. 'But look at the ligature mark. No sign of inflammation.'

'Therefore?'

'She was dead before the rope was put around her neck.'

'Now you're being melodramatic.'

'Why won't you admit what's staring you in the face?' he shouts.

'Staring . . . ?' I glance down at the body but

14

the eyes are closed, thank god.

'The woman's face is blue.'

'It's cold in here,' I insist.

'And there are tiny haemorrhages in her brain and her lungs.'

'Exactly. Consistent with lack of oxygen, caused by self-inflicted hanging.'

'So where's the inflammation round the neck?'

'We've been through this. The hyoid bone is unbroken. So it cannot be murder.'

That shuts him up.

Suddenly his features change. It's like watching Toshiro Mifune in that particularly savage Japanese version of *Macbeth*. His face becomes taut, his eyes narrow to slits. He thrusts out his hands, one in front of the other, the sharp edges facing me like blades. He springs at me like someone demented. One hand stops dead at the side of my neck. If he'd gone just a millimetre further . . .

'Pressure on the vagus nerve stops the heart,' he says quietly. 'Look in the police file. I bet her partner was ex-army, SAS probably, or some sort of survival freak.' He reels his hands backwards. 'Or a karate expert. Like Jackie Chan.'

I remove my half-moon spectacles and place them in the top pocket of my coat. 'You could have killed me. What's your name? Who's your personal tutor? I intend to report you!'

15

He just laughs. 'You're the one who should be reported. Have you thought about early retirement?'

An almighty hubbub breaks out. Before I can quell the riot a deep groan emanates from the floor and does the job for me.

A couple of students haul Spotty to his feet. He's pale and groggy with dark smudges for eye sockets. Supported by his friends like a drunk, he glares at me.

I wag my finger at him. 'Are you sure you're cut out for forensic medicine, young man? It takes a certain type of character, you know. The ability to detach is essential. You failed to detach.'

'That's it, I've had enough,' says Woolly Hat. 'I'm off.' He shoves his headgear back on and strides out, followed by his pathetic cohort.

For a few minutes I can hardly breathe. I feel as if I've been punched in the stomach. Then I rub my aching eyes, put my glasses back on.

The room looks like a butcher's shop. The cadaver is a hollow gourd, its innards scooped out and discarded. There are bloody organs spilling out of the bucket, the floor is slippery with body fluids. The stench of death is overwhelming. Vagal inhibition. I wish I'd though of that. Far less messy. But that night, after the ballet, sheer force of professional habit made me reach for a knife . . .

'I *have supped full with horrors*,' I murmur.

Taking a deep breath I peel off my scarlet-stained gloves and pick up the manila folder. *Threatened to leave abusive partner . . . found hanging . . . partner served in Gulf War . . . extensive collection of martial arts films . . . is death suspicious? Report needed asap.*

I fish my dictaphone from my pocket. I outline the findings of the post-mortem and state my interpretation of the evidence. 'I conclude that lack of inflammation at site of rope marks indicates deliberate compression of neck leading to inhibition of the vagus nerve, stopping the heart and causing death within seconds.'

It takes some time to tidy up and finish my paperwork. When everything is done I stroll out to the car park.

It's cold outside, colder than the mortuary, and already growing dark. A flock of rooks circle high over the grounds and land in perfect sequence on the branches of the tall tree they have made their home. Their cawing cries sound like the cackling of witches on a misty heath.

Or the scrape of knife on bone.

Shaking my head I muse on the events of the afternoon. Young people, these days. Quite frankly, I could cheerfully murder the lot of them.

AND HERE'S THE NEXT CLUE . . .

Amy Myers

Mr Percy Pip had always yearned to be a crime writer. From his careful study of how to break into the market with an eye-catching potential best-seller, he realised that two obstacles lay in his path to stardom. The first was his name, which if displayed in large lettering across the dust-jacket would not instantly attract an enthusiastic readership. The second was somewhat more of a problem. He had learned that rule number 1 in achieving one's goal was to write about what you knew, but so far Percy had never committed a murder.

Percy Pip therefore took steps to remedy both of his shortcomings. Firstly, he selected a *nom de plume* for his new occupation. This would be part-time of course, since rule no. 2 for crime writing was not to give up the day job. When he became a household name, he might reconsider this decision but until then his employers could be reassured of his loyalty, especially as his job dovetailed nicely with his criminal purposes.

Secondly, he began to make meticulous preparations for his first murder. Unfortunately, this would have to be the first of several, since rule number 3, so it appeared from his perusal of booksellers' crime sections, was that a serial killer was an essential feature. The golden days of the lone murder, or even of two (permitted in order to keep the investigation going for 256 pages), were long since over. No, three had to be the minimum, with the necessary clues, preferably gruesome, to indicate that a series was in progress.

*　　*　　*

'What do you mean, crime scene?'

Dr Jonathan Fuller, the director of Mystery Unravelled: Crime-writing Courses Ltd., looked aghast. He had put on several successful workshops all over the country without the intervention of a corpse, and his distress hovered between his own position and wondering who amongst his current group might be a real-life murderer. Janice Dove's dead body had just been removed from the hotel, having been found in her room by his assistant Mavis Sharp, after Janice had failed to appear for breakfast. Since then the workshop's peaceful discussion of the criminal viewpoint in fiction had given way to an all too real influx of police, doctors, and scientists clad in white scene suits.

'Just routine, sir,' the investigating officer said reassuringly. 'Suspicious death, you see.'

'But surely it was a heart attack or perhaps food poisoning,' Jonathan croaked. 'The staff...'

'Poisoning's possible,' was the not so reassuring reply. 'Was anyone else taken ill?'

'Not to my knowledge. After dinner at 7.30 most people prefer to go their own way or retire early,' Jonathan explained, 'but I heard nothing mentioned at breakfast about ill effects.'

Jonathan's weekend courses took place in hired conference facilities in a country house hotel in varied locations. In the current one, in Suffolk, the facilities had seemed the best yet, with his party of two dozen completely separated from the rest of the guests, although this, he realised, would focus the investigation on his own pupils. After all, Janice Dove was known from previous courses to several of the participants here. Many of them were around him now, eager, no doubt, to pick up such gems of police procedure as they could. He found himself automatically answering the inspector's questions. No, this was not the first workshop that Miss Dove had attended. Yes, she was an aspiring writer.

'Such a gift,' he added weakly. 'She showed me her latest rejection slip, on which the agent had written *a personal encouraging comment.*'

The inspector was not interested in rejection slips. 'We'll need all the information you have on Miss Dove. Do you know what she ate for dinner?'

Jonathan looked uncertain. 'I expect it was

20

the stew. It was a buffet. We were moving around—little tables, you know the sort of thing. Most people—'

'Fish,' one of his group, Paul Merlin, interrupted firmly. 'Janice chose the fish. It had *prawns* in it.'

'She had her own vegetarian stew,' Mavis Sharp retorted equally firmly. 'I saw this morning that Janice had been sick. It was *stew*, and plum crumble, I think.'

'Sharp of eye as well as by name, eh?' the inspector said jovially. 'You found the body, didn't you?'

'I did.' Mavis looked modest. 'Of course my profession helps.' She was the author of six lurid whodunits, one of which had actually received a review in a newspaper.

'We make a strong team. Miss Sharp is cosy, whereas I am hardboiled,' Jonathan explained, receiving a strange look for his pains.

'The two types of crime novel,' Mavis explained briskly. 'The Agatha Christie school versus the tough brigade.'

The inspector's brow cleared. 'Rebus!'

As a hat had been thrown into the ring, Mavis felt the need to distance herself from the cosier cosies. 'Of course I am in the *modern* Agatha Christie school.'

Another strange look, this time for Mavis. The inspector decided to move on. 'And all of you were strangers to each other?' He cast a

21

glance over the crowd before him.

'No.' Jonathan steeled himself to speak for his little flock. 'The venue and subject matter of these workshops change, but their value is so great that some of my students come to more than one. I believe there are about eight regulars here today.'

To Jonathan's eye they all still looked unlikely candidates for the role of murderer, and none of them so far as he knew had had any close relationship with Janice Dove, who was in her fifties and hardly likely to catch the eye of an idealistic crime writer looking for a model moll.

Among the eight three were prominent in terms of potential troublemakers, in Jonathan's opinion. One was David Patterson, an ex-policeman in his forties, who assumed his experience was an automatic gateway to publication. He wrote with enthusiasm, but the result, unfortunately, was not fiction. His stories were turgid dollops of 'I proceeded north-west in an easterly direction'.

Paul Merlin was in his early sixties at a guess, an accountant on the point of retiring, with an over-absorbing interest in what he called the psychological approach and Jonathan privately termed the sex-obsessed. He was the ferret breed of student, anxious to display his own superior knowledge while at the same time to winkle out every last drop of knowledge that might be lurking in the

22

recesses of his instructor's mind.

Luke Hayward was twenty-nine, and a teacher with what seemed such a fanatical dislike of teaching that it was clear what drove him onwards towards the promised land of crime writing. A bad teacher, Jonathan decided, the sort who would demolish his pupils in order to rebuild them in his own image. Jonathan prided himself on his ability to pick out the achievers in his audience, a gift acquired from the auctions he conducted in his other occupation. Achievers were those whose willpower would drive them onwards, no matter what the opposition, and no matter whether they were Eton-schooled, state-schooled or unschooled. The chief achiever of the assembled company around him, including Mavis, would in his estimation be Paul Merlin, although he never underestimated the power of the non-achiever to throw a spanner in the works.

'I'm extremely sorry about Janice,' Paul told him earnestly. 'A terrible thing to die amongst strangers.'

'We weren't strangers,' Luke immediately objected. 'We'd all met before.'

'Yes, but we didn't know each other on a personal basis,' Mavis quickly pointed out. Miss Marple always remained detached from her suspects.

'What did kill her?' Jonathan asked, after the inspector had vanished and they were being ushered back towards their own secluded workshop room for interrogation.

David almost visibly swelled with pride. 'We won't know until the autopsy report.'

'*We?*' Luke picked up sarcastically. 'Didn't know you were with the Suffolk police.'

David scowled. 'Once a policeman, always a policeman.'

'I dislike being treated as though we were all potential murderers,' Paul muttered as a gimlet-eyed policewoman opened the door for them to enter. 'How do they know she didn't take the stuff herself?'

'What stuff?' Luke pounced, as he would on an unfortunate sixth-former. 'How do you know it was poison?'

'Even if it was,' David said, 'it could have been an accident.'

Mavis drew herself up. 'It could not.'

'How—' David began.

'Because there was a distinctive supermarket plastic bag at her side full of some prickly fruit, a knife and spoon, and a packet of disposable plastic gloves, not to mention an open window and—'

'Still could have been an accident or suicide,' David interrupted, annoyed at being outranked by a woman.

'And—' Jonathan prompted Mavis to continue.

'A peppermill taped to her chest.'

24

                    *   *   *

There was a certain camaraderie about the Mystery Unravelled crime writing course, held three months later and on this occasion in a Hampshire manor house. Those participants who had attended the previous course, five in all, enjoyed an enviable position so far as the somewhat nervous but excited newcomers were concerned, as they were able to speak with first-hand knowledge of a real life crime scene.

David in particular came into his own, having come by privileged information gained by bribing former colleagues with beer, flattery and, regrettably, twenty pound notes.

Even Mavis condescended to listen avidly, as they awaited lunch on the Saturday morning. 'So what did poor Janice die of?' she asked.

'Hyoscyamine,' David replied smugly. 'Datura seeds grated in the peppermill over, probably, the stew. Clever, wasn't it? I understand there's no forensic evidence to indicate anyone else was involved.'

'So it could have been suicide,' Paul said triumphantly.

'Rather a let-down,' Luke sneered, but was disregarded.

'Then why bother to tape the pepper mill on?' David grunted. 'Daft. I'm just a straightforward cop. Something like that happens in old Agatha's stuff, not in real life.'

Mavis took this personally. 'Only in this case, it did,' she snapped.

'Still suicide,' Paul maintained, anxious to maintain his lead. 'A killer couldn't guess exactly when she would die in order to creep in to attach the pepper mill.'

'The first person to find her could,' Luke said meaningfully. Mavis had criticised the best short story he had ever written. And he knew why: she intended to steal his plot.

Mavis quelled him with a look. 'I knew your thinking was wobbly, Luke, but *really*! Would I go along to Janice's room armed with a pepper mill to check if my victim were dead and then stop to tape it on in order to draw attention to the fact that it was murder?'

Luke rallied. 'Agatha might have done.'

She capped him. 'Agatha always had a rational explanation. I doubt if you do.'

David entered the fray. 'Of course, I'm just a plain cop, but in my experience, the first on the scene often *is* the killer.'

Paul switched tack to leap on the passing bandwagon. 'It's the psychology.'

'Why,' Mavis boomed savagely over him, 'should *anyone* wish to tape a peppermill on to a victim?'

'It's easy,' Paul persevered. 'In the interests of her—or of course his—art.' Two and two for a retiring accountant were permitted to make five.

'Eh?' David looked blank.

'To test us all,' Paul explained. 'If you understood the sexual perspective—'

'Balderdash,' David interrupted. 'It was a joke.'

Mavis seized her chance. 'As I explained in this morning's workshop, the death itself should *never* be a joke. A pepper mill comes perilously close to it.'

The workshop students took this to heart, and the pepper mill at the buffet lunch remained untouched either by hand or in conversation. The wine bottles fared much better. They were all emptied and five more called for, and consequently when the students reassembled for the afternoon workshop, they were some way into discussion of the intricacies of the protagonist's responsibility towards readers before Charles Beeton, one of the five regulars, was missed.

'He'll be here somewhere,' Jonathan said anxiously. 'He's probably fallen asleep.' Charles was a gentleman of mature years and girth, and after the lunch they had all enjoyed, this explanation seemed highly likely. 'But I'll check his room to be on the safe side.' When he arrived, however, he found it unlocked, but empty.

Mavis was not so lucky. En route to the ladies' room in the basement, she stumbled over Charles's dead body. Her scream could be heard by the group in the workshop,

27

growing ever louder as she rushed back to summon help. 'Attack,' she gasped, as she reached the room, panting for breath. 'He's dead. Chest.'

'A heart attack?' Jonathan caught her words as he returned from his fruitless errand, and joined the rush downstairs, already reaching for his mobile phone.

'Attack on the heart certainly,' Luke said soberly, as he reached the body and saw what awaited them. David immediately felt for a pulse, but without success. A knife was protruding from Charles's chest, and Jonathan could not avoid seeing something else too.

Not only was there a distinctive-looking plastic supermarket bag at Charles's side, but another knife, shiny and clean, was carefully taped to his sweater.

'Don't touch the bag,' David ordered, as Luke peered curiously into it. 'Evidence.'

In his element, David took charge, seizing Jonathan's mobile to summon the police; he then deputed Mavis, Jonathan and himself to guard the body while the others should remain together in the workshop room. Any visits to the toilets would be accompanied, according to sex, by himself, Mavis or Jonathan.

The crime scene manager of the police team that speedily arrived fully agreed that the plastic bag was evidence. Inside was a pair of man's shoes, an old fashioned plastic mac that appeared slightly stained with blood, and another packet of disposable gloves. The shiny knife too, he agreed, was evidence though its purpose naturally eluded him, as the knife that killed Charles was declaring its presence so obviously.

'What on earth was the second knife for?' Luke asked, a trifle shakily, after they had been dismissed from the crime scene and rejoined the other students round the table in the workshop room.

'The first one's easier to understand,' David said ponderously. 'Removing it would have covered the killer in blood.'

'But the second?' Luke persisted.

'I think I can guess,' Paul said, with what he hoped was quiet authority.

'Psychologically they carry a sexual implication?' enquired Luke innocently.

Paul stiffened. 'It could be,' he replied defensively. 'However I am inclined to think these are deodands.' He looked round at their blank faces, and added modestly, 'As a solicitor, I have a knowledge of legal history.'

'I thought everyone knew what they were,' Luke immediately put in. 'They're relicts of medieval law which held that the object was a guilty party in the crime and as such forfeit to the crown, sometimes being passed to the victim's family in compensation.'

'Quite,' Paul said patronisingly. 'Not repealed until the middle of the nineteenth century, when a rail company objected to forfeiting one of their express trains. In the case of poor Janice and now Charles, the peppermill and the knife are to be held responsible for their deaths.'

'Try telling that to the Old Bailey,' David snorted. 'No way. It's a copy-cat murder. You'll see.'

*   *   *

They did. Or rather the Kent police did. This time, excluding Jonathan and Mavis, the number of regulars was down to three: David, who said he had a duty to be present because as an ex-policeman he could keep an eye on things; Paul, who was set on proving his deodand theory; and Luke who was set on disproving anything that anyone else suggested.

Jonathan had considered whether it would be wise to hold this course at all, but he had been heartened to find there was no such thing as bad publicity. So numerous were the applications from newcomers that he was forced to turn students away. Mavis Sharp had hesitated about instructing at another course, but on discovering that her young friend Beatrice Worthy wished to sign up she decided she would join her. Unfortunately on arrival at the Kentish hotel, she quickly discovered that Beatrice's motives for wishing to come were mixed. Firstly, she wrung Mavis's mind dry of every detail about the murders at which she had been first on the scene. Thereafter, Beatrice devoted her attention to Luke, and from Mavis's glimpse of the canoodling at the rear of the room during the Saturday workshop, she had broadened her sphere of interest.

David, Paul and even Luke (when he could detach himself from Beatrice) were all eager to outdo each other in the 'My theory about the murders' stakes, and the newcomers were equally eager to detect which of the regulars could have been the killer.

It made for an interesting forum, and Mavis, having recovered from the shock of discovering two corpses earlier in the year, was in her element. Her nose twitched continuously with the sharpness the investigating officer had commented on over Janice's death.

Discussion continued almost until dinnertime on the Saturday, and then resumed over the meal. Jonathan had abandoned the buffet approach to dinner, to everybody's obvious relief, after much earlier debate about Janice's murder. With set places, he could more easily keep an eye on everyone's presence and prevent any lone excursions.

However, after dinner, he could exercise no such control. When Luke promulgated an evening walk, Beatrice eagerly accepted. Mavis gently insisted that she should accompany

31

them, but when she returned after powdering her nose she was annoyed to find that they had left without her. A mistake she told herself firmly, and spent ten minutes chatting to Jonathan, Paul and David before they parted for their separate rooms.

David, through his special knowledge, had told them that the police were as baffled over Charles's murder as over Janice's, even though the Hampshire and Suffolk police forces had consulted their modus operandi files and were in constant contact with each other. Neither the knives nor the plastic mac nor the shoes had revealed any DNA or useful fibres, and thus there seemed little progress, though from time to time one or other of the witnesses was thoroughly grilled.

Jonathan himself had endured several such grillings, which was hardly surprising. After Charles's death, he had feared that the Mystery Unravelled company would be ordered to suspend all further courses, but no such injunction was laid on him although his credit and company details had been checked. What he could not satisfy the police about, naturally enough, was whether any of the participants would have reason to murder any of the others. Was there jealousy over a publishing contract? These students were nowhere near that happy stage, he had explained. Were there any romantic affairs between them? If there were, he would hardly be privy to them, he had reasonably replied. Had he, with his expert knowledge, noticed anything untoward in any of his students' characters, especially the regular ones? Jonathan hesitated over this. Did Luke's edginess or Paul's sexual obsession count? Or David's need to be involved in police work again? He decided not, and did not mention them.

Breakfast on the Sunday morning was a quiet affair with people arriving in ones and twos between 7.30 and 8.30. Some chose to go for a run first 'for inspiration', Luke had explained, since the workshop this morning would be a set exercise of a short criminal story of a thousand words. Others of the group ran nowhere, or in some cases attended early church services. They were fortunate, because it was Luke who therefore came across the dead body of Beatrice Worthy on the woodland path. His white-faced appearance back at the hotel as he blurted out the gruesome details put the latecomers entirely off their Full English breakfasts.

In the all but certain knowledge that this would surely spell the end for Mystery Unravelled courses, if only because no hotel would offer them any facilities in future, Jonathan alerted the police and the hotel manager, and bravely set off with Luke to guard the body. Mavis, rejoicing that it was not she who this time had found poor Beatrice, waited for the arrival of the police.

'Round the next bend,' Luke instructed Jonathan, stopping abruptly on the path. At this stage Jonathan too decided to wait for the police, not sure he could face a corpse again. After their arrival, however, he and Luke followed them cautiously to the scene of the crime, watching from the sidelines as they proceeded with their grim task. Even from where they stood they could glimpse the tongue protruding through blue lips, and blood and froth on the face of what had once been an attractive girl. And even from here they could see the distinctive supermarket plastic bag. They could also see something far more horrible.

Taped to Beatrice's bosom were two severed human hands.

*　　*　　*

On this occasion by unspoken accord, the workshop was abandoned. No one had the stomach for the intricacies of the psychopathic mind (fictional version) when the factual version was all too prominent in everyone's thoughts. Nor was there much stomach for lunch either, particularly for those most concerned in the investigation: the regulars.

The Kent police were assiduously interviewing every member of the hotel staff, and everyone at the Mystery Unravelled course. In addition to Jonathan and Mavis, particular attention was paid to David, Luke, and Paul as the three present at all the workshops where murders had occurred.

Again by unspoken accord, most of the group drifted back to the workshop after lunch, as if a black cloud separated it from the rest of humanity. As it was hard for the newcomers to voice any natural speculation as to the guilty party, there was silence reigning in the room when David returned from a trip to the crime scene. There he had successfully managed to infiltrate the crime scene and circulate for ten whole minutes until ejected by the crime scene manager.

'He left his socks in the bag this time,' David told them. 'And the shoes looked much larger than last time. There was a pair of leather gloves, but no disposable ones.'

'So he went barefoot this time?' Luke asked.

'Or had spare socks with him.'

'What else?' Mavis asked, having had the scene fully described to her by Luke. 'An axe?'

Not having been first on the scene, she felt more objective about this murder, even though it was poor Beatrice. She had her suspicions about this case. Miss Marple always did, and even though Luke was the front runner, David and Paul were still *in the frame.* That phrase pleased her as it showed that she was keeping Agatha's tradition up to date.

'Yes.' David glanced at Mavis's large capable hands. 'But she was strangled manually.'

'So it couldn't have been a woman,' Luke sounded disappointed.

'It could. Sex,' Paul announced darkly.

'Charles wasn't a sex object,' David said scornfully.

'There's sexual jealousy of the young. *And* the change of life,' Paul diagnosed.

Mavis bristled with fury. 'As I explained, Paul, in yesterday's workshop, modern medicine and technology have rendered many crime clichés unusable. Real life has moved on. HRT disposes of such problems far more efficiently than carrying out axe murders.'

'She wasn't murdered by an axe,' Jonathan pointed out in the interests of accuracy. 'The hands were taped on, not the axe.'

Paul nodded solemnly. 'I'm glad you're a convert to my deodand theory, Jonathan.'

Mavis frowned. 'You said the deodand was the object that committed the crime. But the hands were Beatrice's own. They'd been chopped off. Are you saying she strangled herself?' The awfulness of it caught up with her, and she began to weep.

Paul was not to be daunted by tears. 'No, but it's part of the psychology of the killer. We all appear quite normal to each other, but so would the psychopath who committed these murders. Two different faces, one for us, and another one for himself.'

His listeners stirred uneasily, avoiding looking at each other.

Pleased that he had made his point, Paul continued: 'After all, look at Agatha Christie and her famous disappearance. She took time off to pretend she was someone else.'

'But not a psychopath,' Mavis said sharply. 'Poor woman, she was simply—'

'Why?' David cut across the conflict. 'Why the hands at all? It's plain evil.'

'That's just what Miss Marple would have said,' Mavis said, looking at him very carefully.

*   *   *

It was Mavis who by chance did prove to be an achiever after all. Sharp by name and sharp by nature, as the police had said. When she called in at her local police station over a very trifling point of false claims, it was her sheer perseverance and downright bullying that drove them to look into the matter. By subsequent patient tracking of phone records they reached their quarry and then through sheer chance they discovered the murderer of Janice, Charles and Beatrice,

Mr Percy Pip was rudely awakened from a peaceful doze in which he was being presented with the Crime Writers' Diamond Dagger award, and was shattered to find upon his doorstep a CID officer plus a uniformed police constable, holding up ID cards.

'Mr Percy Pip?' And when he nodded, he heard those familiar words: 'We have a warrant here for your arrest . . .'

Percy's face was ashen. He had been given to understand that all policemen were either Plods and thus easily outfoxed, or drunk and disorderly with severe psychological problems. The three investigating officers he had so far met had given no indications to the contrary. What therefore had gone wrong?

'But there was no forensic evidence,' Percy babbled. 'No DNA. I was most careful. They were, I assure you, the perfect murders. All of them—'

He stopped, aware that they were looking at him in a strange way. 'We'll look into that, sir, now you've mentioned it. Meanwhile, we're here to arrest you on a fraud charge, identity theft.'

Percy Pip couldn't believe it. Caught through the mere matter of providing utility bills, driving licence, etc. to establish bank accounts, signatures, accommodation address and rented office and living space, mostly achieved through one simple house clearance. And, he remembered, a false doctorate.

'The identity theft of the late Mr Jonathan Fuller. I have to warn you . . .'

CLOSURE

Carol Anne Davis

Author's note: the pages which follow are extracts from the diary of Dr Rees Ralph Llewellyn who history tells us conducted the post mortem of Mary Ann Nicholls, Jack The Ripper's first victim. The diary, which was found hidden in the secret drawer of a Victorian davenport, has been authenticated by historians and ripperologists.

Saturday 1st September, 1888. Shoreditch Mortuary, Old Montague Street.

The body before me is that of Mary Ann Nicholls, also known to her friends as Polly. Tragedy struck her early when a paraffin light exploded and burnt her brother to death. She married and had five children, but her husband had a brief affair with the midwife who delivered their fourth child. The devastated Mrs Nicholls turned to strong liquor, under which influence she became unreliable and loud. Her relatives disowned her and she became an alcoholic and occasional thief but apparently kept herself very clean, even when living within the grim walls of the Lambeth Workhouse.

A half hour after midnight on 31st August she left the Frying Pan pub and at 1.20am was turned away from the lodging house at 18 Thrawl Street because she didn't have the 4 pence required for a bed for the night. She asked them to keep the bed, promising spiritedly that she would soon be back.

The victim then walked through the cobbled streets of Whitechapel in search of a man who could give her 4d in return for her sexual favours. Heavily intoxicated, she must have merged with the shadows of the warehouses and breathed in the stench from the Winthrop Street slaughterhouse.

At 2.20am she was seen outside the grocers at the corner of Whitechapel Road and shortly afterwards she met her killer in Buck's Row.

He quickly severed her windpipe, she collapsed and he cut her throat. He then slashed at the right side of her stomach—and it's clear from the trajectory of the wounds that he was left handed. He left her skirts raised, cleaned his bloody hands and knife on her clothes and disappeared.

The still-warm corpse was found at 3.45am by a carrier on his way to work. As I live nearby, the police woke me and took me to Buck's Row to examine the woman. I pronounced her dead and arranged for her body to be taken to the mortuary, where I am now conducting the post mortem. It is 10am.

The woman has dark hair and grey eyes.

The mouth has five missing teeth but these are not recent injuries or extractions. She is five foot two inches and looks considerably younger than her forty three years.

On the right side of the face is a bruise which may have been made by a fist or by pressure from a thumb. The same is true of bruises on the left side of the face and neck. The throat has been cut twice, one cut measuring four inches and the other eight inches. Both cuts were to the bone.

The left side of the abdomen has been slashed so that the implement cut deeply into the tissues. On the right side there are four downward cuts penetrating the genitals. The killer may have a rudimentary knowledge of anatomy.

Postscript—On 6th September Mary Ann Nicholls was buried in a pauper's grave in City of London cemetery.

Saturday 8th September, 1888. Shoreditch Mortuary, Old Montague Street.

The body before me is that of Annie Chapman whose body was stripped and washed down by a pauper from the workhouse before I arrived here. She was found at 6am this morning in the recess of a yard in Hanbury Street.

Her life has been a difficult one and this shows in the ravages of her face and body,

41

which look at least fifteen years older than her forty seven years. Mrs Chapman had three children, one of whom was born disabled and whom she had institutionalised. She sent her second child, a girl, to an institution in France—though none of her acquaintances know why—and meningitis claimed her third. Her husband also died and Annie Chapman subsequently succumbed to lung disease, which has seen her in and out of hospital for several years. She supported herself by selling crochet work, flowers and matches and through seasonal work such as picking hops, though has sometimes turned to prostitution from necessity.

The woman went out into the streets in the early hours of the morning to earn money for a bed for the night and was seen in Paternoster Row shortly before 2am.

Some time in the next three hours she met her killer in the dark dingy location of Hanbury Street. He suffocated or strangled her—her face and hands are livid, signalling asphyxia, her swollen tongue protruding through equally swollen lips. He then cut her throat through to the spine from left to right, and attempted to remove her head. The killer also cut open the abdomen, severed the intestines and placed them on her right shoulder. He pushed her knees up to expose her most intimate parts, cut out the top of her vagina and part of her bladder and removed them from the scene.

The woman has brown hair and blue eyes. She has two teeth missing from her lower jaw but these are not recent injuries or extractions. She is five foot tall and was dying of malnutrition.

She has facial bruising and bruising of the breast which is several days old and was apparently sustained in an earlier altercation with another woman. The abdominal and genital regions have been extensively mutilated and the body is almost drained of blood.

As a result of public and press intrusion, the hospital's statement to the press will state that this post mortem was carried out by a Dr Brown (who does not really exist) at a different mortuary. And the body will be buried with the utmost secrecy to avoid undisciplined crowds. I cannot imagine that this maniac will kill a third time, but if he does the police want me to carry out the post mortem and to keep my name from the public record. Otherwise the public and press will never give me a moments peace.

I cannot help but note that these two atrocities have coincided with the showing of Mansfield's play *Jeckyll & Hyde* on The Lyceum. Surely such popular entertainment— combined with the cheap magazines which now clutter our every street corner with their drawings of assassinations—must damage already weakened minds? I am also concerned that gutter newspapers such as *Tit Bits* will get hold of the tawdry details of these murders and make much of them.

Sunday 30th September, 1888. Shoreditch Mortuary, Old Montague Street.

I fear that I was over-hasty in suggesting that two hellish killings would assuage this man's blood lust. Sadly, he has struck again—and again! Alternatively, this may be a crime of identity with the women's sworn enemies or spurned lovers killing them in the same manner as the maniac has killed. There must be many men out there who would like rid of their ageing womenfolk so the body count may continue to rise . . .

The body before me is that of Elizabeth Stride *nee Gustafsdotter*, who I have stripped and washed down. The woman, who has spent time in the Whitechapel Workhouse, was found today at 1am in Berner Street.

The forty five year old's life, according to her neighbours, has been an increasingly fraught one which included giving birth to a stillborn baby. After her carpenter husband died, she tried and failed to support herself entirely by cleaning houses. She resorted to prostitution and has been treated twice in hospital for venereal disease.

The deceased was seen by her latest

common law husband on Saturday but she allegedly left him to partake of alcohol in the Queen's Head pub in Commercial Street. She returned to her lodging house then went out again and at midnight was in the passageway at 40 Berner Street, a long row of dark and desolate houses. Number 40 is used by the International Workers' Educational Club.

It is here—in the shadowy passageway— that her killer struck, forcing her to the ground by grabbing the long scarf which she was wearing and pulling her head back. He then cut her throat from left to right, heard other people approaching and ran off. Mrs Stride was found shortly afterwards by a travelling salesman whose pony shied at seeing her corpse.

The legs were drawn up to the knees and both shoulders were badly bruised, presumably by the killer's weight on her. The victim's left carotid artery has been severed, resulting in her death.

A number of cachous (sweets which smokers use to sweeten the breath) were found clutched tightly in her right hand. Her breath is no longer sweet. The mouth has all of the teeth missing in the lower left jaw but these are not recent injuries or extractions. The stomach contents were of potato, cheese and farinaceous powder, yet it is wrongly rumoured that she ate a last meal of grapes.

To avoid undue public intrusion, the

official version is that this post mortem was carried out by a Dr Phillips. The body is to remain in the mortuary for the time being as the victim was apparently seen with several men in the hours prior to her murder and potential eye witnesses are being hunted down by the police. They will be brought here to confirm whether or not Elizabeth Stride was the woman they saw.

Postscript—Elizabeth Stride was buried quietly a week later at the parish's expense. Subsequently, a group of supposed psychics suggested the identity of her killer. Doubtless this nonsense will die out when we have a more educated class.

Sunday 30th September, 1888. Shoreditch Mortuary, Old Montague Street.

To autopsy two murdered women—doubtless butchered by the same man within the hour!—is indeed an exceptional and sobering task.

The body before me is that of Catharine Eddowes who was found in Mitre Square at 1.45am.

Her life has been fraught with problems and she ran away from home with a much older man, after which her relatives disowned her. The union produced three children but broke up amid rumours of the man's violence and Eddowes own increasing propensity for drink.

The woman, who was age forty six, has auburn hair, hazel eyes and the tattoo TC on her left forearm, which the police tell me are the initials of her common law spouse.

She has supported herself in recent years by begging, hop-picking and prostitution and has recently resided at the Shoe Lane Workhouse where she was known to be argumentative.

In the hours leading up to her brutal death, Eddowes was found slumped in an alcoholic stupor and was taken to Bishopgate Police Station. At 12.55am she was released, having told the police constable that her latest common law husband would beat her. He replied that it served her right.

We know that the victim walked towards Houndsditch, passing one of the entrances to Duke Street. She would have walked along the narrow lane called Church Passage, taking her into Mitre Square.

It is here that she met her killer. He cut her throat, eyes, nose, lips and one of her cheeks, then concentrated his rage on her abdomen. Apparently he then walked through Goulston Street.

The woman has had her left kidney and uterus sliced from her body by the killer. She was suffering from Bright's Disease and the missing kidney will show signs of this. The killer also removed the lobe of her right ear and scarred her under both eyes.

The official line is that a Dr Brown carried out this autopsy.

Postscript—Catharine Eddowes' body is to be taken to the cemetery on 8th October in an open-glass horse-drawn hearse, all expenses, including the polished elm coffin, to be met by undertaker Mr Hawks.

The women have named this The Autumn Of Terror and are afraid to walk the streets after dark, though they throng the murder scenes so thickly in daytime that residents cannot pass, and many are selling seats at their windows which afford a good view of the bloody locations. But the menfolk are armed with heavy sticks and evil tempers so I wager that this maniac will soon be caught and killed.

Thursday 18th October, 1888. Shoreditch Mortuary, Old Montague Street.

Today, I am autopsying two children who died of an as yet unspecified disease, but my thoughts keep returning to Catharine Eddowes murder, the reason being that on 16th October, a parcel containing half a kidney (and which showed signs of Bright's Disease) was delivered to the chairman of the Whitechapel Vigilance Committee. The letter read *'From Hell . . . Sir, I send you half the kidne . . . prasarved it for you.'*

Its authenticity aside, it's clear that we need to increase the literacy of the working classes. The move away from the classics and Latin is to be decried, especially as it corresponds with a move towards popular music appreciation and other simple subjects. I fear that if we follow on down this road, we will end up with ostensibly academic courses in inn-keeping and gardening!

This state of affairs is not helped by the current standard of journalism in most of Great Britain's 170 newspapers, many of which are attributing ghoulish quotes to non-existent persons. It's rumoured that one such journalist has even sent written communications in a mis-spelt hand, signing the postcards Jack The Ripper. Can our press sink any lower than this?

Wednesday 14th November, 1888. Shoreditch Mortuary, Old Montague Street.

I believe that we need a more educated police force to track down this hellish slaughterer. Incredibly, most of our constables have no qualifications yet are pitted against criminals who have a native cunning.

The body before me is that of Mary Jane Kelly who was found on 9th November 1888 on the bed of her room in 26 Dorset Street.

She has known hardship, becoming estranged from her parents and six siblings at a young age. She married but her husband was tragically killed in a pit explosion. She later became a prostitute and moved from one lodging house in the East End to another, eventually ending up at 26 Dorset Street, which backs on to 13 Miller's Court.

The woman, who was age twenty five, has long blonde hair, blue eyes and a fair complexion. She is five foot seven and has—or rather had—well proportioned limbs.

At 11.45pm on the day of her death, she was seen walking drunkenly with a man in Dorset Street. Moments later neighbours heard her enter her room and start singing one of her favourite songs, *Only A Violet I Plucked From My Mother's Grave*. She continued to sing Irish songs—her parents were Irish though they relocated to Wales when she was a child—for some time, before going out again at 2am where she unsuccessfully asked a male acquaintance for sixpence. Moments later she was seen with another man walking back in the direction of her room.

At around 3am, two neighbours heard a cry then all was silent. It's believed that Mary Kelly was sleeping with the sheet over her face at the onset of the attack. The killer cut her throat from ear to ear, slicing deeply down to the spinal column. He removed her entrails and placed them on the bedside table, cut off her nose and slashed the remainder of her face until it was quite unrecognisable. He also sliced off both of her breasts and placed them by the side of her liver on the table.

The body has been so badly mutilated that it took a team of surgeons six hours to piece it back together. The heart and uterus have been excised and all of the flesh has been cut from the right thigh and right buttock. There are numerous other cuts, though, strangely, the woman's chemise has been left in place.

For the purposes of keeping public order, full details of these atrocities will not be disclosed to the press or the public (who are already telling falsehoods about there being a three month foetus in Mary Jane Kelly's womb) and the post mortem will be attributed to a fictitious Dr Bond.

The body is to be kept in the mortuary whilst an attempt is made to track down Mary Jane Kelly's parents and siblings.

Thursday 15th November, 1888. Shoreditch Mortuary, Old Montague Street.

The identity of the killer continues to intrigue the man in the street, and they suggest everyone from a man called Leather Apron to an insane medical student to a mad midwife. One wag even hinted that it might be the gifted painter Walter Sickert. Several also blamed it on gangs such as the Old Nichol Mob. But in the end the killer turned out to be a boy . . .

51

For I am the only man in Whitechapel—nay, the whole of England—who knows the identity of the slaughterer and I will hide my writings away so that they are only discovered many years after my death by some author with too much time on his hands. By then the case will be long forgotten but may be of some passing interest to a local historian.

In short, the boy that they call Jack The Ripper has a desperately poor pedigree, born to a common prostitute and an unknown father. His mother soon abandoned him to the Lambeth Workhouse where he eventually became my assistant, opening up the mortuary for the police at all hours and washing down the bodies for meagre pay.

Workhouse boys are incorrigible thieves, so I wasn't surprised when I saw young Joseph absentmindedly cleaning his hands on a piece of Catharine Eddowes torn apron. I naturally assumed that he had taken it from the clothing he'd removed from her corpse. Going through his jacket pockets, I found Elizabeth Stride's scarlet posy and assumed he'd also stolen it from the mortuary before I saw her body, though I could not imagine what a virile young boy would do with a flower.

But later I picked up the handkerchief which he'd dropped in the sluice room, and a piece of labial tissue fell from it. Gentle reader, I could remember the ghastly mutilations which Mary Jane Kelly had endured and knew that her labia had been excised at the murder scene. It was one peculiarity too many and I suddenly realised that the man they called Jack The Ripper might already be in my sights.

I could, in theory, have gone to the police—but imagine the public derision when it was found that this very mortuary had been harbouring the murderer. The cartoonists and journalists would have had a field day and I'd have been the laughing stock of the town. And, as I mused on my alternatives, I felt a creeping excitement which I'd never felt when slicing cold, dead flesh.

So I waited in the shadows of the Lambeth Workhouse yesterday evening, waited until 2am when he crept out into the chill autumn. For the first time in many weeks, the East End was cloaked in fog so I was able to keep close to him as he glided soundlessly through Whitechapel's grimy streets.

At last he espied an elderly hag who was standing on the corner, craning away from him in search of succour. He crept towards her with his knife raised—and I leapt forward and grabbed his left arm, pulling it downwards so that the blade cut deeply into his own throat. I cut again and again, acting so quickly that the old woman was unaware of our brief but incredibly vital struggle. Then I fled, leaving Joseph dying on the damp, cold ground.

Friday 16th November, 1888. Shoreditch Mortuary, Old Montague Street.

Early this morning, the police came to my door and asked me to formally identify the body and perform the post mortem. I shall do so within the hour and suggest that the killer is a drunken male, undoubtedly an oaf.

We are all born of women and surely should treat them with more respect—but is that same respect necessarily due to the numerous ragged boys who clog our workhouses and steal from us on street corners? I'm beginning to realise that I did society a service when I sliced through Joseph's soft white flesh. And there was such an unexpected satisfaction in watching his body writhe and his blood spurt that I may have to seek out another tender boy and do it again . . .

ANNE AND CLARE

Liz Evans

Anne

I'd promised myself I wouldn't do this again, but a compulsion seems to take over my hands and makes them move of their own volition towards the bedroom cupboard.

The towelling sleep-suits lay on the bed like misshapen frogs; arms and legs bent into V shapes. Small woolly hats; minute bibs with aquamarine 'A's embroidered on them; knitted bootees; a soft shawl the blue of duck eggs. Luckily this is a Catholic country where blue for the Madonna is used for baby girls, so the clothes are suitable for either sex. The second shelf holds the nappies, feeding bottles, steriliser, powdered formula, and cleansing wipes. All bought for cash at separate shops over the past month. Finally the necessary ugliness on the bottom shelf. Thick plastic sheeting, two rolls of strong parcel tape, surgical ties, and a stainless steel filleting knife.

Clare

I love the feel of sun on my skin. If I close my

eyes and breath deeply, I'm sure I can detect the warm, spicy, scents of North Africa on the light southerly breeze. Logically I know it's probably my subconscious supplying the smells that go with blue skies, sunlight, and white-washed Moorish villages.

The architecture here is fake of course. A speculative builder's attempt to design a pseudo-village that will blend into the Southern Spanish coastline. This area is over-run with acres of empty apartments awaiting those who want second homes in the sun or to live the retirement dream. I can be invisible while I'm here, and unremembered when I leave.

The shrill buzz of my watch alarm reminds me it's nearly time. Before I go inside, I walk over to the balcony rail and look around. Blank-eyed, shuttered, windows stare back at me in all directions. The narrow cobblestone alleyway below is deserted. If this had been a real village there would be old women in rusty black clothing, with faces like walnut shells, shuffling up the streets; toddlers playing outside front doors; and the smells of cooking drifting from ovens set up on rooftops to escape the stifling heat inside. The only thing on the roof terrace opposite me is a blue and yellow 'Vende' board. This is a sterile place. It seems ironically appropriate.

A twinge in my back reminds me why I'm here. Unconsciously I smooth my linked hands over the expanding bump and cradle the weight. Thank heavens it won't get any larger now. It's almost B-day.

Anne

I swear the bump has grown several inches over the past few days. It must be nearly full term. I wish I knew the exact date, but I can't ask too many questions. I don't want to become her friend. I don't even know her name.

For the baby's sake I need to judge the moment correctly. The longer it stays inside her, the stronger it will be. On the other hand, if I leave it too late, she might give birth naturally. I've followed her several times into local towns and she's never visited a clinic. I decided she must be into natural child-birth. It seems to me a desperately selfish idea. It's not as if the baby has any choice in the matter. But no matter how determined she is to squeeze the thing out to meditation music and organic candles or whatever, I'll bet once the pain kicks in, she'll be screaming for *Los medicos* on her mobile. I've never understood the reasoning used by those who snatch babies from maternity wards. Do they imagine everyone will shrug their shoulders and carry on with their normal lives? The only way to successfully take a child, is to remove one that will never be missed.

She's gone back inside her apartment, so I swing the bedroom shutters wide. The gaps between the slats make a handy peep-hole to keep an eye on the terrace below. The morning sun floods into the room and I catch a glimpse of myself in the mirror over the chest of drawers. What picture do you get when someone says 'mistress'? Someone young and curvy? Long-legged and firm busted? A tumble of shiny hair and come-to-bed eyes?

My face stares back at me; square and heavy-jawed, framed by short coarse brown hair. The image is cut off at the chest, but the wide shoulders and big arms tell you what the rest of the package is like. 'Junoesque' Clive used to call me. Maybe that's what appealed to him; the attraction of a contrast. His wife was small and skinny; a washed-out, simpering thing, making a virtue of her helplessness. I've always hated being this big, but I can't deny it's going to be useful. Moving the remains will be easy.

Clare

I heard the shutters upstairs opening as I was closing mine. She often does that. Sometimes I feel like we're a pair of figures in those weather clocks; one coming out as the other goes in. She's the only other resident in this complex and it was just my luck she's living directly above me. I was afraid she'd try to be

58

friends; the last thing I wanted was girlie chats over wine on the terrace. Fortunately she seems to desire my company as little as I want hers.

Locking the shutters, I plugged in the laptop, connected it to my new mobile, and switched on the video link. The plain beige-coloured wall opposite appeared on the screen. It had a slightly fuzzy appearance as if the contrast on the screen needed adjusting. In this case, however, it was due to the film of gauze that I'd fixed over the lens. I left it on while I went into the bedroom and took the wig out of the bag. It takes only a second to yank it on and flick it into place. A cloud of fair hair settles around my shoulders. I complete my alternate look with a pair of rimless spectacles.

I run a quick check on the blocking software before connecting to the internet. If anyone tries to trace the origin of this call, they'll find themselves being bounced around the globe from ISPs in Europe, South America, and the Far East, before finally hitting the net equivalent of a brick wall. I wrote the program myself.

As soon as I go on-line Francesca's face appears on the screen. 'Clare, you're late. Is everything alright? We were worried.'

'Everything's fine. Hi Rick.'

Her husband moved into view. He has his normal slightly dishevelled, just got out of bed, look. My heart gives a small skip before I remember.

'Morning tad.' He used my old nickname. Tad, short for tadpole, because I was the smallest and youngest of our group in the care home. 'The reception on this thing is still a pain.' He tapped the screen as if that was likely to clear it. 'How's my boy?'

'Expanding.' I turn sideways so they get the full effect of my enormous belly.

'*Is* it a boy?' Frankie says eagerly. 'Have you had a scan?'

'I told you I don't want to know the sex. It could be a girl. Does it matter?'

'No,' Frankie says immediately. 'You know it doesn't. But you *have* had a scan? You are going for your check-ups regularly?'

We have this conversation every time. She knows I won't answer.

'Please let us know where you are Clare,' Frankie pleads. 'We won't interfere. You needn't even see us. If we just had a contact address, or a telephone number?'

'You know the deal, Frankie. I have to do this alone.'

'But it wasn't what we *agreed*. You never said you'd be going away. You just *disappeared*. I thought we'd go to ante-natal classes together. Plan things. What if anything goes wrong?'

I heard a muffled murmur in the background. No doubt Rick pointing out I

60

hadn't been persuaded before, so why would I change my mind now? He pretends to be laid back about this whole pregnancy thing, but I know he wants this baby as much, if not more, than Francesca. He wants to send his genes marching on into the future. Frankie told me, while he was out of the room, that he's already put up a toy fort in the back garden and ordered a baby carrier with blue chequered upholstery. So much for not caring what sex it is. Son of Rick is plainly the preferred option here. Taking advantage of the interruption, I speak before she can start with the pleading again. 'How are the preparations going at your end?'

'We've finished the nursery. Watch.' The video swoops and pans over pale yellow walls with nursery characters dancing around at cot level. The blinds are lemon and the furniture is white picked out with more primrose. There's a mobile of small birds turning gently in the breeze over the spot where the cot will eventually stand. 'Do you like it?'

'Whatever you think's best. It's your baby.'

'Thanks. Thank you so much Clare. You know how much this means to us, don't you?'

Oh yes. I know that all right.

Anne

I need some more batteries for my torches. The electricity here has a habit of going off at odd times and if the apartment downstairs is the same as mine, then there are no windows in the bathroom. I've decided to use that room because it's fully tiled. It will be easier to clear up afterwards.

There's a garage shop on the roundabout at the bottom of the complex. Walking down the hill I'm surrounded by the flowers of hibiscus, frangipane, and busy lizzies. It's hard to believe it's only a few weeks after Christmas.

Clive and I travelled a lot on business but we were always in England for Christmas. His wife insisted they spend it at home—*'for the children's sake'*.

'I have to go along with her. She's always been highly strung. Clinically depressed mostly. I must think of the children. You understand, don't you Annie?'

And of course I did. He couldn't leave his children with that neurotic witch, could he? And the wife always got custody in divorce cases. So we waited whilst his daughters grew up and I spent my Christmases with a turkey ready-meal for one, and the fantasy of the family we'd have one day: rosy cheeked, blonde children, in their pyjamas, opening presents before a roaring log fire on Christmas morning. Except for that one year when I hugged the secret of a tiny, acorn-sized, promise growing inside me.

He persuaded me to have an abortion in

January. It wasn't the 'right time'.

It was this Christmas that convinced me I'd picked the right girl. She had no visitors and she didn't go out. Like me, she's a yule-time orphan. No one will miss her.

Because I was thinking about her, it took me a moment to register that she wasn't in my head but actually standing in front of me in the shop. The assistant is packing a carton of eggs and two croissants into a carrier for her. He's got that special smile that people seem to reserve for pregnant women. We exchange a small nod since we can't very well pretend we haven't seen each other. The assistant says, 'Soon you will be bringing the little one in?'

'No. Afraid not. My rental is nearly up. I'm leaving shortly.'

For me this is both good and bad news. It's good that her disappearance won't be questioned. But it means I have to act soon. I added a bottle of surgical spirit to the batteries. I don't want the baby to pick up an infection from her skin.

Clare

The woman from upstairs was in the garage shop. For a moment, I had the stupid idea that she'd followed me. I've seen her several times in places I hadn't expected to; last month I could have sworn I caught sight of her Fuengirola. For a while I thought Frankie and

63

Rick had hired a private detective to track me down. But it's obvious from Frankie's questions she thinks I'm still in the UK. Commonsense tells me it's just a coincidence; there are only so many places you can shop around here.

Rather than go directly home, I crossed over the road and walked down to Casares beach. It's virtually deserted and I have the bay to myself. Even the beach café is closed this early in the season. It was a café like this one where Rick and I worked the summer I was eighteen. We spent our nights serving lethal cocktails to tourists and our days in bed. Rick was the love of my life. And I was his. Along with Tanya, Rosie, Katya, Carmen and Sheena as it turned out. But I was a late developer; Rick was my first one and I naively assumed we were in a monogamous relationship until Katya put me straight. By that time it was October and summer had died in more ways than one.

We kept in casual touch for the next twelve years; hence the wedding invitation. It was odd seeing him in his morning suit, looking shy and uncertain. 'Who'd have thought it, eh Tad? Me, married man and—hopefully—family guy. Surrogate willing.' He read my expression. 'Frankie had cancer. She's had a complete hysterectomy, ovaries as well.'

'And you don't mind?'

'Sure I mind. Until she told me we couldn't

have kids, I didn't realise how much I wanted them. But I want Frankie more. The fact she can't carry my kids isn't a factor. We'll find someone else to carry them. They'll still be mine, biologically.'

I hadn't intended to, but I find myself walking along the edge of water, following the curve of the bay around to Sabinillas. The extra weight and soft sand make it hard to keep my balance and I find myself having to place my feet very carefully. A couple with a bunch of dogs appear from somewhere. When an over-enthusiastic terrier tries to jump up at me, I have to twist and dance out of his way. It turns me around, and I discover that her-upstairs is a few hundred yards behind me on the wet sand. Damn it, perhaps the wretched woman *is* following me.

Anne

She went for a walk along the beach. Following her, it's hard to believe she's pregnant. She's carrying no extra weight on her back. From behind the only clue is that ten-to-two waddle. She nearly lost her balance when a dog went for her. I don't suppose a fall on wet sand would have been dangerous, but it gave me a nasty turn. If she goes into labour out there, it will be too late. Some interfering idiot will call an ambulance. My baby will become her baby. I can't let that happen.

Clare

They've changed their minds on the names again.

'We've both decided we prefer Lucca for a boy. What do you think?'

'Lucca's fine.'

'You are coming home for the birth, aren't you?' Frankie asks. 'We can come and fetch you. Just tell us where?'

Before I can reply, Rick's hands appear on her shoulders and he moves her away from the camera. 'Hi Tad. Listen, I know you don't want us to hassle you on this, but I do have a stake in this baby. We would really appreciate it if you let us be there at the birth. How about it?'

He produces that quirky, little boy, grin, that always got him whatever he wanted from me. The hot flush of need spreads through me. Maybe that's why I first suggested this. The chance for one last time of glorious sex in a warm bedroom while the sun threw afternoon shadows on the white ceiling. The reality turned out to be a highly unromantic gift of lubricating jelly and a turkey baster.

'No. I have to do this my own way. When the baby is here, I'll call you. If you don't hear from me for a couple of days, you'll know things are moving.'

The blast of the door bell startles us both. It's so unexpected at this end that for a moment I think it's his, until Rick says. 'Who's that?'

'No idea. I have to go.'

Switching off the laptop, I check the spy-hole. Her-upstair's face looms large and fish-eyed in the circle. What the heck does she want?'

Anne

After the incident on the beach, we both walked on into Sabinillas. She stopped at one of the bars along the promenade. I passed as if I hadn't noticed her and continued on to the Sun Sol supermarket. I bought a selection of fruit, a bottle of wine, and several fruit cordials. I need an excuse for calling on her. I want to check that bathroom.

Clive always admired my meticulous planning. I'd draft every itinerary down to the last detail. Nothing was ever left to chance. It's the secret of success, you have to have a method, think things through, leave nothing to chance. As soon as I made up my mind to do this, I made plans for the disposal of the body. Can you tell me the logic behind cutting out a baby and leaving the mother's body on full view looking like an alien has just burst out of her stomach? It stands to reason it's going to trigger a full scale police alert.

Clive's company covered the globe in cheap boxes, to enable Clive and family to live in a large, solidly constructed mansion. At least it means I know my way around a site. They don't work Sundays here. I shall leave her in the foundations somewhere and pour concrete. When the workmen turn up, there'll be a row about who poured the stuff when it wasn't in the schedule, but they'll eventually decide to work round it. Builders never make work for themselves, if they can avoid it.

Selecting several peaches, a couple of oranges, and a bottle of cordial, I walk downstairs.

Clare

I only just remembered to take my wig off in time. I had to hide it behind my back when I opened the door to her-upstairs. She'd brought me some fruit and bottle of raspberry stuff. My near fall on the beach seems to have nudged her conscience. I have an open invitation to call her, any time of the day or night, if I think the baby's coming. However it turned out she had an ulterior motive; she wanted to know when I was leaving because she thought my apartment would suit a friend. There's dozens of similar flats outside, what on earth does she want this one for? Anyway, I told her I'd be gone by the end of the week. God, she's ugly. I wonder if anyone ever

68

fancied her?

Anne

Clive left his wife two weeks after their youngest girl's sixteenth birthday. The following week, he suggested it was time we ended our relationship—both personal and professional. He gave me a generous severance payment; like I was a very expensive whore on contract. When his divorce came through he married a bimbo of twenty six who could have been his wife's double. I was forty four and already menopausal; bastard, bastard, bastard!

I tried all the usual routes for the childless. Privately funded IVF at dubious clinics. UK and foreign adoption agencies happy to consider me if I'd be prepared to take a teenager, or a handicapped child? No I wouldn't. I wanted a baby; a soft warm body that would look at me with unconditional love.

And finally, an illegal adoption from Romania; complete with a fake British passport.

'Baby boy, ready in six weeks,' the broker had explained. 'His mother not want. Ten thousand pounds cash, complete package. Half now, half when you have baby.'

I flew out with the passport and baby clothes hidden in the bottom of my suitcase. I'd already chosen a name: Aaron George.

There were four of us on the trip. Another middle aged woman and a thirty-something couple. They collected us from our hotel in a ramshackle mini-bus and drove us out into the country. Somewhere, well away from the town, the bus was stopped by a collection of scruffy men with bad teeth and knives conspicuously sticking from their waistbands. They explained that the police had become aware of this business deal so it was not safe to proceed. As they had expenses however, they felt it was only fair we handed over the other five thousand pounds. I guess they realised we weren't going to complain to the Romanian Office of Fair Trading. The other three cried on the way back; at least I held out until I was back in my room.

It's odd how fate works out. I'd accepted I'd never have a baby now. I'd driven down here because it was where I'd planned to take my son. With just his baby clothes and the fake passport as a reminder of his ghost, I was going to say goodbye here. And then and I opened my shutters and there she was on the terrace—ripe and plump—just like the peaches.

Taking the filleting knife, I test its sharpness on the fruit. Their suede skin feels like warm flesh; it splits in a straight line and the flesh bursts out. I think it's time.

Clare

This will be my last video call before I go off-line for the birth. I get things set up and pause for a minute to picture the final call, when I introduce Rick to his son. I already know it's going to be a boy. I imagine myself cradling the small bundle, wrapped in his little knitted blue suit and the cutest pair of bootees you ever saw. I can visualise Rick's face as he sees his baby for the very first time.

I'll let him look for a few minutes. And then I'll let him watch as I put my hand over it's mouth and slowly smother his fucking kid to death.

Anne

She didn't open the door when I rang. Her car is still parked outside, so she hadn't left yet. Maybe she'd collapsed or something. I have a horrible picture of her haemorrhaging my baby out.

'Hello? Are you all right in there? Do you need any help?' I hit the door with a balled fist. There's no letter-box, I can't even peek inside. 'Hello, hello. Are you okay?'

To my relief, I hear the lock being turned and the door swings open. For a moment I think all my planning has been for nothing; the one thing I hadn't allowed for has happened. She's invited a friend to join her. Then she

71

spoke.

'What do you want?'

'I, em . . . didn't recognise you.'

She looks puzzled and snatches off the spectacles and wig, thrusting fingers through her light brown hair so that it stands out in soft spikes. 'I forgot. I'm trying out a new look. Did you want something?'

I held out my bag. The wine bottle is protruding from the top. The knife is safely out of sight in the bottom. 'Since we're both leaving, I thought we could have a goodbye drink. One glass won't hurt the baby.'

'Thanks. But it's not convenient. I have things to do.'

Packing no doubt. 'Just a quick glass.' I can see the refusal forming on her face, so I force my way into the room. It's another advantage of being this size. 'I'll pour shall I? Are the glasses in here?' The kitchen is just a galley off the sitting room, I'd got the cupboards open and two large wine glasses out before she could object. I pour out and, as I'm righting the bottle, I leave a trail of liquid over the unit surface. 'Oops, sorry. Have you got a cloth?'

She turns away to snatch sheets from the kitchen roll dispenser and I pull the knife out of the carrier. I intend to stab her high in the back where it will miss the baby, but the knife gets tangled in the plastic of the bag. I'm holding the blade above my head when she swings back. She looks upwards. 'What are you

. . .' I bring it down hard into her chest and hear the air grunt out of her lungs.

Clare

'Where did you get it?'

'Theatrical costumier,' I've already unhooked the back fastening and now the full weight of the pregnancy suit is hanging from my neck. Ducking my head, I slip out of it and it joins my ripped dress on the floor. The thick padding and canvas backing had taken most of the force of the thrust and boning had deflected the blade. I was going to end up with one hell of a bruise over my ribs. 'You add padding as you want it. I only intended to wear it in here when I was on-line. But I started to like the way it made me feel. People treat you differently when you're pregnant. You're special. A bringer of life.'

'So there was never a baby?'

'No.' Despite the fact I'm standing here in my underwear and she's the one clutching the knife, I feel like the one in control. She looks pathetic sitting at the dining table with tears sliding down her face. 'And there never will be for me. My bastard first boyfriend gave me gonorrhoea. By the time it was detected, it was way too late. They hollowed me out; womb, tubes, ovaries, the lot.' I had the op in Australia. No-one back home knew. How do you tell people you're diseased; a sterile piece

73

of meat? Infertility from cancer is noble; clap isn't.

I told her about Rick and Frankie and the surrogate baby. 'I paid a pregnant junkie for her pee. Twenty quid and you too can have positive pregnancy test. I wanted Rick to spend months looking forward to the birth. I wanted him to see his son. And then I wanted him to watch while his kid was smothered and feel the worse pain he'd ever felt. The kind I felt when they told me I'd never have a child.'

'It wasn't the girl's fault. Don't you feel guilty about her?'

'You've just tried to murder me and you're asking if *I* have a conscience?'

'I'm sorry. I just so needed . . .' She didn't finish but I knew exactly what she was feeling. The emptiness that no-one can understand. 'How were you planning to kill a baby that doesn't exist?' she asked.

I opened a drawer in the living area and heard her catch her breath. I did the same the first time I saw the doll. *The most lifelike ever created*, the advertisement had said. And it was. The flushed skin, the tiny fingernails, the downy eyelashes, you'd have sworn it was alive. Particularly if you were viewing it through the obscuring curtain of a gauze covered lens. I switched on the laptop and camera and stood before it, the baby in my arms. With a hand cradled under it, I could make the head and legs appear to move. I fired up an audio program on the disc and a baby's cries filled the room. I'd rehearsed this sequence endlessly. As the cries reached a crescendo, I put my fingers over the mouth. The sound changed, muffled whimpers, gradually faded to silence.

'They'll call the police,' she points out. As if I might have overlooked that fact.

'They'll look for Clare Nicola West, long blonde hair, wears glasses. But I was married briefly in Australia; I have a passport that says I'm Nikki Fox, complete with a new photo.' I shrugged. 'And if the police ever do catch up with me, it'll be obvious there never was a baby. Just a nasty practical joke from a barren witch. What's your defence going to be?'

As I say it, I realise I may have over-calculated my power. She's still the one with the knife and I'm the only witness. Dumb move Clare.

Anne

I think this is my favourite time of day. Early morning when the courtyard is pleasantly warm before the Moroccan sun scorches it and the only sounds are the trickle of the small fountain and calls to prayer. I ease open the map and use the coffee pot and a dish of ripe apricots to weight it down.

Nibbling on a fresh croissant, I scan the jigsaw of countries until I hear footsteps on the flagstones and look up. 'You shouldn't walk around barefoot, you never know what's crawling around out here.'

'Don't nag,' Clare says with an affectionate grin. Helping herself to an apricot, she sucks out the flesh and looks over the map. 'I saw that girl in the Souk again. Eight months gone at least. And off her face on whatever. It would be a kindness to the kid.'

'No. We agreed. It's too close to home. We'll take the ferry from Ceuta and look elsewhere. Croatia perhaps. Or Greece.'

We both turn towards the house at the sound of indignant yell. Clare is quicker than me. 'My turn.' She comes back cradling a wriggling bundle who is trying to climb down and walk by himself. Aaron is nearly eighteen months old now. It really is time we found him a brother or sister. And we know the plan works.

THE NETHER WORLD

Paul A Freeman

I breathe on my hands to warm them, then fix a hook into the top of the manhole cover. Positioning my feet either side of the iron lid, I heave. The cover comes free and I inch it aside until the aperture beneath is revealed in all its mystery. The upper rungs of a ladder are all we can see clearly. They disappear into oblivion.

Detective Constable Helen Alcott leans across, forcing me out of the way. Her face is now directly in line with the steaming sewage gases escaping into the frigid night air. 'What a pong!' she says, wrinkling her nose.

Detective Inspector Harold Moore pushes his subordinate aside and shines a torch into the dark, gaping shaft. 'Are you sure this is the right place, Mr Jenkins?' he asks me. 'The sewer isn't backed up here.'

Sure enough, there's a gentle flow of fetid liquid running along the runnel beneath the ladder.

'The Sanitation Department's had a cluster of blockages reported in this general vicinity,' I reply. 'The cause of the blockages must be somewhere close by.'

The two police officers glance at each

other and exchange a look of grim understanding. They know what we're likely to find and they're not looking forward to the discovery. In the moonlight they appear pale, and as they suit up, D.C. Alcott shivers—though not because of the cold.

'Ladies first!' I volunteer, but my jocular offer is not taken up.

Therefore, I'm the first to leave 'Topside', as we sanitation engineers call the surface. I secure my tool belt. Then, I lower myself into the portal leading to that strange, subterranean world of passages and galleries below our feet.

Each of us wears a hard hat equipped with a lamp, and as we descend into the darkness, shafts of light leap about crazily, making fantastic, eerie shadows.

'Are you sure you're up to this, Mr Jenkins?' asks D.I. Moore. There's the suggestion of a tremor to his voice. 'After all, it's your first day back on the job, sir.'

With a splash I jump off the bottom rung of the ladder and smile up as the reluctant police officers follow me into what I call my Nether World. We make a strange trio, dressed as we are in the jolly orange coveralls of the Sanitation Department. However, unlike mine, theirs bulge at the hip pocket, an indication that D.I. Moore and D.C. Alcott are taking no chances.

'I'll be fine,' I reply airily to the detective

inspector's question. All the same, I finger my right thigh—a dead giveaway that I'm *not* fine. It's my first trip below since Sewer Man, the country's most wanted serial killer, stabbed me and left me for dead down here. 'Don't worry about me. I'm just as eager as you two to catch the son-of-a . . . gun,' I say, remembering there's a lady amongst us. Yet my words are all bluff and show. In my mind I'm replaying my near fatal brush with death.

*   *   *

Victims of the killer nicknamed Sewer Man started showing up a couple of months ago. They were dismembered, stuffed into sewer outlet pipes. No one would have cared that much, for the victims were vagrants, tramps, bag ladies—the scum of polite society, really. However, their body parts were blocking outlet pipes, thereby affecting the everyday lives of those respectable citizens living Topside. For one thing, sewage was backing up and overflowing onto the streets. For another, the stench of diluted urine and faecal matter made those respectable Topsiders heave up their guts.

Which brings me back to my one-on-one encounter with the mysterious Sewer Man. After a second body was discovered (and after the police had made a perfunctory sweep of the sewer system), another suspicious sewage backup occurred. There was an off chance that Sewer Man had been at work again. So, to show they were taking the situation seriously, the municipality sent me—their Chief Sanitation Engineer—underground to investigate. And to make sure I wasn't shirking, I was accompanied by an ambitious and adventurous young councilman.

As we worked our way towards the area of the blockage, we came across the occasional rat-gnawed finger or toe—proof that Sewer Man was up to his old tricks again. These clues eventually led us to an elevated outlet pipe. It was sealed closed with the head and torso of an unfortunate bag lady, like a cork stopping up a champagne bottle.

'What was she doing down here in the first place?' asked the horrified councilman before disgorging his breakfast.

I explained: 'When it gets too cold to sleep out in the open Topside, transients come down here to the Nether World. They relish the warmth given off as bacteria munch their way through human waste.'

Leaving the councilman to a second bout of nausea, I wandered off in search of Bag Lady's arms and legs. It was then that Sewer Man, lurking in the darkness, chose his moment. The councilman didn't have a chance. By the time I could respond to his screams, he was dead, his head virtually sawn off his shoulders, his blood further moistening the already slimy floor.

The sight of the carnage before my eyes must have distracted me. For how else could Sewer Man have sneaked up from behind? With one hand over my mouth he quietened me, and with a serrated blade in the other he stabbed me deep in the thigh. The attack was swift and silent. I didn't even glimpse my assailant.

How I managed to crawl Topside without bleeding to death, I'll never know. The upshot: Sewer Man's tally was now four dead, one wounded. And it stayed that way for nigh on a month, too, while I recovered in hospital. Perhaps the city's vagrants thought it better to freeze to death Topside, rather than risk the warmth of Nether World where Sewer Man might be stalking them.

Yet, when I was released from hospital and lay at home recuperating, Sewer Man struck again. Once more the city was afflicted by the all too familiar scenario of backed up sewers. This, plus the fact that the fourth of the five victims had been an upright councilman, resulted in me being pressed into service by the police, to guide them through the subterranean maze that comprises the city's sewer system.

*   *   *

Myself and the two police officers make our

way along the elevated walkway of an arching tunnel. A river of sewage flows inches from our feet. Detective Constable Alcott is disgusted by my dark, claustrophobic Nether World. She treads carefully, as though walking in a Topside park where dogs run off the leash. As a rat scampers past, she squeals louder than the rodent and presses herself against the tunnel wall.

'Rats and roaches,' I inform D.C. Alcott, 'are the sanitary engineer's only company in Nether World. And before you ask, there aren't any crocodiles in the tunnels, flushed down the loo by inconsiderate pet owners. That's an urban myth.'

D.C. Alcott looks relieved, so I add cheekily, 'There might be the odd alligator, though.'

D.I. Moore chortles at his colleague's unease, and once she's done cursing us, we continue on our way.

Even though my thigh throbs interminably, I remain in upbeat mood. 'The blockage is somewhere up ahead,' I explain. 'Somewhere around the main gallery.'

Knowing we're nearing our goal, we become more alert. All joking is put aside. We strain our eyes and ears for any sight or sound. We hear the tinkling trickle of sewage water and the scurry of tiny rodent feet—but that's all.

At last we reach the gallery—a vaulted,

brick atrium at the heart of the sewer system. Sewage water is pouring in from the outlet pipes that ring its circumference. In a swirling vortex the brown, soup-like fluid disappears down a sink hole at the centre.

'This is where all the city's sewage collects before being sent to treatment plants,' I yell over the cacophony of noise.

'Not *all* the city's sewage,' D.I. Moore corrects me, shining his lamp up at two of the gallery's outlet pipes.

Just as the councilman did while in my care a month ago, D.C. Alcott vomits at the horrible sight before her.

'Sewage Man's getting more confident,' says the detective inspector. 'He's nailed two victims this time.'

Indeed, plugging each of the two outlet pipes is a human torso. The heads (one male, one female, and both still attached to their trunks) are staring out lifelessly over the gallery that has now become a crime scene.

'Seems those two were living down here,' D.I. Moore conjectures, indicating two mattresses and a bundle of clothing lying on the elevated walkway below the human remains. 'What do you reckon? A husband and wife?'

D.C. Alcott manages a nod of agreement before throwing up again.

'What's that beside their clothes?' I ask.

It looks like a pile of firewood, but when

D.I. Moore moves closer and realises it's a heap of neatly stacked human limbs, he almost loses his stomach contents, too.

As the police officers compose themselves and pull on latex gloves to examine the various evidences, I take a back seat. This is their investigation and I'm superfluous to their crime scene. Yet, while I'm observing them, I notice a movement out of the corner of my eye. I turn and my lamp catches a shadow flitting into a side passage.

Not sure exactly what I've seen, I leave D.I. Moore and D.C. Alcott to their task and slip away to investigate.

The passageway is narrow, with a slippery floor. A stream of sewage water runs down the middle and as I watch out for my footing, I lose sight of that enigmatic shadow. The passage reaches a junction and, taking my courage in my hands, I put my head around the corner and look to my left. Nothing! Then I swiftly turn my head to the right and give a start that has more to do with terror than with surprise.

A man, about my height and dressed in an identical orange coverall, is no more than five yards away. His dark eyes are glowering at me from a featureless face. It's him. I recognise him now.

'Have you brought me more offerings?' asks Sewer Man. 'I hunger for company in this Nether World of darkness.'

I nod, dumbly.

He points towards the pouch on my tool belt. I open the Velcro clasp, but instead of my screwdriver, I pull out a blood-encrusted knife with a serrated blade.

'Kill the policeman first,' commands Sewer Man, this evil mirror image of my genial self. 'Then take your time with the woman. Slice her up nice and leisurely. And don't get any ideas about a guilty conscience—not like you did over that councilman. Just remember that when you stab yourself, you're stabbing me, too.'

DIRTY, EVIL GREED

Karline Smith

Bethel Town, Parish of Westmoreland, Jamaica, West Indies

Thursday 29th July, 1976. 17.30 hours.

Cherry-Lynne came on Sundays; Chevonne on Monday, Adele Tuesdays, Wednesday was Terri's turn, Thursday Cameira, Friday Donna-Marie and Saturday Isabella. Whatever their backgrounds, Indian, Chinese, Lebanese, Portuguese, Uncle Beckford wasn't fussy. His nine-year-old nephew watched their comings and goings curiously.

Beckford 'Sweet-Boy' McKinley was the sole inheritor of his wife Avia's fortune acquired through JJ Ginger Beer, one of Jamaica's finest, and suddenly he was the most popular guy in town.

Cameira Chin's boyfriend dropped her off to her sugar daddy's Westmoreland home. She stepped out of his newly-sprayed pride and joy 1967 Triumph, wearing her short school uniform skirt, which showed off two beautiful long peanut-brown legs, and a blouse that was way too small for her well-developed grade-eleven breasts. Her hair was parted in two long ponytails. Swaying seductively on tall platform shoes, she walked towards the huge house.

Beckford met her at the back entrance, watching her with licentious green eyes surrounded by lightly tanned Caribbean skin. She was his favourite, especially as he was rumoured to be the father of her two-month-old baby daughter. Laughing, like his last winning number on the lotto had come up, he carried her straight up to the master bedroom on the first floor. The boy heard the sounds of frenetic lovemaking. The king-size cast-iron bed he had shared with his late wife beating furiously against the polished wooden floor and walls. Then the telephone in the main reception room began to ring. There weren't many people in the district with a telephone. Beckford had had one installed the day after Avia died.

'Hello?' the boy spoke into the phone, his voice echoing on the line as if the person was in another dimension of time and space. The caller wanted to speak urgently to the boy's uncle so the boy knocked on Beckford's door nervously. Annoyed at the interruption, Beckford's curse came out like a whine. 'Chuh . . . come . . . come in,' he said. As the boy entered the room, his eyes round and glued to the huge protrusion between Beckford's thighs, under the sheets, Beckford's mood altered. He smiled playfully. 'Come here little man.'

The boy took two shaky steps forward, holding the phone for Beckford to plug into the extension socket. Beckford threw the phone down carelessly. He was pushing some white powder under his nostrils, sniffing hard, and giving a sharp moan. 'No. Come more closer . . . 'pon de bed . . . that's right.' The boy sat next to his naked uncle, feeling sick, not wanting to look. Beckford caressed the boy's cheek. 'What yuh 'fraid for? Open yu eyes. Look at her. She beautiful, isn't she?' He laughed roughly, lighting a cigar. 'Here tek some of dis.' The boy took the cigar. Coughing as he inhaled, he handed it back to his uncle who exchanged it for a shot of rum. 'Drink it slow.' The boy, eyes still watery, took a careful drink and coughed some more. Beckford laughed, like a strangled hyena, slapping his thigh heartily. 'Little man, tonight is de night, ya becomes a big man.'

Suddenly the boy leapt off the bed. Pleasure quickly turned to confusion as Beckford traced the boy's terrified stare to the handgun in the girl's hand, aimed directly at his chest. Naked, with her hands steady and direct, Cameira Chin backed away from the bed slowly.

'Hey, bitch, come pull gun pon me? What is this? Bwoy, run go call sergeant Robinson. Quick!' Beckford switched his attention back to the girl, stuttering. 'Whah—what yuh want? Money? Jewellery? Heh? How much money?

N—N- Name your price.'

The girl cocked the hammer. Beckford started to weep deliriously. 'Please, heh, please don't shoot me . . . please. I will do anyt'ing. I *beg* you. Please . . .'

Smiling slowly, Cameira Chin squeezed the trigger with delicate precision.

The .45 bullet ripped through muscle, bone and flesh.

The silk white bed sheets spread dark crimson like a bloody eclipse.

She then angled the gun towards the hysterical boy.

*   *   *

Six Weeks Previously . . .

Still, so silent. Not even a breeze blowing along the dusty road. The boy had been vigilant for the last five minutes, which seemed like forever, with the clear glass jar poised steadily over the unsuspecting victim. In all his nine years, he had never seen one as huge as this. Covered in shades of brown and black speckles, it was the perfect addition for his small collection of spiders, bullfrogs and lizards, hidden in a perforated shoebox under the space between the veranda and the pimento tree. His heart slammed hard against his ribs excitedly, momentarily stalling the breath in his lungs.

Sandy, the boy's Labrador puppy, started

yapping curiously. But after a swift rebuke from her master, she became silent. Sweating lightly, the boy slammed the glass jar down over the scorpion on the ground, trapping the arachnid inside. He turned the glass over and screwed the lid shut.

His joyful laughter climbed all the way to the sky, rolling with the distant sound of thunder in the green Westmoreland hills, in the Jamaican Mid-West.

*   *   *

'Bwoy? How many times I have to tell you to come straight home from school?' The raw slap across the face took him by surprise. Miss Avia, bony-looking and black-skinned, was waiting for him at the top of the road that led to the place known as home, a vast seven bedroom white house set in an acre of land, 'And didn't I tell you to stop encourage that bag of fleas to come to the house?'

The boy adjusted his school satchel over the shoulder of his khaki school uniform nervously. He was in deep trouble. If he had left the scorpion, he wouldn't have been late. And he could not force himself to get rid of the beautiful dog he had found at the crossroads near Miss Jessie's shop. He hoped the letter he was about to give her would save him the torturous pain of a thick, heavy leather belt across his back and legs, burning through his flesh, until his mind faded to darkness. Yet, only a fifth grader, he was top of the school with the best exam results in the whole history of the school. Principal Thomas had already submitted his application to the Education Board for the boy to take his Common Entrance Examination a year earlier. There was no doubt. He was destined to go to one of Jamaica's top secondary schools.

'Ma'am, see, I make you proud.' The letter stayed in his shaking outstretched hand. Her dark eyes roved over him oddly. Uncle Beckford joined them from the house, looking tired and haggard. Miss Avia turned around and looked at him. The boy saw the strange look that passed between husband and wife. Miss Avia turned and walked away.

'Yu sister . . . Kara, she . . . dead.' His uncle said solemnly, 'Little man, I'm so sorry.'

The school letter fell from the boy's hand.

He watched it flutter away in the breeze, like a little bird flying away freely.

And he felt the first wet drops of a heavy storm falling on his face.

*   *   *

Thursday 29th July, 1976. 21.00 hours.

'The Westmoreland Homicide Unit is investigating the circumstances surrounding the gun murder of two unidentified persons, one male and one female, on Lily Rose

91

Gardens, Bethel Town, this evening. Reports from the CCN's Metro Officer are that about 6:35 p.m., the gardener, who lives in the grounds of the house, heard explosions coming from inside the house. Following the explosions, a young man, in his late teens or early twenties, was seen running from the house. The police were summoned and, on their arrival, a youth was found with gunshot wounds, outside. Reports are also coming in that a nine-year-old boy has also been shot, but it is unknown whether the boy survived at this present time. Residents are said to be shocked, and have described the scene, as a house of horror. It is understood that the deceased man's family belong to the well-known ginger beer company Johnnie Johnson, operating since 1850, whose co-director Avia McKinley née Johnson, said to be the murdered man's wife, died only recently. We will give you an update as soon as we have more information. This is Jasper Emmanuel McFarlane, reporting for Radio Jamaica, live, at 9.02 p.m.'

*   *   *

Circles, spreading, until they faded with each new stone thrown in the sparkling water. This was the boy's sanctuary; a tranquil place near the river, yet distant from the echoic voices of washerwomen and people bathing. Dressed in

92

cut off jeans and a red t-shirt, he was safe here, throwing stones in the river, lying for hours with books he had borrowed from Westmoreland's main library, sprawled out in the long grass on his front, Sandy curled asleep beside him, safe from Miss Avia's beatings. It was already late afternoon.

'Momma?' It was just the sound of the bush rustling fooling him. Momma had passed two years ago and that's why they had ended up with his uncle and his harsh wife Avia. Momma never, ever beat him. She was beautiful, patient, and loving. His longing for her was as intense as the day she passed and now his elder sister Kara had gone there was a void in his soul that would never be filled. Before Kara died, he had not seen her for weeks. Uncle Beckford and Miss Avia had said Kara was ill and couldn't be disturbed. Perhaps the same sickness took Momma.

A deeper rustling sound from the bush brought him out of his mournful trance. Looking around quickly he saw thin, five-year-old Willie from next door, watching him inquisitively.

'What you want, Winkie?' The older boy asked, closing his book and squinting in the bright Saturday afternoon sun. Sandy stirred awake and yawned.

'Miss Avia seh yuh fe go ah Miss Jessie shop and buy sugar and milk. Here, see twenty dollar. She seh mek sure you bring back de change and don't buy no sweetie or she gwine tear de skin offa ya red backside. And me name is Willie. Not

Winkie.'

The boy recited the rhyme that he knew Willie hated.

'Wee Willie Winkie runnin' through Westmoreland town, upstairs and downstairs in his mother's nightgown, tapping at the window and pissin' through the lock . . .'

Willie tossed the money at the water's edge and sped through the bushes, laughing.

The older boy fished the wet twenty-dollar bill out of the river and gave chase.

*   *   *

Thursday 29th July, 1976. 21.01 hours.

Sergeant Danville 'Biggs' Robinson, unlit cigar dangling from his dry chapped lips, closed the door firmly on his green series III Land-Rover. The vehicle was parked outside 34 Lilly-Rose Gardens, Bethel Town, five miles from the main police H.Q., just after nine p.m. A radio reporter from R.J.R was covering the incident live for their hourly news bulletin. As the family were renowned in the district, there were also print journalists from The Jamaican Gleaner and The Star. Danville heard the radio journalist talking about a 'house of horror' as he stared intently at an unseen audience.

Danville spat on the ground. A small crowd of locals had gathered and he heard one or two muttering about a curse on the McKinley family, a rift that went back to the poorer side of the McKinley clan, from Clarendon and Port Royal. At times like these, rumours about curses or *Obeah* were always rife.

Danville had been informed that the bodies were still in the house. The McKinleys' gardener, a man in his sixties, had just given a statement to Police Constable Watson. A male medic was treating a third person, a young man of twenty, in an ambulance nearby. He had received shots to the shoulder and arm but was still alive and conscious.

The blue and red lights of two patrol cars sliced through the pitch-blackness like a supernatural phenomenon. Above the hum of human life, Danville heard the rhythmic song of the crickets, and saw fireflies dancing in the main beam from Watson's police car headlights.

Danville was also accompanied by his youngest son, O'Neill Jacob Robinson, a graduate in Psychology and Medicine, who had just completed Phase 1 of the G.E.P. Law and Police Procedures, and was now on Phase 2: Detachment. His detachment included shadowing a local police station, which just happened to be the station where his father was the Commanding Officer.

Danville had not wanted O'Neill to continue the apparent family tradition of entering the Jamaica Constabulary Force.

Initially, he had been pleased when his son had said he wanted to become a Physician, for he had already lost two other sons to brutal gunmen via separate bloody and violent incidents and did not wish his only remaining son to suffer the same fate. He didn't know when, or what, had changed his son's mind, but O'Neill had been persistent. At 21 years of age, O'Neill was tall, brown and exceptionally handsome. He walked self-assuredly, some might say arrogantly, alongside his father. As both men headed towards the house, Danville sensed that O'Neill was tense. Danville lit the cigar, inhaled, and then blew out leisurely, studying his boy.

'You ready?' He asked.

Swallowing deeply, O'Neill nodded.

*   *   *

'Shop!' The boy hit his palm loudly on the counter in the traditional, yet improper to an outsider, way of informing the shopkeeper Miss Jessie he wished to be served, but there was no sign of her. The local mini-mart was empty of people and nearly empty of stock. Due to the current political simmering, coupled with the export of foreign products, there was a shortage of basic consumer goods such as soap, flour, cooking oil, and rice. The crime rate, spawned by widespread unemployment, was high and destabilizing activities from outside and within,

was threatening to leave the country bankrupt, and on the verge of a state of anarchy. There was demoralisation seeping from every corner.

'Pressure Drop' by Toots and the Maytals poured from a battered radio chained to the wall in the corner. The music stopped as the DJ cheerfully announced that the time was three twenty in the afternoon and the temperature outside was ninety degrees and still rising.

The boy looked down at the pint of goat's milk (Miss Avia was allergic to cow's milk) and then suddenly remembered the sugar. He walked away from the counter just as a local woman entered the shop. As he sauntered down the aisle towards where the sugar was stored, he saw the shelf with the comics. He could barely contain his excitement. Miss Jessie had finally done it! She got some comics he had requested.

The boy picked up a comic called The X-Men and skimmed through the pages. He was desperate for the comic but he had no money. Disheartened, he put the comic back and turned to walk towards the counter. Suddenly he froze. Someone, on the other side of the aisle, had mentioned his dead sister's name. His heart raced, pumping blood around his body furiously.

'Kara . . . just start High School last year an' was doing good. She was good friends with me lickle granddaughter, Lorna.' Miss Jessie's distinctive rasping voice continued. 'Same thing happen to the live-in maid they had, a fifteen-years-old Chinese girl from Savannah-la-mar.

Hear seh she get the work to help out the family the next thing she get pregnant . . . I hear the baby was for Beckford . . . and when her belly started to show Miss Avia fling her out . . . warn her that no decent household in Westmoreland going to employ her again as a maid becauh she going to spread the word that the girl is a worthless, man-stealing whore . . . Avia seh the girl was after Beckford from day one . . .'

'But a twelve-year-old little girl who just start High School? Eh? His niece? Eh? His own flesh and blood for God's sake? What Avia got to say about dat?'

'Avia? Avia know all along what Beckford was doing to dat child. Them try fe keep it quiet but my friend Macey is a friend of Avia's brother, Doctor Johnson and him wife Coretta, and she seh when the girl give birth after three days and nights of labour, the baby dead. The girl body just blow up like when pumpkin over ripe and after five minutes she just dead . . . too late to get de minister . . . Blood . . . everywhere . . . blood . . . God rest her soul. She must have died in pain and agony . . . and Lord, Lord . . . Lord so much sin.'

*　　　*　　　*

Thursday 29th July, 1976. 21.05 hours.

Five hundred dollar bills, scattered around the room, like paper in a tornado. That was the

98

first thing Danville Robinson noticed. His eyes travelled over the death scene, flitting impassively from one thing to the next, a myriad of significant actions. A half-smoked cigar on the floor. An overturned bottle of clear white rum. Blood splattered over the walls like a red sea mural painted by a demented artist. The small, bloody and bare footprints of the boy zigzagging towards the front door in frantic shock. Cocaine scattered everywhere like snow. The tumbled-over drinking glasses and clothes shed in a hungry-for-sex trail towards the bed. The young girl, lying naked, with punctured holes from gunshots in her chest and face. The older man, nude, skin salt-white drained of blood, one leg kicked akimbo, the other tucked at an awkward angle beneath the body, looking as if he had attempted vainly to get up and run. His eyes were glaring wide in a petrified gaze probably at the exact moment when he had opened his bowels.

Death knows no dignity.

And even if he closed his eyes, Biggs knew he could smell it too, blood, fear, greed, sex and death.

Beckford Louie McKinley. A friend since '65. Who came to the club regularly to fraternise, play dominoes, smoke speciality hand-wrapped flavoured cigars, and to talk about their favourite subject, politics, Edward Seaga versus Michael Manley and the sorry state of the country. *Who's a fucken sorry state now?* Danville puffed heavily on his cigar. It was bad that his close associate had died in this horrible way.

He turned to ask O'Neill what his initial thoughts were.

O'Neill was hunched up in a corner, one hand on the wall supporting his shaking body, vomiting out his soul.

* * *

Avia Gloria McKinley sat under the cool shade of the screen-netted veranda, in her cane swing chair, swinging, waiting . . . annoyed. She had been waiting almost an hour since she sent mahgar Willie next door with the message for the boy to get the milk and sugar from Miss Jessie's. She would never have taken in her sister-in-law's children if Beckford hadn't beaten her into agreeing. She knew he wouldn't be around to take responsibility for the children, leaving it all up to her. All he did was work late each night and then come in drunk from 'business meetings', like tonight. Well the boy would get it today and get it good. She had pulled a perfect thin branch from a tree nearby for him and his blatant disrespect.

Miss Avia was not poor nor was she unintelligent. Wealth was in her family, owing to their unique recipe for ginger beer. From day one, her family had been against her marrying the

100

destitute but stunningly handsome Beckford McKinley, even if he was tall, and light enough to pass as white. She had loved Beckford from the first time they met. And once Beckford had married into money he suddenly became incredibly fashionable, always dressing in the latest flared trousers, platform shoes, jewellery and tight fitting open-neck shirts, with his hair styled in the up-to-the-minute Afro hairstyle and sideburns. He worked out in the gym frequently, which made him look fifteen years younger than his forty-two years. And at twelve years his senior, Miss Avia was often mistaken for his mother!

She guessed her family were right when they warned her that his peasant family would plague her with constant begging. She soon learned how to ignore them and the threats of Obeah that followed.

Five years ago, when she thought she was entering the menopause with no chance of having children, they had Levi. Overjoyed, Miss Avia had had grand ambitions for her only son, college, The Norman Manley School of Law at the University of the West Indies. But Levi was far behind his peer group and despite assurances from her brother, Doctor Abel Johnson, that everything was OK she knew, felt it from somewhere deep inside, that everything wasn't. When the child was three-years-old, on a loud stormy day, she pushed him outside and slammed the front door, hoping he would call out to her and scream to be let in. Fifteen minutes later, when she opened the door, Levi was still standing there, not making a sound, stone cold and wet. Tests at Kingston's University Hospital confirmed he had autism. Miss Avia had given birth to a half-wit who was nowhere as bright as her sister-in-law's son. In fact, he was what local people call 'fool-fool'.

Avia blinked. The sun was blocked by the figures of a woman and a young girl standing on the veranda. They were dressed in old black long gowns and boots, which she found strange for 1976. They asked for directions. Then she recognised them. The woman looked at her coldly. 'Why yu keep troubling my boy, Avia, eh?' Suddenly, the woman lunged at her with a machete. She was unable to move just as the woman brought the sharp cutlass straight towards her head. Avia woke up from sleeping on the cane chair and found herself on the veranda floor, her eyes watery, perspiring heavily, her heart beating.

There was nobody on the veranda.

*   *   *

Thursday, July 29th 1976 21.34 hours.

'Am I right in confirming that the dead girl was your girlfriend? A Miss Cameira Nicole-Anne Chin? And you are Richard Orion Alvarado, aka Ricky?' The ambulance was cramped, the air stale. O'Neill was taking notes. The prisoner, sitting up, strapped to a drip, handcuffed, and sweating from the pain, said nothing. Danville Robinson gave him a sharp backhanded slap across the face. 'Answer me bwoy or the rest of your life stops here.' The male medic implored them to hurry up, as the young man needed urgent hospital treatment for his gunshot injuries. Danville gave the medic a stern look. He really didn't give a *raas* if the youth bled to death. He had seen many things in his forty-six years, twenty-six in the force but never such carnage in this quiet and decent part of town. 'Friend, may I perform my duty as a law enforcement officer without further interruptions please? This person is a murderer.'

'Murderer? Me? Me is no murderer.' The youth said hoarsely but bitterly. 'Talk to de bwoy. Him plan everyt'ing but I never know seh him set we up too. When I come back, at 6.30 de front door was open. I walk in and see Cameira and Mister 'Kinley shot up. I run outta de house fe go call somebody but the bwoy buss two gun shot inna me. Why yuh don't 'terrogate him? Why yuh nuh ask him? He tief my daddy ring from me too. My daddy dead and pass it on to my mother. She pass it on to me. Eh? Ask him nuh?'

Danville kissed through his teeth and hit the prisoner again, so hard blood oozed from his split lip.

'Yu hear dat O'Neill? Our *friend*, here, is

tellin' us that a small, frightened God-fearing boy from a respectable well-known middle-class family, is a murderer! Dat him *plan everything*. Dat he is a murdering, thieving Einstein . . . aged *nine*. Kiss me neck!' Danville laughed suddenly and stopped just as suddenly. 'Be a man, tek yu responsibility and admit what you are. Nuttin but a dirty, worthless, murdering, nager. Look at that child. That boy got nobody now. His mother died two years now, sister and auntie not long ago and now his Uncle. He has no one.'

O'Neill looked at the boy. Another medic was attending to him. Wrapped in a sheet, the boy was shaking jerkily, tears streaming down his face, crying for his dead uncle. The hard-faced young man before him was a larcenist. He was also illiterate, poor and of no fixed abode. He'd been locked up twice on two public and violent disorder offences. Now, it seemed, he had graduated to the big one.

Danville spoke coolly, containing his inner rage. 'My friend, you are unemployed. You have no means to raise the infant you and Miss Chin have just had. And obviously, *obviously* without any money and desperate, you both hatched the plan to rob her former employer. The safe has been ransacked. As a former employee, *she* knew what was in the safe. The boy has said his uncle kept a handgun in there also. The boy tells me seh he pretended to be dead after she shot him. And that shortly after, you, Ricky Alvarado returned to collect ya money and yu woman.' The boy had told him shakily that the couple then had had sex next to the dead man. They quarrelled about the money. She shot Ricky twice. But Ricky managed to retaliate with the gun from the safe. The gardener's statement corroborated much of the boy's account and the old man was able to verify the identity of Cameira, the arrival of Ricky and the background of the two. Basically, Ricky Alvarado didn't stand a chance. 'My friend you are barking up the wrong tree if you think *I* am a fool.'

It was a clear case of dirty evil greed.

Danville Robinson arrested Richard Orion Alvarado on two counts of homicide, armed robbery and one of attempted homicide.

Ricky Alvarado was facing the automatic death penalty.

With luck, he would hang within time.

Robinson spat and looked towards the staring medic. 'Patch up the pussy'ole and mek we lock him up.'

*   *   *

Still recovering from her disturbing dream, Miss Avia walked into the formal dining room. She saw the pint of goat's milk on the dining table, and the packet of white refined sugar next to the pile of freshly washed and crisp sun-dried laundry. She also saw the twenty-dollar bill she had given Willie to give the boy. She wondered when the boy had returned and how he had managed to slip into the house past her as she slept on the veranda. More importantly, how did he purchase the items without spending the twenty dollars? Why was this boy so damn contrary, like his Uncle, Beckford?

'Bwoy? Boooooooyyyyyy-ooohhh?' Wherever the boy was it seemed he was not in the house. She could feel her blood pressure rising. Deciding it was time for her regular soothing evening shower, Avia walked into her beautifully tiled blue and white bathroom, tiles imported from abroad and the envy of her friends. She started to undress before realising she had not traded the towel in the bathroom for a fresh one. At that point, she made a mental note of hiring another new maid, preferably not young or pretty. Maybe a young man though she supposed that Beckford would probably try to bed him too. Evening was approaching. She could hear the crickets. A veil of darkness was descending.

Eyes closed tight, Miss Avia was enjoying the stimulating water from the overhead shower pouring over her body, remembering her dream. Why yu keep troubling my boy, Avia, eh? The dream was an omen from the boy's dead mother. It was a powerful dream and very realistic. It made her think about the curse she had heard was on the family. The dream tugged at her conscience. Why yu keep troubling my boy, Avia, eh? Maybe it was telling her to change the way she treated the boy or something would happen to her. *Why yu keep troubling my boy, Avia, eh?* Avia's heart pounded. It was unusual for her to feel fear, but even as she showered, she could feel the hairs on her arms rise. She would make amends later—bake him his favourite sweet potato pudding and allow him to keep the twenty-dollars, or take him to their second home by the beach in Negril for the week to help him get over the recent death of his sister.

As she reached blindly for the soap, a sudden pain made her wince. It felt like a knife cut, painful and sharp on her left wrist. Turning off the shower, she opened her eyes and saw it, right next to the soap. A huge scorpion. A bee sting had nearly killed her several years ago when she'd suffered a rare allergic reaction to it. Since that near-death incident she always made sure the house was free of such things. The bathroom window was closed. There were no gaps under any doorway big enough for anything to crawl through and she always slept surrounded by mosquito nets. Her wrist was turning into a dark red bruise, which would soon become black. She felt that familiar dizziness swooping through her head.

Miss Avia pulled her clothes onto her wet skin as rapidly as she could, trembling violently, her heart trouncing against her fragile ribs, desperately trying not to panic. Her throat was swelling. Her eyes felt as if they were throbbing and bulging. Her body felt as if it was turning to

107

ice. Barefoot, she lunged at the bathroom door, and tried to turn the handle yet the strength to even pick up a dime was fading from her body fast. She collapsed on the floor just behind the door.

Suddenly she could hear movement in the living room. 'Beckford? Beckford . . .'

A dog barking. Thank God! The boy was in the house!

'Bwoy, come quick. A scorpion bit me. You know what to do if that happens . . . Open the door . . . Send for Doctor Johnson.'

From the corner of her eye she could see the scorpion, sensing her movement and vibrations, heading towards her.

'Bwoy!! Help me! Where are you? Open the door! If yuh nuh get in here when I get out . . .'

The bathroom door opened slowly. Vaguely, she saw the boy looking down at her.

She started to grunt, grabbing his ankles.

The boy prised her fingers away from his feet.

He left the bathroom and closed the door firmly.

BEDSIDE MANNERS

Martin Edwards

'I've never done anything illegal before,' the woman says, fiddling with her necklace.

This seems unlikely to me. She is forty five if a day, and works as an accounts manager for a motor car dealership. But I am accustomed to the little ways of my clients. *Clients*, yes, it is five years since I last cared for a patient. Now I have found my true vocation. Yet there is this about serving clients. They are always right.

So I treat her to my reassuring smile and say, 'Trust me, there is nothing illegal about going out to the theatre.'

'You deserve a break,' the red-faced man tells her. 'After all you've done . . .'

'This is all about freedom,' I say, in my best bedside tone, as I glance at the clock on their mantelpiece. 'So you will be leaving in five minutes?"

'Yes, yes,' the man says. 'We need to make sure the girl on the desk gets a good look at us when we pick up our tickets. If any questions are asked . . .'

'There will be no questions.' Again I smile, exuding confidence. 'Trust me.'

'Of course, Doctor. But just in case . . . if anyone does ask, there will be witnesses. We were in the foyer of the theatre before seven o'clock. Like I said before. It's a fall-back position.'

Absurd. But I humour him with an approving nod.

The woman hesitates. 'I must go upstairs.'

The man's unhealthy face—he is a candidate for a stroke, if ever I saw one—creases into a frown. He throws me a doubtful glance. 'I'm not sure . . .'

I nod towards the staircase, encouraging her. 'Why not? You wish to share a precious moment.'

She scuttles off, heels clacking on the treads. Her lover ventures a rueful smile.

'She'll be all right, Doctor. It's just nerves, that's all. This is what she's wanted for years.'

'I understand.'

And naturally I do. This is a pleasant house, on the outskirts of the village, its value inflated by the promise of a soon-to-be-built by-pass. Who would not wish to own it, and to have that ownership unfettered by obligation? My gift to them, as to all my clients, and all my *subjects*, is freedom.

The man seeks to engage me in conversation, embarking on a story about his ill fortune in business during the years when he managed a public house. I reply in monosyllables. My priority is to compose myself and prepare my heart and mind for the task that lies ahead.

Soon the woman is back with us. Head bowed. Is she murmuring a prayer?

The man claps her on the back. He has decided that contrived jollity is the right note to strike. 'Well, then. We'd best be off.'

'Yes.' It is barely a whisper.

Suddenly she glances at me and I see dread in her eyes. Dread of what is to happen. I have seen that look before, on other faces where previously I had seen nothing more than greed. But this is not a greedy woman. She is weak, that is all. The man in her life has cajoled her into doing something against her better judgment. Not for the first time, I suspect.

'Everything is going to be all right, isn't it, Doctor?'

I am a model of calm and goodwill. 'As I explained when we reached our arrangement, my method is tried and tested. I need not trouble you with details, but you may rely on me.'

'The laws in this country are an absolute disgrace, anyway,' the man says. 'In a civilised society, what we're doing would be applauded.'

'What the Doctor is doing,' the woman says hastily.

He offers me his hand. It is large and sweaty. 'Well, I'll say it straight. I couldn't do what you do. You deserve a medal.'

The woman twitters to the same effect, pays me fulsome compliments. As she runs out

111

of breath, she adds, 'I'll never forget the help you have given to us, Doctor.'

'And to . . .' I begin.

'Yes, yes!' Her eagerness is pathetic. 'That's what matters most, of course. We aren't thinking of ourselves.'

'Well, then.' The man hands me the copied keys. 'You will . . . dispose of these?'

'As we discussed.' I cough discreetly. 'If I might ask you for the envelope?'

Slowly, as if hypnotised by my expression, he takes a fat envelope from the pocket of his tweed jacket and hands it to me.

'If you don't mind . . .' I tear open the envelope and flick through the fifty pound notes. The final instalment, paid in full. 'Thank you.'

'It's the least we can do,' the woman says. 'We owe you so much.'

The man's face is flushed, irritable. Despite all that we have said, he is far from certain that I shall keep my word. But he has no choice but to trust me. I am anxious for them to be away now. I need time alone.

'Goodbye, then.'

To my surprise, the woman steps forward and presses cold lips against my cheek. A kiss of gratitude. Then the man takes her hand and within moments they are gone.

As I hear their rusty little car splutter down the drive, I help myself to a nip of brandy from my flask. Only one, mind. I have no intention of repeating the mistake I once made in the hospital ward.

I allow myself an hour of quiet reflection. For all my experience, each case for me is special. Unique. This is the difference between my past and present careers. One operation is, frankly, much like another except in those frightening instances where an error is made. Nowadays, however, each assignment feels like the first.

I consult my watch. The sedative will be wearing off. This is one of those little details that mean nothing, in truth, to my clients, but everything to me. It is time to pick up my case and climb the stairs.

The room has that musty smell so familiar to me. It clings to the old and infirm. Outside, rain is slapping against the window-panes. Within, the only sound is a hoarse rattle of breath.

Silently, I move to the bedside and open my case. The subject's eyes are closed. I bend over her.

'Molly,' I whisper.

I touch a fleshy shoulder through the thin cotton nightdress. She is by no means reduced to skin and bone. No wonder the GP said she was good for few years yet.

'Molly, look at me.'

No response. I pinch her shoulder and she gives a little moan. Her eyelids flutter. Yes, she can see me. I hear a stifled noise. Is she calling the woman's name? It is impossible to make out the syllables.

I shake my head. 'Just you and I are in the house. They have left you in my care. You are . . . mine.'

This is the moment.

I lift the small, rose-scented pillow from the case and hold it a couple of inches from Molly's nose. All the time my eyes are fixed on hers. They are grey and rheumy and filled with incomprehension. Also with terror, of course, there is no disguising the terror.

She knows what is about to happen, her mind is not dull. And she knows that there is nothing that she can do.

'I am about to set you free,' I whisper. 'Free from care, free from pain.'

All too soon it is over. I do what I always do, I have perfected my method over the years, though I cannot bring myself to describe my *ritual* in words. Some things must remain private, they are so special.

When I have tidied, I pat the envelope in my pocket. The man assumes that this is all about money, but he is as wrong as the woman who regards me as a candidate for sainthood. As wrong as my former colleagues, whom I baffled because they could never understand the thoughts rippling through my mind. No doubt they were afraid to understand; perhaps I was not so different from them as they liked to believe.

The truth is, we all have our little frailties. My weakness isn't anything so crass as greed. I first succumbed in my original career, but only now am I able to indulge myself to the full and luxuriate in this exquisite, this matchless pleasure.

THE LAST GET-TOGETHER

Robert Barnard

Christine wasn't surprised to see Jude crossing towards her through the palatial spaces of Milan Centrale railway station. The little group always ran into each other in the days leading up to the reunion. Milan was like that—sprawling, but with quite few people-centres. So though their homes these days were Istanbul, Milton Keynes and all stations to Umeå, they all took these meetings very much in their stride.

'Hi, Christine. You don't look a day older. Well, maybe a day. So this is the last time, eh?'

'Yes. It's been good, but I think we're right to call a halt.'

'As soon as it began to attract talk it was doomed. Personally I think it's a bit craven, but then—several of us have sold out to respectability.'

'Don't look at me. I'm considered a bit of a weirdo in Harrogate.'

'Well, Harrogate . . . But I wasn't looking at you. You always took your own line.'

'It will be lovely to see Marcia and Tonio again. That's what this has really been all about: a celebration.'

'Hmmm . . . Yeah, of course. See you,

116

Chrissie!'

And as she went down into the Metro Christine congratulated herself on being right: the happy marriage of Marcia and Tonio *was* what all this was really about—a marriage that had lasted for twenty-five years and was still, patently, a cause of love and contentment.

The class had been a year at Mme Vincent's finishing school by Lake Leman when they had come for a final treat to Milan, with trips to Verona, Bergamo and Mantua. It was at Mantua, when three of the girls (as they then were, but only just) were having lunch in the open air in a ristorante by the Virgil Park, that Marcia had met Tonio, who was waiting at their table. He gave them all impeccable service, but he had eyes only for Marcia. The next day he turned up at a restaurant only half a mile from their hotel in Milan, much to everyone's surprise except Marcia's. The restaurant was owned by his uncle, and his family seemed to have restaurants everywhere including Britain. By the end of the week they declared they were engaged. For the last twenty years they had owned and run the best Italian restaurant in Cheltenham, helped financially by Tonio's uncle and hindered in every way possible by Marcia's horrible family. Yes, it was this glorious success that they were celebrating, Christine thought, in those every-five-years reunions in Milan.

And not that other, revolting, hideous

117

business.

She said as much when she met Philippa in the Museo Poldi-Pezzoli, a favourite place of the more cultivated members of the group, and Philippa had agreed.

'Of course it is,' she said. 'Whatever people say.'

Christine shivered.

'I don't regard journalists as people,' she said.

As they walked through the richly-filled rooms Philippa giggled and said: 'Do you know, I still haven't seen the "Last Supper".'

It had been the first mix-up of Mlle Bourget, their tour leader. Well, not the first, because they had been supposed to go to Florence but somebody had muddled up the booking and they had had to change plan at the last moment. But Mlle Bourget had insisted they all go together to view the Leonardo, and when they got to the refectory at Santa Maria delle Grazie they were met with a blank refusal from the Gorgon behind the ticket office glass—a woman armed with rudeness and an impermeable conviction that rules had to be obeyed: individuals had to book tickets by phone two days in advance, and parties, which clearly they were, two weeks in advance. Nothing could shake her, and finally Mlle Bourget's pitying tones gave way to shrillness.

'Then we'll go to the Brera. There are

plenty of Last Suppers there.'

It became a much-quoted and giggled-over riposte over the next few days. But they had got back into the bus and were driven to the Brera Gallery where they did indeed see Last Suppers by Rubens, Veronese and others, all with appealing dogs underneath the supper table that the girls said they *adored* and an atmosphere generally more lively and agreeable than the postcards suggested prevailed in Leonardo's version. Even years later one or two girls could stop a conversation with the remark that there were *much* better Last Suppers than the one at Santa Maria delle Grazie.

It was that same night, during the serving of dinner, that the other matter—the one that more cynical minds suggested was commemorated in the five-yearly reunions, was first mooted. It was while Mlle Bourget was away phoning the woman who was to guide them round the Cathedral the next morning that, in the absence of her formidable respectability, the proprietor of the Hotel Moroni first revealed his true colours. As soon as she slipped out the girls began their excited chatter, amorous and artistic, that the first two days of their final treat inevitably evoked, and Signor Moroni, prowling round with plates of lemon sorbetti and chocolate mousse interposed his voice.

'What you-a young ladies want-a, you

119

want-a a bitta fun, eh? Not all this hart and stuff-a, but bitta fun. You growing girls-a. That's-a what all girls want-a.'

Christine could remember staring at him coldly, the only look in her adolescent arsenal that seemed appropriate. Other girls giggled, or looked at each other with expressions of horror. The fact that Signor Moroni was a man in his sixties had not been disguised by his hair dye, nor was the fact that his protruding gut was belted in and probably corseted hidden from the girls' penetrating inspections. His habitual expression was an oily leer, and even when he had confided in two of the girls that he was a lonely widower they had been conscious of a sharp look from the corner of his eye to see how they took it.

'The cheek!' said Andrea after dinner. 'To imagine we'd look at anyone old enough to be our grandfather.'

'I've always fancied older men,' said Thomasina, who hailed from Aberdeen, 'but I draw the line at the over-thirty-fives!'

The next night Mlle Bourget did not oblige by leaving the table at any point, but Signor Moroni had prepared for this. Instead of distributing plates with the food already served out on them, he set warm plates in front of them and brought round serving dishes with Ossa Bucca or whatever put on them, and then with vegetable dishes. He did not make the mistake of propositioning every girl, but he did

120

make his aims clear to two or three of them.

'You want a nice-a time tonight? Good time with someone who knows-a all da tricks? You know-a where my door is.'

After dinner, when Mlle Bourget went off to occupy a much-trumpeted seat for Gluck at La Scala they inevitably got together over coffee outside in the twilight at a nearby bar. Mirth was unconfined, though Christine, through her laughter, was worried as well.

'*How* can we have ended up in a place where the proprietor is aiming to get us all into bed with him?' she demanded.

'Easy,' said Jude. 'The piss-up over the booking at Florence. They had to take what they could get, and the only place that was able to take a classful of young ladies was just the sort of seedy dump that no finishing-school would normally touch with a bargepole. Hence Moroni.'

It seemed to make sense to the girls.

'I suppose so,' said Christine. 'I expect we shall cope. It's not as though we've never been propositioned before.'

'No, it's not,' agreed Jude. 'Though Swiss men . . . '

They all agreed that the Swiss men who had tried it out (successfully in some cases) had almost all been incipient bankers with statements of income and expenditure forever in front of their eyes who were hardly more exciting as lovers than Signor Moroni.

'Still,' said Thomasina, 'at least they were young, and interested once we'd established that we didn't want more than a good meal and an evening's fun.'

'Well, Moroni is *interested*,' said Philippa. 'You can't deny that.'

'He shouldn't be at his age,' said Andrea. 'He should be sitting at home in warmed-up slippers before the telly, watching one of those endless game shows they have here.'

'Quite,' said Philippa. 'He should be punished for his presumption.'

They all laughed, but Jude said 'Right.' She rather gave the impression she was thinking seriously how.

The next night Signor Moroni got round to Jude in his propositioning of the whole party. Jude was quite attractive really, everyone agreed, but not in any obvious way, so it was not surprising she was fairly far down on his list. He was becoming increasingly specific.

'You come-a to my room tonight, pretty lady? We have bit of jig-jig in my bed, eh?'

Jude hardly left a pause before she replied.

'Tonight I'm busy. We're all busy. Let's make it tomorrow.'

The smile on Signor Moroni's face lasted the rest of the meal.

This called for something stronger than coffee, and Simone slipped out to the supermarket for a bottle of brandy which they handed around as the discussion began in

122

Jude's room over what they would do.

'The only possible thing to do is nothing,' Christine said. 'If Jude goes along and then disappoints him there's the danger of his turning nasty and—well—you know—taking what he wants.'

'I'd like to see him try,' said Jude.

'Well, maybe you could cope, but there'd be an awful fuss, and nastiness,' said Philippa. 'We'd all hate that.'

'Speak for yourself,' said Jude. 'Oh admittedly Old Mother Vincent wouldn't be pleased, and my father would spit fireworks. But Vincent can't *do* anything much, can she? It's the end of the year, and we're about to slip out of her grasp. She won't even want to deny her precious diplomas and scrolls to any of her so-called graduates. We're her best advertisement.'

'But what about your father?'

'It would be worth it just to see him die of apoplexy when he heard what we were accused of.'

'Do you really want to go?' Christine asked incredulously.

'Not exactly. What I want is all of us to go.'

They looked at her, some literally open-mouthed.

'Be bloody crowded,' said Marcia.

'One at a time,' said Jude. Jaws fell open again.

'But—' 'You can't mean—' 'Be serious—'

'I am serious. The biter bit. It's the best humiliation possible. See how many he can get through. I would have said three maximum. After that, total humiliation.'

'He just wouldn't open his door.'

'Of course he wouldn't. But an evil old lecher like him would feel the humiliation just as much as if we were there to witness it.' She looked round at the other girls. 'You all on, then?'

'I am certainly not,' said Christine. 'It's a horrible idea, disgusting. Cruel to him and intolerable for us.'

'Well, we'll put you last on the list,' said Jude. 'He'll be well past it by then.'

'You will not put me anywhere on any list,' said Christine, chin up.

'The lower end of the list is purely theoretical. Let's get the upper end in shape.'

'No one wants to—' began Christine.

'Speak for yourself!' came several voices.

So once Christine had stormed out and back to her room they drew up a list with five enthusiastic names on it and the rest left a jumble at the end.

'By then we might be in the mood for anything,' said Simone.

And in the course of the next day their mood certainly changed. Christine went after breakfast and stayed up at the Castello all day, visiting the various museums and taking in almost nothing of what she saw. She felt disgust for her classmates and hoped that staying on her own all day would be a firm statement of disapproval that would influence them when night came. None of them noticed, however. They did this and that, especially shopping, in various groups punctuated by lunch together in the Victor Emmanuel Gallery. Without exception the mood of all of them began to fizz, raising the excitement quotient of the whole group. It was going to be a hoot!

Dinner that night was tense, but in a comic sort of way. There were many bursts of laughter, but at nothing very much. Mlle Bouget noticed nothing. She was selected to guide these jaunts for her cultural know-how, not her human understanding. In fact she knew as little about adolescent girls as the average bachelor of eighty. When they broke up after dinner she said: 'Early start tomorrow, girls. Be sure to be in bed by half past ten.' All the girls except Christine knew that half past ten was the time that Jude had whispered to Signor Moroni when he proffered the dish with the sauté potatoes on. That had been agreed over lunch.

'I hope you've given up your disgusting plan,' said Christine, looking from one to another with pain in her eyes.

'Now, Christine,' said Jude, bustling up as if she was a difficult child who found it hard to fit in, 'just you go upstairs and put yourself to

125

bed, and don't even *think* about it. A good night's sleep is just what you need.'

And just what I'm not likely to have, thought Christine bitterly. She had already had interrupted nights when every creak of the floorboards—and the Hotel Moroni was a nineteenth-century building with built-in creaks—had suggested that someone in the group might be taking the proprietor up on his invitation.

That last night was the worst of all. It began at ten-thirty when she heard a long walk from a room at the end of the landing—Jude's presumably—the whole length of the corridor to the unnumbered door to Moroni's flat at the other end. The walk was accompanied by such weird creaks it sounded like a piece by Stockhausen. Twenty minutes later there was the walk back, interrupted by a soft knock on a door, then another, shorter walk along to the flat, a knock, the sound of a door opening and shutting.

And then again. And then again.

Christine was unsure how often it happened, because at times during the night she fell into a troubled sleep. When she woke up in the morning at six o'clock she lay awake expecting to hear the last girl taking the walk, but of course the horrible joke must have finished hours ago. She had a half memory of a long consultation in the corridor, voices at whisper level, but she couldn't make up her mind whether this was in one of her waking fits or one of her dreams.

Breakfast was a hurried, silent affair. Signor Moroni never appeared at breakfast, and the help-yourself tables were serviced by two elderly and silent women. After it was done the girls scrambled upstairs to their rooms, closed their already-packed suitcases, then ran down the stairs and out to the bus taking them back to Switzerland.

'You'd have thought he'd have come to see us off,' said Marcia.

The bus journey, however, was not the escape from pressing worries that they had all hoped for. At lunchtime Mlle Bourget phoned the school at Bonneville and spoke to Mme Vincent. She came back looking worried.

'Something very tragic has occurred.'

'*Very* tragic? Not just tragic but very tragic?' asked the irrepressible Jude.

'*Very* tragic,' said Mlle Bourget firmly. 'Signor Moroni has been found dead in bed. Clearly a heart attack.'

'So what's the problem?' asked Marcia.

'The Italian police are asking that we turn round and go straight back to Milan.'

'Why? What's it to do with us?' persisted Philippa.

'Of course it has nothing to do with us. The incompetence of the Italian police is legendary. So this doesn't surprise me.'

'It's the *com*petence that surprises me,'

muttered Jude.

'Mme Vincent has decided that we should return to the school. Each young lady should collect the rest of her belongings, and the coach will continue to various European cities. Each young lady will have instructions what to do before returning to England at the time already appointed, early next week. On no account are parents to be worried by early returns. Now, let us get immediately on the bus and head for the border.'

They were stupefied into silence for a while. Most of them, at any rate, were stupefied. Christine tried to decide which of the girls were not really surprised at the news. Jude, of course. Philippa probably. Andrea. She ruled out Marcia entirely, what with her engagement to Tonio and her remarks about Moroni coming to see them off. They only really started talking when they reached the border.

'It's not a crime, sleeping with someone,' said Philippa.

'Mme Vincent is making such a fuss because she knows if it gets in the papers the school will be finished,' said Thomasina.

That was a sobering thought. The school's clientele was almost entirely British, being based on a period in Mme Vincent's youth when she was governess to girls of 'good' family there and had made numerous contacts. The merest whisper, then, would have been fatal. After a pause Marcia said:

'If Mme Vincent is wise, she'll send us all home now.'

But Mme Vincent, being wise, did no such thing. She was aware that sending pupils home before the appointed end of the school year would inevitably arouse questions. She had a better plan. When the coach reached Bonneville the girls were, as per instruction, rushed to their rooms to collect their possessions, given replacement air tickets from various European airports, then bundled back on to the coach with details of the hotels, twelve separate ones, where they would spend their remaining days. The Italian policeman who had telephoned Mme Vincent had been unable to conceal concupiscence and a lecherous relish at the reasons for Signor Moroni's death. Mme Vincent smelt several rats and blenched at the possible threat to the school's reputation. The girls were to be scattered to the four winds to prevent the Italian police questioning them.

On the coach which was taking them to their first destination Christine said: 'If it all comes out, I'll take the blame. I'll say it was my idea.'

'Why should you?' demanded Marcia. 'You were the one who stood out against it. All the rest of us went along to one extent or another.'

'Not all of you, I'm sure. A lot of you wouldn't have gone along the corridor when it came to the pinch. Anyway, most of your parents would create blue murder if they knew. My father trusts me absolutely. He would *know* I could never do a thing like that.'

But it never came to that. And now, at their last reunion, they could talk about the matter quite calmly.

'I would have gone along,' said Marcia to Christine, as they walked around the Brera and looked at the dogs again. 'I was sixth on the list. I would have gone.'

'But *why*, Marcia? When you had Tonio. And had just got engaged?'

'I knew he had a roving eye, so I knew I had to let my eye wander as well now and then. We've run our lives together on that basis . . . It hasn't been a bad marriage.'

Christine thought this was a sad summing-up of what she had always thought was a brilliantly successful union. But who was she to make judgments?

So at the time, summer 1980, the girls were delivered around like parcels to various German, Dutch and Belgian hotels. They whiled away the time till their flights home mostly on their own. Christine did come across Jude in Schipol Airport, and while they were waiting for their respective planes she did raise the possibility of an occasional reunion—'not every year, but say every five years. In Italy.'

'Not a bad idea,' conceded Jude. 'Keep an eye on each other. Don't forget your promise?'

'My promise?'

'To say it was your idea and you who slept with Moroni if it all gets out.'

'Oh that. Right.'

But that was obviously all academic by then. The Italian police had been foiled by the quick thinking of Mme Vincent. And after all, what had they done? Sleeping with an elderly lecher was not a crime, though Christine continued to think of it with distaste. It was a pity some of the girls had talked about it as a punishment, not a reward, for his lechery. That almost made it a revenge killing.

They could not have foreseen how the events of June 1980 would begin, little by little, to become talked about, known, in Italy at least. Weeklies such as *Buon Giorno*!, *Avanti*!, and *Ciao*! didn't even exist when the death of Moroni occurred. But when they did start up the whispers that had started in local Milan newspapers were recycled and embroidered on. Moroni had left a roomful of pornography, much of it involving young girls. Cheekily he had left it to the Milan Public Library. Very soon whispers went around that a class of girls (age unspecified) had abruptly decamped from the hotel just before the news of the death broke. Soon lip-smacking policemen were supplying more accurate information in return for anonymity and unspecified sums of money. Soon it was known that the class of girls were in fact eighteen or nineteen years old, came from a finishing school, and that more than one were thought to have been involved. Eventually the news leaked out that the girls held a reunion from time to time in Milan.

'It's fortunate that Tonio's relatives are all in the restaurant trade,' said Marcia to Jude in 2005. 'We can meet at different places each time, and no one gets wise to us.'

'And always the most delicious food,' said Jude, a practical soul and a *bon viveur*.

'Yes,' said Marcia thoughtfully. 'To anyone outside it would look like a celebration of the poor man's death.'

'You sound like Christine, the ghastly little hypocrite. The "poor man" was a sleaze merchant and brought it on himself. Nobody asked him to fuck us—he should have known he couldn't last the course.'

We knew it, thought Marcia. We girls knew it. What does that make us?

They always had a private room in the chosen restaurant. That way they could talk uninhibitedly without fear of it being reported. Italian waiters were getting a lot more English these days, Marcia reported authoritatively, but fortunately it all concerned food. This time it was Da Bruno's, owned by a cousin of Tonio, and renowned for its antipasto and its calorific deserts. The waiters recognised English women and hardly needed telling they were of the Jude Galloway party, dining in the private room. Most of the waiters saved their private lascivious grins for when the door had closed behind each one. Tonio brought Marcia, then went his own way, as he always did when in Italy. Christine in the past had thought this sweet and tactful, but since Marcia's revelations she could only see it as a symbol of a marriage built on a swamp.

'What a time we had!' said Thomasina, when they had finished their gins and tonic, had a mountain of antipasto delicacies, and were well into the splendid Sicilian wine. 'We were trail-blazers. Probably trips like that are commonplace these days, but not then: an engagement, all sorts of little encounters which most of us have kept secret—'

'Or semi-secret,' said Andrea.

'Well yes. And then there was the—what shall we call it?—'

'Climax?' suggested Jude.

'*Bonne bouche*. For some of us the climax never came, remember. But it was still quite a thrill.'

'Not for all of us,' said Jude. 'Miss Steel-Knickers wasn't thrilled.'

'You've never quite forgiven Christine for that, have you?' said Andrea. She had a voice whose loudness she always underestimated.

'For what?' asked Christine, vegetarian option half way to her mouth. Then she nodded dismissively. 'Oh, never mind. I know. I don't see how one need forgiveness for something one hasn't done, but still . . . I've never regretted it.'

'You will,' muttered Jude. Andrea looked at her in surprise.

'What did you say?' she asked. Jude left a few moments' silence.

'Do you know, I've hated Christine almost from the first. That air of total innocence ceased to be appealing very quickly, and then I started asking "Why can't she be like us?" Why did she have to proclaim her utter moral superiority all the time? As if she was surrounded by a halo of light, and we were in the darkness.'

'Oh, you're exaggerating,' said Andrea. 'She's just a normal nice girl.'

'Maybe. To me she's something mid-Victorian. And from fiction, not reality. Altogether too good to be true.' She looked at her watch. 'Won't be long now.'

'What do you mean won't—' But Jude had put her finger to her lips.

'Listen.'

Outside there was the sound of scuffling. Footsteps were heard, then shouts from the waiters, a fight developing. All the girls started looking at each other, and Christine's face wore the distress of foreboding. Then the door burst open and there scrambled into the private room a motley crew—all men, many holding cameras with flash attachments, some clutching notebooks, and some at the back still fighting with the waiters. As they approached the table Jude got up and in their alarm all the other girls did the same. She went down the table till she came to Christine, then she put her arms around her and kissed her. She turned to the jabbering crowd of men.

'Christine has promised to tell you how she thought up the whole idea,' she said.

Then she went back to her place as a look of horror suffused Christine's face and she became surrounded by the gang of shouting, demanding, excited men. Jude sat down again beside Andrea, satisfaction instinct on her face.

'They'll crucify her,' she said.

ALL SHE WROTE

Mick Herron

The Head of Section had Daisy's report right there on the desk. Marked *eyes only*, it began without preamble:

*   *   *

The General is uglier than he appears in photographs. His face is pockmarked and cratered; ruined by an adolescent inflammation, I suppose, and up close presents a palette of angry purple outbursts. He has thick black curly hair—too black to be natural. Vanity is not the prerogative of the attractive. His teeth are yellowing, and his eyes, too, have that same unhealthy light, as if he were a carrier of something we don't yet have a name for. When he speaks, it is in a voice used to command but of a slightly higher pitch than might be expected. When he walks, it is with neither grace nor lightness. His reputation as a man of subtle moves could hardly be less deserved.

The Imperiale, on the other hand, is everything its brochure promises. Its rooms are large and cool, with overhead fans that beat like a metronome, so that you fall asleep in the comfortable knowledge that the building's heartbeat never falters. The lifts are splendid, and in constant working order, and the lobby is a marketplace for information. I never crossed its tiled floor without registering at least three furtive conversations in corners. As for the bar—which occupies a patio overlooking the bay, and is lined by friendly palm trees—this is where the foreign correspondents gather, pretending they're relaxing. All wear sunglasses, even in the shade, and an air of expectation hangs heavily over the tables, as assorted possible headlines compose themselves in journalists' heads. Last year, both Greene and Hemingway stayed here. I expect it will turn up in a novel before long.

On my first afternoon, the General walked through the lobby while I was reading an English paper. His gaze rested on me for a long while. I kept my expression blank, I trust, though his inspection was unpleasant.

It might seem odd that Rubello keeps a suite at the Imperiale, but it is somewhere he feels secure: far enough from the President's palace for him not to feel overshadowed; close enough that his driver can deliver him there in ten minutes. When on the premises, he keeps only a brace of guards with him. The Imperiale is regarded as neutral territory by all, as any horror taking place within its walls would harm the island's tourist trade. Besides, the General has little to fear from the correspondents. Most of them only leave the bar to waddle as far as the casino. They tend to be on their next-to-last legs, their stomachs as padded as their expense accounts.

*   *   *

I have been told that a report should *cover the background*—that was the phrase. Cover the background. So. The General is General Marc Rubello, 52 years old: much loved by the army he commands; much feared by the people. Feared, too, I think by our own dear Majesty's Government—or at least, feared by our American cousins, and therefore held to be fearsome by us. It's no secret that Rubello's rival for the Presidency, Chief of Police Andrea Nabar, is the horse Whitehall and Washington back. As far as the islanders are concerned, the race lacks a favourite. Nabar is much loved by the police force he commands; much feared by the people. But less likely to steer east were he to take up the reins of power.

There is a saying I've heard: better the bastard on your side than the bastard on the other. I won't ask you to forgive the vocabulary. There is worse to come.

As for the President himself—the former President, I should call him now—he was the weakling son of a stern leader, with rarely a thought to call his own. Presidents' sons should never be Presidents themselves. They either splash about, helplessly out of their depth, or indulge in wars to exorcise their fathers' ghosts. There was never any doubt that the Presidential Palace had a temporary resident. It was simply a question of which bastard would replace him.

*　　*　　*

The assignment was straightforward: I was to pose as a guest at the Imperiale, and 'gather information'. When would Rubello make his move? Would he aim for a bloodless coup, or take the opportunity to exterminate opposition? Given that this included the police force, civil war would result if he took that route, and Her Majesty's intelligence services like to know in advance about such events. I assumed similar information was being gathered regarding Nabar's intentions. As it turned out, I underestimated the degree of interest being shown in the General's rival.

It's a peculiar affectation—to pose as something you truly are. For whatever my motive for being there, there's no doubt I was a guest at the Imperiale. I had a room on the third floor, and a balcony overlooking the square. There was nothing unusual in being a tourist there at any time of year, and political unrest was never spoken of in front of visitors.

There were always groups of soldiers and policemen on street corners, but they were largely keeping an eye on each other, and taking turns beating up beggars and thieves. Tourists were off limits; rarely, if ever, arrested.

And as far as my actual task went, I was not without resources. The Service has long had an asset in place at the Imperiale. Maria is a maid. She has heavy eyebrows, and for some reason this lends a certain foreboding to many of her utterances. The first time we talked she launched, without invitation, into a discussion of Rubello's vices.

'The General is a man of fearsome appetites.' She was looking at me directly when she said this. 'When he takes a lover, this requires his full attention. The same when he takes a prisoner.'

'Is there a difference between the two?'

'You might say not. Sometimes I see them leaving in the morning. They look as if daylight will strike them dead.'

'You have no sympathy for them.'

'They come asking favours. They leave having suffered more for those favours than they expected.' She shrugged. 'Life is hard.'

'I imagine he does not have to look far for his conquests.'

'He is a powerful man,' Maria said. 'And many people require favours.'

'And you?' I asked. 'You have not . . .

attracted his attentions?'

She laughed. 'I am not his type.' She was still looking at me. 'You are the type he enjoys.'

I remembered the gaze he'd bestowed on me the previous afternoon, and suppressed a shiver.

'And you have fair skin,' she said. 'He likes fair skin.'

I did not want to pursue this topic.

'Daisy,' she said.

'Yes.'

'It is a pretty name.'

I smiled uneasily. 'Thank you, Maria.'

She became businesslike. 'Anyway. You have device, I understand, yes?'

The sudden change of subject threw me, and for a moment I had no idea what she meant.

'Listening device? To hear the General's conversations?'

'Oh. Yes. Yes, I do.'

'I tell you when is safe to put in room.'

'I thought—'

She waited me out.

'I thought perhaps you would put the device in place.'

But she was shaking her head before I finished speaking. 'No. That I cannot do.'

'But you would have a reason for being in his suite. If I were caught—'

'If you are caught, you are a lost tourist. If I

141

am caught, I am a dead maid.'

It seemed unarguable. My only rejoinder—that I would have to be a very lost tourist indeed to end up in the General's suite—failed to reach my lips. There was a limit to what Maria was prepared to do for her stipend, and this exceeded it.

I said, 'I have never done this before.'

I'm not sure why I told her this.

She said, 'No. But do not worry. I tell you when is safe.'

*   *   *

She tell me when is safe. That should have been a comfort, but over the next days, I felt anything but secure. The game of being a tourist—of taking the dangerously overloaded bus into the hills to the famous caves; of wandering the market, buying coins from 'centuries-old pirate hauls'—felt like its rules had changed. Those soldiers: were they eyeing their police counterparts, or watching my every move? That pair of policemen, pacing behind me—was that coincidence? The second evening I dared not venture out of my room, which was very un-tourist behaviour. Not appearing at the bar, was unheard of, without a doctor's certificate.

That night I slept badly. It seemed I heard noises in the hillsides; beasts engaged in combat over the same dry bones.

But in the morning, Maria was waiting when I went for breakfast. 'Tonight,' she said.

I looked around. There was no one in sight. Nobody cared I was talking to a maid. 'Is it safe?'

'He goes to the casino. Every week, this day. He leaves at nine, returns at two, three. You have all evening.'

'It won't take ten minutes.'

I was fairly certain of this. I had been shown many times how to plant a bug.

She said, 'You are not scared.'

It didn't appear to be a question. I answered, anyway: 'A little scared, yes. I've never done this before.'

The eyes beneath those heavy brows glanced briefly towards heaven. 'You go in at ten, yes? I wait on stairs. I keep guard.'

'What about his soldiers? Don't they watch his room?'

'They watch his back. They go to casino also.'

She bustled off, on maidly tasks. I had no appetite for breakfast, and returned to my room.

* * *

I don't remember much about that day. I examined the eavesdropping device I had been equipped with, I'm sure of that—it was smaller than a watchface—and practised attaching it

143

to the mouthpiece of my telephone. After a few dry runs, this took no more than a minute. I would also have to search the General's suite. There might be documents or photographs that I, in turn, should photograph. The camera I had used as a tourist was of the normal size, but the one I had been supplied with for this purpose would fit in a pocket. This, too, I practised with. The rest of the day is a blur.

The balcony. I expect I sat on the balcony, looking down on the square below. All those people milling about. One way or the other, my mission would affect their lives—did that responsibility weigh on me? I don't think so.

At 9.55, Maria knocked softly on my door.

'It's time?' I asked her stupidly.

'He not here for hours. Now is safe.'

I nodded, meaning it as thanks. Then I took the stairs to the fifth floor, and the General's suite.

The hallway was empty, Rubello's guards nowhere in sight. As Maria had said, they watched his back and not his rooms. I knocked on the door. No answer. If there had been, I'd have fainted on the spot. I looked over my shoulder to see the top of Maria's head, a few stairs down the well, then used skeleton keys to open the door, my heart pounding louder than any overhead fan. The room was cool. It faced the bay, and the balcony doors were open, the curtains fluffing in the breeze.

Noises drifted upwards: gossip from the bar, and distant music.

I stepped to the phone, but could not unscrew the mouthpiece.

It was something from a dream—the gate that comes no closer, no matter how fast you run; the corridor that stretches endlessly ahead. No matter how hard I twisted, the mouthpiece remained immoveable. Downstairs, disassembling the phone had been the work of seconds; here, it felt like one of Hercules' tasks. From the patio, conversation drifted: I heard laughter and singing. The laughter might have been aimed at me.

But I had hours. There was surely somewhere else I could place the transmitter. The trouble was, I had been given no alternative instructions; no standby location. The bug was small, but not invisible. I could fix it beneath a table, but it might be found by a maid other than Maria. And would not overhear both sides of a telephone conversation.

After what can't have been more than ten minutes, but felt as many weeks, I cursed my luck and gave up. But there were still the General's papers to look for. I was halfway to the desk when I heard voices from the hallway. I think my heart stopped at that moment. Before it could start again, I did the only sensible thing of my life. I dropped the transmitter on the floor, and with my foot nudged it under the bed.

The door opened.

*   *   *

This is my report. I have covered the background. There are things that happened you do not need to know.

*   *   *

Up close, the General is uglier than he appears in photographs. His face is pockmarked and cratered; ruined by adolescent inflammation. When he speaks, it is at a higher pitch than might be expected.

'How did you get in here?'

'The door was unlocked,' I stammered.

'No. My door is always locked. Did Maria let you in?'

He knew about Maria.

I shook my head. Nodded. Shook my head.

'So. You come for a favour, yes?'

I had no other answer. 'Yes.'

'You are a tourist. For my people, I do many favours. What favour can I do a tourist?'

'I am a writer,' I said. 'A journalist.'

'You have no press card. You are not registered as a journalist. Your visa, it says tourist.'

I nodded again, dumbly.

'I noticed you in the lobby. I asked about

146

your papers.'

'I plan to become a journalist,' I amended. 'I hope to sell a story soon.'

'But you do not belong to a newspaper.'

'No,' I said.

'I see.' He considered the matter. 'They call this freelance?'

It was a glimmer of light in the darkest of rooms. I groped towards it. 'That's what they call it, yes. Freelance. I hope to write a story and sell it to a newspaper. And then I will be a journalist.'

'I see. And so you come to my room.'

'I . . . I was hoping for an interview.'

'We have many journalists here. Many stay at this hotel. You want an interview? I give interviews every week.'

I said, 'You give the same interview every week.'

He smiled at that.

'I was hoping for something a little more . . .'

My mouth was dry. Vocabulary failed me. This man had tortured prisoners to death.

He said, 'Something a little more private.'

' . . . Yes.'

'Something a little more intimate.'

' . . . Yes.'

'So you become a famous journalist. First to interview next President of little island paradise.'

I said, 'Yes.'

147

He nodded. He unbuttoned his jacket. Through the window behind me, laughter and song still drifted.

'So,' he said. 'I do you this favour. What will you do in return?'

Without waiting for a reply, he picked up the phone I had been unable to master. 'No calls,' he said.

*   *   *

Some men use sex as power. I don't need to tell you that.

Perhaps the worst of it was, I could not pretend to be there against my will. If the General knew I was a spy, he wouldn't waste time on a trial. He would have put a bullet in my head, and had me carted through the lobby in a basket. When your men loot villages on your word, the disposal of a body is a domestic trifle. His type or not.

And besides, besides, besides—even if my wants had aligned with his, he was not the man I would have chosen to enjoy them with. He takes his pleasures as roughly as he treats the island he would rule. He expects his commands to be fulfilled instantly. And there is no apparent limit to the degradation he inflicts.

Sometimes I see them leaving in the morning. They look as if daylight will strike them dead.

                    *   *   *

That night, as we both know, Chief of Police
Andrea Nabar seized power in a bloodless
coup. No shooting, no explosions—a polite
signing over of power by a dimwit long
stupefied by presidential responsibility. I
stumbled from Rubello's suite at six; by ten
past, the General was under arrest. His 'No
calls' was more than a suggestion to the
switchboard—long practice had established it
as code for total privacy. The armed guards on
the stairwell brooked no interruption. The first
inkling they had of regime change was the new
Presidential guard arriving, with heavy
artillery.

And we both know too that what happened
to me was deliberate. It was no accident I was
chosen for this mission doomed to fail; no
accident I was the General's *type*. And no
accident he returned early from the casino that
night. Maria was not simply our asset; she
would hardly have been suffered to continue
working (indeed, living) if she were. She was
also the General's pander. Intelligence assets,
like whores, indulge more than one master.
Some while after she glued his telephone's
mouthpiece to its receiver, she had told
Rubello I was there. That she had done both
on your orders did not interfere with his lusts.

Rubello was well and truly occupied while
the island's future slipped into his rival's

hands.

And me? Once able to do so without obvious pain, I took a flight home. To write this, my first and last report.

What should I have expected, working for a Service whose practice is deception?

May you, and all who work for you, rot in hell.

*   *   *

The Head of Section laid the folder on the desk and paused for a moment. Then she sighed, picked up a pen, and initialled James Daisy's report.

And that was all she wrote.

GOING BACK

Ann Cleeves

Susan had thought she would recognise the place immediately. The pictures in her head were solid and precise. She revisited them regularly, saw them like photos. The grey line of houses surrounded by grey hills. The school playground only separated from fields by a low stone wall, so the wind blowing across it chapped their lips and turned their fingers blue. The tubular steel climbing frame, where she'd hung from her knees, her skirt falling over her upper body and the three girls in the corner of the yard, sniggering and pointing, shouting at the boys to look. *We can see your knickers! We can see your knickers!* The chimney-shaped stove in the junior classroom, which the caretaker filled with coke and which belched out sulphur-tasting fumes. Her mother's mouth crimped in disapproval.

But everything was different. The village had become a fashionable place to live, within easy commuting distance of Leeds. You could tell that rich people lived here. The school had been converted into a picture from a glossy magazine. Through plate glass windows you could see a pale wood mezzanine floor and exposed beams. Susan wondered if there was

151

any chance of seeing inside, of smelling the wood and touching the heavy fabric of the curtains. Changes to the School House, where she'd lived, were more modest, but the lines of the severe square box had been softened by a conservatory and hanging baskets. In her memory she saw the house through drizzle and fog. Her mother's resentment at being forced to live there had imposed its own micro-climate. Today there was the pale, lemon sunshine of early spring.

And she was back. A fiftieth birthday present to herself. What did they call it? Exorcising ghosts.

So she stood for a moment trying to find her bearings. She sensed Tom's impatience, but this was her time. Let him wait. She stared fiercely down the road, then closed her eyes and laid the pattern of houses over the landscape of her memory.

'They've widened the lane,' she said. 'The verge was deeper then.'

He kept quiet. He knew it was important not to say the wrong thing.

When they'd moved here from Leeds, her mother had called it a cultural desert. It had been her father's first headship and he'd had no real choice in the matter. He hadn't fitted in at his previous school and had been told by the director of education to apply. He had no vocation for teaching. In the war he'd been happy, had hoped the fighting would go on forever. Afterwards, what could he do? The government needed teachers and would pay him to train.

Her mother had met him when he was a mature student and had rather liked the idea of marrying a teacher. It was a respectable profession. Perhaps she pictured him in a gown taking assembly in an oak panelled hall. Susan thought she couldn't have been aware then of the reality—the poor pay, the grubby children who wet their pants and carried nits. Her father didn't have the academic qualification to teach in a Grammar School. He was reduced to drilling the four times table into the heads of bored seven year olds, to supervising the half-dressed prancing to Music and Movement on the wireless. It was no job, he said, for a grown man.

And this, he had to admit, was no real headship. There were only thirty children, fifteen infants and fifteen juniors. He took the juniors in one classroom and Miss Pritchard took the infants in the other. Susan's mother never liked Miss Pritchard, who was plump, comfortable and vacuous. She liked nothing about the village at all. All she could think of was moving back to the city.

The house was always cold. Even in summer the damp in the walls and the floor seeped into your bones. The wind blew over the Pennines and under the doors. Susan remembered the building in black and white, like the fuzzy pictures on the television in the corner of the front room. Her parents sat every evening in silence watching television, surrounded by their utility furniture, the few good pieces of china her mother had inherited from a well-off aunt, an inscribed tankard which had been given to her father when he left his last school. And always, sometimes even drowning out the voices on the TV, there was the sound of the sheep on the hill. Like a baby crying in the distance.

Susan had escaped outside, to ride her bike down the lane and play on the climbing frame in the school yard. Always on her own. Nobody wanted to be friends with the teacher's lass. They were frightened she'd tell on them. She saw them sometimes, the other girls, Heather and Diane and Marilyn sitting on the pavement outside the council houses down the hill, their heads together over some game. She never went to join them. She knew she wouldn't be welcome and besides, her mother didn't like her mixing. But she watched them. She always knew what they were up to.

She had been so strong then, so easy in her body. She'd walked miles across the hills. There'd been handstands against the wall, reckless slides across ice on the playground, cartwheels. Her mother hadn't approved. If she saw her daughter on the climbing frame she'd rap on the kitchen window to call her into the house.

'What's the matter?' Susan knew how to play the innocent. She'd had to learn.

'Behaving like that. Showing your underwear to that boy.' The boy was Eddie Black, a slow, gentle fifteen year old who lived in the cottage next to the school. He spent much of his time in the garden, in a wire mesh aviary, caring for his birds.

Susan wondered why that was so wrong. Why was that different from doing Music and Movement in front of her father? Or his coming into her bedroom when she was dressing. But she said nothing. She knew it was impossible to argue with her mother when her mouth was stretched in that thin-lipped way. When the sherry bottle was uncorked on the kitchen table and the first glass was already empty.

One evening stuck in her memory. It had been just before Easter and her mother had gone into Leeds to a concert. The Messiah. She'd driven herself in the black Morris Minor. An adventure, but an ordeal. She'd never enjoyed driving. When she returned she was a different woman. Susan thought, if she'd bumped into her in the street, she wouldn't have recognised her, the colour in her cheeks, the way she stood. Susan had sat on the stairs wrapped up in the candlewick dressing gown listening to her mother's voice.

'Let's move, Philip. Please can we move back? A fresh start.'

155

She hadn't heard her father's answer, but the next day nothing had changed and the move was never mentioned again. She couldn't tell if anything was different between them.

And me? Susan wondered. What was I feeling in this house I don't know anymore? Nothing. I crept around on the edge of their lives, frozen and silent, trying above all not to make things worse. In school it was the same. Making myself invisible so they wouldn't poke and pinch and jeer. I only felt alive when I was outside, when I was running or climbing. Or watching.

'Well?' Tom asked, breaking into her memories.

'The gate into the field's in the same place.'

It could even be the same gate. It was green with litchen and sagging on its hinges. The same sound of wind and sheep. The quarry had finished working even before her day. Now only a tractor would go through occasionally. This was rough grazing and took little work.

'We used to have sports day in that field, the flat bit near the gate. The quarry's up the hill.'

She said *used to* but as far as she could remember it had only happened once. Her father must have made some arrangement with the farmer. They'd all trooped out through the open gate. No uniform sports kit. It wasn't that sort of school. She was the only

156

one with an airtex shirt and navy blue shorts. Heather wore a cotton dress, very short. The fashion. She was in her last year of juniors and already had breasts, which bounced as she ran. Not that she'd put much effort into the running. It had been a simpering show. She'd looked around her making sure they were all watching. But Susan had won the race. She'd crossed the line even before the boys. *That'll show them,* she'd thought. Flying across the field, she'd felt triumphant. This small world was hers. Let the other girls say what they liked. And of course they'd had plenty to say. Real girls didn't run. Not like that.

Now, middle-aged, she felt the first twinges of arthritis in her shoulders and her knees. She was overweight and unfit. All her movements were tentative. She'd never have that freedom again. The confidence to balance, arms outstretched on the top bar of the farm gate. That sense of running over the uneven grass. She caught her breath to prevent a wail of loss and regret.

Soon after Sports Day, Heather Mather had gone missing. At first everyone thought she'd run away, hitched a lift into Leeds or sneaked onto the Secondary Modern bus. She was a flighty thing. 'Too old for her years,' said Mrs Tillotson, the widow who took the Sunday school and played the out of tune organ in the church. A policeman came to the school and talked to them all in turn, looking very big and clumsy sitting on one of the children's chairs, his bum hanging over each side. They hadn't laughed at him. They knew he was trying to be friendly. Her father had stood at the front of the class, watching and frowning. Even if Susan had wanted to tell the policeman what she knew about Heather Mather and where she was, it would be quite impossible with her father listening in.

Then, when Heather didn't return, the word in the village was that Eddie Black had taken her. Eddie lived with his mother and though he'd left school, he didn't work. Susan knew Eddie hadn't taken Heather. He wouldn't know how to hurt her. He was painfully careful when he held his birds, and once when Susan had tripped and fallen, grazing her knee so it bled, he had cried. But everyone in the village said he'd taken her. One night someone threw a rock through Mrs Black's bedroom window. The next morning Eddie woke up to find that two of his birds were dead. Their necks had been twisted. He stood in his garden and looked round him, bewildered, his mouth slightly open, as if he couldn't really understand what had happened.

Heather never turned up and her body was never found. The police wanted to charge Eddie with her murder, but decided that they had insufficient evidence. Even in those days, more was needed than neighbourhood gossip and a gut feeling that the boy was odd. They needed a body.

Beside her, Tom coughed. He didn't want this to last all day. He wanted to be home in Durham, before it got dark. He knew it was important, but he was a great one for routine. He liked to get his dinner on time. Susan untied the frayed baler twine which attached the gate to the post, lifted it on its hinges over the long grass and they walked through.

'This way,' she said. 'Mind though, it's a bit of a walk.'

Heather Mather had boyfriends nobody knew anything about. Not a real boyfriend. Not a lad her own age to have a giggle with, holding hands on the way down from the hill. Games of doctors and nurses in the shed at the bottom of the garden, brief forbidden kisses and flushed red faces. The other girls played games like that, but not Heather. She *was* too old for her years, as Mrs Tillotson had said, and when she thought no-one was looking she had a watchful, wary look. Sometimes Susan thought, if she hadn't been the teacher's daughter, they might have been friends. Heather's boyfriends were older. They were men, not boys. She got into their cars and drove off with them and when she got back she lied about where she'd been. Even to Marilyn and Diane.

Uncle Alec took me to the pictures in town.
And Uncle Alec lied about it too.
It were a good film, weren't it, love?

159

His arm around her, protective, as they stood on the short strip of pavement, the only pavement in the village, outside her house. Alec Mather, her Dad's brother, who worked as gamekeeper on the big estate, who was tall and strong and carried a gun. Who had a dog which would do anything Alec told it, which would go through fire for him, everyone said, but which snarled and bared its teeth at anyone else. Susan tried for a moment to remember the name of the dog. Why wouldn't it come to her, when everything else was so clear? Soon she gave up. She had other, more disturbing memories.

It hadn't been Alec's car Heather had climbed into, her skirt riding up, so she nearly showed *her* knickers, the first time Susan had watched her. It could have been one of Alec's friends who was driving. He was about the same age, dark hair, greased back, a tattoo on the back of his hand. And later, when he dropped Heather back in the lane down to the church, Alec was there to meet them. When Heather wasn't looking (though Susan was, hiding at the top of a high stone wall, which surrounded the churchyard) the stranger seemed to hand him money. Alec slipped it quickly into the pocket of his jacket. The wall was nearly three feet thick, covered with ivy and overhung with branches. Susan could remember the smell of the ivy even now, as they walked across the field, up the hill towards the quarry. This was the first of several encounters she witnessed over the months. Sometimes the men were strangers and sometimes she recognised them. Money usually changed hands.

Would she have described this to the friendly policeman when he came to the classroom to ask about Heather, if her father hadn't been there, listening in? Perhaps she would. Then everything would have been different. Her whole life. She wouldn't be here, walking up the hill with Tom on an April afternoon.

After that day she watched Heather more closely. She listened to the women talking after church. Heather's father had gone away to work. He'd got a job as a cook in the merchant navy. Alec spent a lot of time with the family to keep an eye on things. It only made sense.

And one afternoon Susan watched Heather climb into her father's car, the teacher's car. It was soon after Sports Day, at the start of the school holidays, one of those rare hot, still days. In the house there had still been a chill caused by the rotting walls and her parents' antagonism. Her father said he had an NUT meeting in Leeds and her mother wanted a lift into town. He'd told her it wasn't possible. He'd promised a lift to colleagues from the villages on the way. There wouldn't be room in the Morris for Sylvia too. She'd sulked, fetched the sherry from the side board, which she only did at lunchtime when she was severely provoked. Outside it was airless. Susan felt the sun burning her bare arms and legs, beating up from the tarmac of the playground. She went to her nest on the churchyard wall not to watch, but to find some shade.

She saw Heather first. She was on her own. No Alec. No Marilyn and Diane. She walked slowly down the lane, her head bent, looking down at her sandals. In September she'd move on to the big school and already Susan could sense that gulf between them. It was very quiet. There was a wood pigeon calling from the trees behind the church and the distant, inevitable sheep. Then a car engine and the Morris Minor, squat and shiny as a beetle, drove solely past. It stopped just beyond Heather. She didn't change her pace or look up, but when she reached the passenger door, she opened it and got in. Despite the sun reflected from the car's bonnet, which made her screw up her eyes, Susan was frozen. She wanted to shout out. *Hello. Heather. Look at me. Come and play.* Anything to stop her climbing into the car. But the words wouldn't come. The car pulled slowly away, backed into the church entrance to turn, then drove off.

Alec was there when it returned. He was leaning against the wall, turning his face to the sun, so close to Susan that she could almost have reached out and touched his hair. The dog was with him, lying on the road, its tongue out, panting. Her father was alone in the car. The window was open and she could see his face, very red. He was furious.

'You cheated me,' he said. It was a hiss not a whisper. Alec hadn't moved from the wall and if her father had spoken more softly he wouldn't have been heard. Susan thought he sounded a bit like one of the little boys in the infants' class, complaining about a stolen toy. *It's not fair.* That was what her father meant, even if he didn't say it.

'She came with you, didn't she?' Still Alec leaned against the wall, his arms folded against his chest, that smile on his face.

'But she wouldn't even let me . . .'

'That were down to you, weren't it? She's only a slip of a thing.'

'For Christ's sake, man.'

'Anyway, that were the deal. Ten pounds. No going back now. Any road, it's already spent. Where is she?'

'Up on the hill. Near the quarry. We went for a walk. I thought . . .' He didn't finish the sentence.

'Aye well, I reckon she'll come down in her own time. I'll have a word. Make her see sense. You can fix up to take her out later, if you like.'

Her father didn't reply. He didn't mention the money again, though money was always tight in their house. It was one of the things her parents fought about. He wound up the window and drove off. She wondered where he went. Not to the union meeting. He wouldn't have had time to get to Leeds and back. Later though, when it was dark outside and they were watching the television, he talked about the resolutions they'd discussed at the meeting and the men he'd met. Susan would have been entirely taken in if she hadn't known he was lying. She wondered how many times he'd lied to them before. It was as if everything was a game and nothing was real any more.

Heather didn't go home that night. That was the day she disappeared.

Susan thought she couldn't have been the only person in the village to know about Heather's men friends and how Alec organised it all. They must have seen the strangers' cars, realised there were nights when the gamekeeper had cash to spend in the pub. But nobody spoke. When the police asked questions the villagers talked about shy Eddie Black. Otherwise they kept their mouths firmly shut. Alec's dog had a mad eye and Alec had a fierce temper, even when he was smiling. They didn't want to know what had really happened to Heather.

Susan knew. When her father had driven off and Alec had sauntered back to the village, towards the house he shared with Heather's mum, she'd scrambled down from the wall, pulling away the ivy in her haste. Despite the heat she'd gone to the hill, running all the way. She hadn't opened the gate into the quarry field that day, she'd climbed it. Then, she'd been young and strong. From half way up the hill, she'd seen Heather lying flat on her back at the edge of the old workings. At first she'd thought she was asleep, but as she approached, scattering the sheep in her path, she'd realised that the girl's eyes were open and there were tears on her cheeks.

Heather heard her coming. She must have done. By then Susan was out of breath, panting, and there'd be the sound of her footsteps and the sheep loping off. But she didn't sit up until the very last minute.

'Oh,' she said. 'It's you.'

'Who were you expecting?' Susan demanded. 'Alec? My Dad?'

'Your father? He's pathetic.'

That was what they always called *Susan*. It was the jeer that followed her around the playground. *You're pathetic, you are.* Shouted in turn by Marilyn, Diane and Heather. It was the word that made her fight back.

'Not as pathetic as your Dad. Moving out and letting Alec take up with your Mam. Not as pathetic as you, going off with all those men, just because he tells you.'

She was shocked by her own courage. She'd never stood up to one of them before. Heather was stunned too. She got to her feet but didn't say anything. Susan thought she might run down the hill and home. But she didn't. She just stared.

At last Heather spoke. 'If you say anything at school, I'll tell them about your father. I'll tell them he made me go off with him.'

'I wouldn't tell them!' Susan moved forward. 'I never would.' In her head she had a picture of the two of them, sitting on the pavement outside the council houses, friends brought together by the shared secret. Besides, who would she tell?

Heather must have seen the step towards her as a threat. She backed away, lost her footing, slipped. Susan might have been able to save her. She was strong. And there was a moment when she almost did it. When she almost reached out and grabbed the girl's arm. If she saved Heather's life, wouldn't she have to be her friend? But she decided not to. She wanted to see what it would look like. What Heather would look like rolling down the steep bank until she reached the overhang and fell into nothing. What sound she would make when she hit the stones below. It was as if all the watching had been leading up to this moment. And it was all very satisfactory, very satisfying. There was the expression of panic when Heather scrabbled to save herself and realised it was useless, the moment of flight, the dull thud. And then her undignified resting place amongst the rubble of quarry waste, her skirt around her waist, her legs spread out.

Susan would have liked to leave her there for everyone to see.

But that wouldn't do. Someone might have seen Susan get over the gate into the field. Then there'd be questions she didn't want to answer. And Susan wanted to get closer to the body. She was curious now to see what it looked like. She peered down over the lip of the cliff to the face of the quarry where the stone had been hacked away. It was a difficult climb, but not impossible for her, not so very different from scrambling down from the church yard wall. Only in scale. At the bottom she took a minute to catch her breath. She stood over Heather, who didn't really look like Heather at all now. Then she rolled her close into the cliff face and piled her body with the loose rocks which lined the quarry bottom. That was more exhausting than the climb back. When she reached the top the sun was very low. She took one last look down the cliff. Because of the angle it was hard to see where Heather was lying and even if you could see the place it would look as if there'd been a small rock fall.

When she got in her mother told her off for being so filthy. *When are you going to start acting like a girl?* Her father talked about the union meeting. They watched television. There was shepherd's pie for tea.

The policeman came into school to ask his questions and later she wished she'd told him what had happened. She could have explained that it was an accident. She could have said she'd panicked. They'd have had to accept that. They'd have given her help. But perhaps by then it was already too late. The trouble was she'd enjoyed it. The moment when Heather fell had been so exciting. It had the thrill and the power of running across the field in sports day, of crossing the line first. It had caused sparks in her brain. She'd wanted to recreate that buzzing sensation. She'd thought of nothing else. That was why she'd killed Eddie's birds. But birds aren't like people. It wasn't the same.

Tom wasn't much fitter than she was and it took them longer than she'd expected to walk up the hill to the disused quarry. Since her time they'd put up a fence and a couple of notices saying it was unsafe. It wasn't as deep as she'd remembered.

'That's where she is,' she said. 'Under that pile of rubble at the bottom of the cliff. That's where you'll find Heather Mather.'

'So,' he said. 'The scene of your first crime.'

'Oh no,' she was offended. 'Heather was an accident. Not like the others.'

She liked Tom. He was her named officer at the prison. She'd refused to speak to the detectives and the psychiatrists who'd tried to persuade her to tell them where Heather Mather was. Her first victim, as they called her. The first of four before she was caught. All pretty girls, who simpered and pouted and made up to older men.

Tom spoke into his radio and she could already see the police officers who'd been waiting in the van coming through the gate. She let him take her arm and steer her down the hill. He'd be ready for his dinner.

THE BLOGGING GAME

Yvonne Eve Walus

The next blog I find screams purple text on a black background, a killer on the eyes. I feel no remorse. The owner deserves everything I have in mind for her. Her entry for today is all about rain.

> *The world is a painting, slowly soaked in water, diluted, blurred. The earthworms are tongues of purple paint squashed out of their earth-tubes. I take a sip of hot chocolate. I rub its silk into my palate. This is not chocolate. This is me. I taste myself on my tongue.*

Wow, I love your blog! I write in my comment. **You have the soul of a poet.**
That's all that I need to play The Game.
Rule # 1: If she bites, she's mine.

*　　　*　　　*

The summer sun beat down on South Africa's capital city with its life-sucking sizzle. Lieutenant Wilma van Rooyen looked at the documents in front of her, wiped her moist forehead and popped another piece of a melting Cadbury slab into her mouth. The cloying sweetness made the heat even worse.

I really should stop, she thought. Then she broke off another piece and held it in her fingers as she read the crime scene report.

The victim, a thirty-five-year old single woman, was found dead by a guard in her Moreleta Park security village after one of the neighbours reported a suspicious lack of activity on the premises. In the old days, the report would have given the victim's race, but in today's post-apartheid era, the race had to be deduced from the name and the photographs. In this case, Nakti Singh. Indian.

There were no signs of a forced entry or assault, which was a welcome change from all the armed break-ins that too often resulted in the death of the robbed residents. Nakti Singh's body was slumped forward onto the keyboard of her computer, the machine still running. The officer in charge was meticulous enough to include the last web page viewed by the victim: a blog site.

Found clutched in the victim's left hand was a mirror. An empty used syringe lay on the floor next to the computer stand.

A thorough search of the flat failed to produce anything out of the ordinary: no illegal substances, not even a gun—that traditional item of most South African households.

The post-mortem report came next. Death

by an overdose of heroin, a single needle mark. Van Rooyen skipped all the units and numbers. She was hardly interested in the exact weight of the victim's liver. She looked at the summary: good health, not pregnant, not sexually abused, no suggestion of struggle.

Case closed. There were so many others awaiting her attention. Cases of accidental shootings with one's own gun. Cases of being killed in your bed for your laptop. Cases of brutal rape followed by even more brutal murder. She should be getting on to them.

And yet, the tidy—almost too tidy—case of Nakti Singh's death, wouldn't let Lieutenant van Rooyen be.

She leafed through the papers again (oh, when are they going to enter the 21st century and go electronic). And there it was again: good health, a single needle mark, no drugs found on the premises.

Of course, it was still possible for the victim to be a user. She could have smoked grass at school, swallowed acid at parties, then one day finally decided to try the taboo of heroin.

Lieutenant van Rooyen looked at her hands. The entire slab of Cadbury was gone, her fingers licked clean.

*　　　*　　　*

What I love most about The Game, is winning. I know it would be nobler to say that it's the ecstasy of the chase, the mental masturbation of playing the right words, the sportsmanship. But I would be lying. I play to accrue victories.

> *Ppl tag me to list down 5 wierd things abt me. I'm finally doin it today. So here goes nothing, in no ptclr order*
> *love my long hair its great.*
> *I h8 the smell of cocoa—*

The blog goes on and on, I have trouble focussing on its txt-speak, its meaningless babble. And yet deep inside I know. This will be the next one. Not because I like the writing—but precisely because I don't. It'll be a real challenge to find the right words to make this one want to play.

I phrase my reply carefully. The adrenalin pumps thick in my ears. I can taste the thrill of The Game. One strike and I'm out. If I choose the wrong phrase, The Game is over.

It's easy with the poets, the writers, the wordsmiths. They understand the power of words. And they can't resist mine.

But how does one hook the others? The word-barbarians who don't understand the first thing about grammar or story-telling? The navel-gazing self-centred hordes who impose their verbal diarrhoea on the world?

My fingers fly over the keyboard: **You have the soul of a true romantic. I feel I know you already. Have we ever met? In another lifetime**

perhaps?

All women are alike. Accountants, interior decorators, housewives. In London, or Mumbai, or Idaho. Black, white or completely green. They all have the same lowest common denominator: no matter how much they deny it, deep inside they are all waiting for their prince to ride into the ordinariness of their lives in his white BMW and take them far-far away to fabulous riches and eternal love.

It's so easy. Just give them the words they want to hear. Cheap cubic zirconia words, as effective as diamonds.

*　　　*　　　*

Had Lieutenant Wilma van Rooyen not been on duty that evening, Anna Barnard's death would probably have been signed off as a heroin overdose. Anna was a twenty-year old with a history of drug abuse. Her body was found by her live-in boyfriend in their bathroom, the syringe still clutched in her fingers. The boyfriend was distraught. He claimed that (a) Anna had been clean for months, and (b) she hadn't had any money for smack.

'That's odd,' muttered van Rooyen to her colleague. 'Why would she take her laptop into the bathroom to shoot junk?'

'Wanted to write a blog entry while she was high, did she?'

A blog entry? Wilma van Rooyen frowned. The Indian girl, what was her name, Nalini? No, Nakti.

'Kobus,' said van Rooyen, 'get me all the O.D. cases in the Gauteng area for the last two years.'

'You're kidding, right?'

Wilma sighed. Clearly, she'd been watching too much American TV. This here was Africa.

'Just bring whatever files you can find in central storage. We'll go through them together. And Kobus?'

'Ja?'

'Catch.' Van Rooyen tossed a few coins into the air. 'Grab us a couple of chocolate bars on the way. They will go nicely with all the file dust.'

*   *   *

I can't find a good one today. The blogs on my to-do list all seem too similar to the last five. Rule # 4: never get bored. That's a good rule: I'm ready for a degree of novelty.

Not too much novelty is permitted, of course. Rule # 3: settle on one M.O. and don't change it within the same run of The Game.

My M.O. for this run is blog comments. I did emails in a previous run of The Game, but the intimacy of email made it far too easy: you can say things in email that you can't in the open forum of blog comments.

Rule # 2: Keep playing, don't take more than three days to select your new partner. In desperation, I visit one of the South African blog rings and start clicking at random. The first one I find has an interesting title, 'A journey through the time' by somebody called Betelgeuse, but the blog turns out to be in Afrikaans.

Another one, Clouded Mind, shows promise with its paranoid prose and its cries for help, but when I notice all the bi-polar links, I decide against it. Mentally ill people are simply too unstable to play The Game.

I press the Next button. The blog has to speak to me. I know I'm doing it all wrong by searching this way. The Game is about words, not about fate. I don't like the entropy that results from chance. But my finger keeps moving.

Next.

Next.

Next.

At last. This blog is clearly written by a man, I know it from the tone. I'm both excited and a little apprehensive: I've never played with a man before. But the entry speaks to me, so it's settled: this will be my new Game partner.

What is it with the media? I _know_ that the average person is pretty damn thick. So one part of me says 'yeah, okay, fair enough, dumb reporting for a dumb audience'. And another part says 'But, but, but . . .'

Wow, cool blog! I write. **You have the mind of an analyst.**

Hmmm, that may not be sufficient. So I add: **But you should have put a comma before the quotes.**

Yes, that should do it.

* * *

The Colonel was not impressed.

'So this guy, what? Kills you by writing comments in your blog?'

Lieutenant van Rooyen grit her teeth so hard her jaw hurt. 'That's how he makes contact, sir, by writing a comment. He goes by the handle *Game Player*. The blog author reacts to his comment with a comment of her own, he responds in kind and so the conversation continues until his last, fatal, comment.'

'Don't these women know the first thing about Internet safety?'

'Sir, his victims feel safe, because he doesn't suggest a meeting or even a phone conversation. They only ever speak on the blog, never divulging their personal details.'

Van Rooyen knew what the next question would be, but she knew better than to interrupt when it came.

177

'So how does he find them?'

'Through the blog, sir. Most people assume your blog identity is anonymous provided you don't have your name in it, but that's no problem to any smart hacker. Once *Game Player* figures out the victim's identity and finds her postal address, he sends her a little parcel of heroin in the mail.'

*   *   *

Rule # 17 of The Game states plainly: if you fail once, you must stop.

But, having failed, I now realise that the rule is ambiguous. Firstly, it doesn't specify *what* I must stop: the whole run of The Game or just the pursuit of this particular victim. And secondly, I initiated The Game with women in mind. Failure to entice a man to play shouldn't really count as such.

So perhaps I am allowed to go on, after all. If I don't, I'll have to find a new Game with a new M.O. And then so much preparation will go to waste: the carefully worded letters on genuine letterheads, the catalogues, the boxes that look as though they've come straight from the marketing room of a big corporation.

Sometimes the heroin is disguised as a skin-rejuvenator: 'Just one drink from the fountain of youth and your wrinkle worries fade', or a vitamin injection: 'Preserve your health forever', or a slimming product: 'Your weight just disappears'. All of the statements are true, too, in a way, and that's more than I can say for real advertising.

My ultimate fantasy is to be able to attach 'My words kill you' as a slogan to one of the heroin parcels.

*   *   *

It didn't take Wilma van Rooyen a long time to learn how to create her own blog on her home computer. For good measure, she created ten of them, all in the line of duty. It's not as if she had anything else to do, though: no boyfriend since longer than she cared to remember, no hobbies, and the TV sucked.

She rewarded herself for every blog with a chocolate from a Dairy Box. An old radio ad suddenly echoed in her mind. A wedding night, a Dairy Box, an eaten praline and the recurring line 'You're so selfish!'

Wilma smiled. Perhaps it was just as well she didn't have a boyfriend.

Then her smile faded. She recalled another ad for the Dairy Box. A queen, her knight bringing gold and perfume from afar. The queen not impressed . . . until he pulls out a Dairy Box. The closing line: 'Oh darling, you shouldn't have.'

Perhaps she shouldn't have. But now it was too late. The bait was cast.

The internet is a superb thing: it has something special for everybody. The pervs can download free photos of whatever stokes their desires, the lonely can talk to other losers, the liars can play out their fantasies. ('I'm a 22-year old blonde with big boobs,' yeah right. And I own a corporate empire yet have enough time on my hands to chat online every night.)

Anyway, the internet allows people like me to talk to other people like me. There's a man in America who—if he's to be believed—can hypnotise his fellow Game players to commit suicide. I was sceptical at first, but the way he described it sounded plausible enough. He conducted an internet relationship with a nineteen year old for a whole year. He found out a lot of personal details during that time, all her secret fantasies and fears (it's insane what people tell strangers online). One day, during their phone conversation, he hypnotised the girl into jumping out of the window by making her think it was a diving board at a school gala. 'Jump, your father's watching,' he apparently said. And jump she did.

Anyway, I'm still debating the precise small print of The Game's rules on our forum, when I stumble upon her blog.

There it is, in black and white—or in black

and beige, to be precise. The list of names of all the girls who played with me, together with the dates of my victories.

I am acutely tempted to answer, to leave a warning comment on the blog.

You have the soul of a policeman, I chuckle as I imagine writing it. **In a way, we are almost soul mates: I also ensnare**.

But of course, that would be unwise. So all I do in the end is trace her contact details, her likes and dislikes, her entire personality. It's right there in her blog, and she doesn't even realise that a single sentence on her profile page tells me more about her than meeting her face to face would.

*   *   *

It was another hot Friday afternoon. Wilma van Rooyen could feel her uniform stick to her skin as she stepped out of her car to buy a piece of grilled chicken for her supper. On the way, she emptied her post box. A bill from Telkom, a postcard from a girlfriend who was enjoying her holidays skiing in Switzerland—the snow looked freezing and Wilma imagined the pleasure of rolling naked in its virgin cool. Oh, bother, a note from the post office about a parcel.

She was just in time. The post office was closing already.

'Here you are,' said the grumpy woman

behind the counter.

The parcel was small, official-looking. Wilma opened it when she got home. Inside was a promotional note from Cadbury inviting her to sample their latest flavour in the Luxury Range, and a large bar of chocolate. Wilma studied the colourful wrapper. Beautiful. Thick swirls of chocolate against a rich gold background, the name of the bar embossed into the silky paper.

Alas, as soon as Wilma touched it, warm liquid chocolate oozed out of the foil, covering the exquisite golden wrapping with its melted goo.

Wilma shrugged. The chocolate company must be mad to send out promotional items in this heat. She licked her fingers absent-mindedly, then threw the entire parcel into the bin.

THE END OF A SERIES

Jürgen Ehlers

'This might well be the beginning of a series.' Stolle spreads both files on the desk in front of his colleague.

Meyers shrugs. To him it looks rather like the end of a series. Two bank robberies, in November and December 1951, and nothing since. Nine months quiet. 'It's rather a long time ago. It's over,' he says.

'Still unsolved. And within our *Polizeidirektion*, Meyers.' Lüneburg Police are responsible for the whole area down to Soltau and Fallingbostel, some 65 kilometres to the south.

Whatever, Meyers thinks. Another two hours and my weekend starts. The robber won't strike now.

*   *   *

It is Saturday, September 6th, 1952. For the man who is driving a stolen car into Buchholz the weekend has started already. He couldn't sleep last night, but now he is wide awake. Everything has gone smoothly and he is confident that it will continue like that. This time he is far better prepared. Nothing to

183

worry about. And if anything should go wrong he still has his gun.

*   *   *

'I don't understand this.' Lotte Schönbohm sighs in despair. She has spread out the forms in front of Blaschke so that Dieckmann cannot see them.

'Don't worry, dear,' says her colleague. 'You've got a whole year. You can apply up until August 1953.'

'Yes, that's what they say now, those politicians.'

'I suppose our government will keep their promises . . .'

Lotte nods. But she thinks: if they all apply—who's going to pay for all that? How many displaced people are there? Millions, that's for sure. It's impossible that they will all get compensations. She is afraid of being late. As soon as the Burden Sharing Law [The Burden Sharing Law provided financial support for the repatriation of ethnic Germans expelled from neighbouring countries following the end of WWII.] became effective, she had collected the questionnaire. And now she doesn't know how to fill it in.

'Blaschke?' asks Dieckmann.

Hurriedly Lotte puts her papers aside. But Dieckmann has seen them anyway. 'That's something you can do after work!'

Lotte blushes. She doesn't want to risk her job. Bank clerk, that is quite something, isn't it? Anyhow—better than nothing. Lotte rushes back to the counter. 'Who is next?'

Blaschke throws an angry look at Dieckmann. Asshole, he thinks.

In the counter area there are four clerks and six customers. Friedrich Dieckmann, the cashier, looks at his watch. Not quite ten. The morning is not even half over. Dieckmann is 64, he has been working in the bank for 45 years. He casts an eye on Lotte, who is busy with a customer. Lotte Schönbohm—she has just turned twenty, just finished her apprenticeship. Good-looking girl. And Blaschke, that whippet! It's clear that he is after her. Or trying at least. Blaschke is more than 20 years his junior. Dieckmann sighs silently and returns to his banknotes. He sorts and counts them. The economy is picking up, good for the banks, good for business!

Dieckmann is bundling the notes to be put in the safe. 18,000 DM—a nice little sum. At that very moment the door is thrust open, and a man storms in, his face hidden under a black scarf. *A raid*, thinks Dieckmann, *my god, this is a raid! What shall I do?* But there is nothing he can do. The man pushes the customers aside. 'Stop it!' one of them shouts, trying to catch his sleeve. The man knocks him down, leaps over the counter and draws a gun. Dieckmann freezes in shock. The robber starts stuffing his bag. Nothing but banknotes, masses of banknotes. All in nice bundles. The band says Kreissparkasse Harburg, Buchholz branch. That will give him away, Dieckmann thinks. If he doesn't get rid of them, they will catch him immediately. Then he realizes that the safe door is ajar. Why didn't he shut it? To save time, of course. Now he will get into trouble. The guy is waving about with his gun and herding them into a corner. 'My god', thinks Lotte Schönbohm. 'Today of all days! All that money! Just as if he had known!' And then: 'For heaven's sake, Blaschke, what on earth is Blaschke up to?'

Blaschke has taken cover behind his desk. This is it. The chance of a lifetime, he thinks. Such an opportunity will not come again. Whilst the robber is plundering the safe, Blaschke sneaks off to the window, unbolts it and jumps out the very moment the robber is finished with the safe. He's bagged the money, runs to the window and jumps. Blaschke is frightened to death, when the man lands on the lawn right next to him. That's it, he thinks, closing his eyes. But the robber takes no notice of Blaschke, instead he runs past him and jumps into his car. A cream-coloured Opel Olympia. And off he goes. The whole raid has taken no more than a minute.

Dieckmann reaches for the phone and rings the police. 'After him!' somebody demands. That is just what Blaschke does. He

186

jumps on his motorbike and roars off. I'll get him, he thinks, I'll get hold of him. Praise and acknowledgment from everyone. Richter, Fricke, all the Harburg management. And what will Lotte say!

But he stands no chance. He should have bought that NSU long ago. Why on earth hadn't he done it? His K50 only manages 40 km/h. In Buchholz that is no problem. In town the guy must drive slowly, too, but as soon as they reach the outskirts, the Opel accelerates. Blaschke can still see him, but the gap is widening. If he is heading for the *Autobahn*, the hunt will be over anyway. But he is not heading for the motorway. He turns left instead. The B3, towards Harburg, Blaschke thinks. But before they reach the *Bundesstraße*, he turns right again. And now it appears that the robber is no longer in any hurry. He seems not to have noticed his tail. In fact, Blaschke is making ground on the Opel. He is heading for the forest, Blaschke thinks. Probably planning to hide the money. Blaschke sees his chance. I can do Jiu-jitsu, I will catch him, he thinks.

*　　　*　　　*

In the meantime, the police have arrived. But they are on bikes, with no chance of pursuing the robber. They have to call Lüneburg. The *Kriminalpolizei* from Lüneburg arrives in less than an hour. They have sent out telexes to all

187

major police stations in Hamburg and Niedersachsen. The Elbe bridges and all access roads to Hamburg are being blocked, all cars checked. But it seems that the robber has not turned towards Hamburg. He seems to have made for the Kleckerwald forest. *Kommissar* Stolle says: 'Meyers, that is your job! If the robber is still hiding in the forest, we will certainly find him.' Meyers sets out for the Kleckerwald. The manhunt is on.

*   *   *

'We will catch him,' Stolle says. 'Eventually.' It has turned out that no immediate arrest is possible. He is trying to assess the situation. What exactly has happened?

The cashier shakes his head. 'I can't believe it. Why on earth did I leave the safe door open? Why?'

'That doesn't make any difference. The guy was armed, he would have forced you to open it.'

'And all the money gone . . .'

'Yes,' says Stolle. 'All the money indeed. 18,000 you say?—That is what struck us, too. A town that small. How many inhabitants do you have?'

'Not even 7000.'

'And so much money in the bank.'

'Normally it would be much less, of course. And I had already counted it. Most of it,

188

anyway. An hour later, and it would have been taken to Harburg, to the central office.'

On the floor in front of the counter lies a small piece of brownish cardboard. Stolle picks it up. 'Has anyone of you lost this?'

Nobody has. It is a railway ticket.

'The robber. It must have dropped out of his pocket when he pulled his gun,' the bank manager suggests.

'Possibly.' It is a ticket for the Osthannoversche Eisenbahnen issued today. Soltau–Lüneburg, return. 'Tell me, who knew about the money?'

'Everybody—This is a savings bank. Every customer can see what's going on, and if I count hundred DM bills, everbody can see there's a lot of money.'

Stolle shakes his head.

'This wasn't something a customer would do on the spur of the moment. This was planned well in advance.'

'Then I don't know.'

'Really?—How many tellers do you have here?'

'There are four of us. Dieckmann, the cashier, Blaschke, Lotte Schönbohm and me.'

'Just four,' says Stolle. He considers that. 'That Blaschke,' he says, 'how long has he been with you?'

'Just about two years, the same as Lotte. You don't think that he might have something to do with this raid, do you?'

Before Stolle can answer, Meyers bursts in, red with excitement. 'He's gone!'

Stolle had not been expecting anything else. 'What about Blaschke?' he asks.

'Waiting outside.'

'So he didn't make it?'

'He was stopped by the barriers. When the train had passed, the Opel was gone.'

Probably better like that, Stolle thinks.

*   *   *

Stolle and Meyers retreat to talk things through. 'Those jobs last year,' says Stolle. 'Do you remember? All the same pattern. A single guy, masked, armed, jumping over the counter, leaving through the backdoor or back window, all without saying a word . . .'

'The same man, possibly.'

'Presumably. But something was different this time.'

'The haul. He's never raked in so much before.'

'No. Three thousand in Fallingbostel and not even two thousand DM in Schneverdingen. And here close to twenty thousand.'

Stolle says: 'I wonder. The car, with Hamburg license plates. Something with BH, they say. Probably stolen in Hamburg. He wants us to believe that he's from Hamburg. But I doubt it. I doubt it very much.

Fallingbostel, Schneverdingen, Buchholz. All around the Lüneburger Heide. And that Soltau ticket. What's on the Heath, apart from sand and sheep? Lots of military. The Brits. Any number of soldiers, probably bored to death, living in poor conditions. And at the same time they see that our economy is booming. Their former enemy getting rich again. The German miracle, as they call it. Might give some of them some funny ideas . . .'

'Shouldn't someone contact the Brits?' Meyers asks.

'Yes. Someone should. The Landeskriminalamt, I suppose. We must report this to Hannover.' Stolle is not inclined to deal with the British Military Police himself.

Why not do this ourselves, thinks Meyers. They must have somebody who speaks some German. But that is Stolle's decision, of course. 'What are the odds that somebody picks just the right moment before the money is being transferred to Harburg . . .'

Stolle shakes his head. 'He must have known about it. One of them who's working here in this bank, one of them must have talked. My guess would be Fräulein Schönbohm.'

Meyers shakes his head. 'No, I can't believe that.'

'We'll have to keep her under surveillance,' says Stolle.

'It might just as well have been one of the

others,' Meyers insists. 'That mad motorcyclist, what's his name, that Blaschke, or . . .'

'Yes, everything is possible,' snarls Stolle. 'Not very likely though. Lotte Schönbohm is the only female staff member, and the robber was a strong young man. Either he has approached her and sounded her out, or they are hand in glove. We will have to find out.'

'I'll take care of that,' suggests Meyers.

'We both will,' contradicts Stolle. At this point he doesn't quite trust his young colleague. *Höflichkeit und feingefühl*— tactfulness and understanding of the people's problems are demanded by the British 'Instruction on the Re-Organisation of the German Police'. Meyers has too much tactfulness and understanding. Especially with regard to young women.

*   *   *

When they return to the counter area, Lotte Schönbohm is just about to go home. They notice that Dieckmann's eyes follow her, longingly.

'I suppose it's not all that easy for a young girl here in a little backwater like Buchholz,' Stolle suggests.

'Oh, she knows how to amuse herself,' Dieckmann growls. She has refused to be taken home by him. He feels snubbed.

'Has she got someone steady?' enquires Meyers.

Dieckmann hesitates.

'It isn't Blaschke, is it?' prods Stolle.

Dieckmann shakes his head. 'No, not Blaschke. She goes with a Brit. For some months now. Someone called Evans, I think.'

'Evans,' says Stolle. Shit. Now he has to make that call. 'May I use your telephone?'

Dieckmann has blushed. He feels like a traitor. Couldn't the police have asked Lotte instead of him?

*   *   *

On the phone he sounds reserved, tells the German to send the files so that they can check everything carefully. But then he reacts. Evans may be a common name, but not so common he can't identify the chap.

And now he is standing in front of him. Lieutenant Evans. A young upstart, Roberts thinks. An upstart with a record. Armed robbery, it says. Lengthy investigations, no conviction.

'Take a seat.' Roberts points to the visitors' chair. He leafs through the file in front of him, until Evans gets visibly nervous. He looks into his face. 'Buchholz,' he says. 'Tell me about Buchholz.'

He jerks. 'Buchholz?'

'Don't fool around,' says Roberts. 'You

know Buchholz very well. You have raided the local savings bank this morning . . .'

He shakes his head. 'No, Sir, I . . .'

'Yes, you did,' says Roberts coolly. 'And not only Buchholz. Three bank robberies at least. I might just as well hand you over to the Germans.' Roberts waits until that has sunk in. Then he continues: 'But I won't do that. I'd rather not. This is not just a personal favour. We are representing the United Kingdom, and whatever we do or not do reflects on our country. And as you know, we are not especially popular here in the Heath. Our tanks damage the roads, our soldiers seduce the girls, and now we are even starting to rob banks? It's not on, Evans.'

'No.' There must be evidence, thinks Evans. Strong evidence, or else Roberts wouldn't talk to me like this. But he has no idea what that evidence might be. Except perhaps Lotte. Might she have talked? His girl Lotte?

'There are two options. Either I hand you over to German police, or you apply for relocation. Right now. I've got the form ready. In fact, I have already filled it in. There's only one thing for you to do. You have to sign it. Here.'

Evans hesitates for a moment. Then he signs. His hands are shaking.

That went rather well, thinks Roberts. I don't have much up my sleeve. But this solves all the problems. He says: 'You're a free man, Evans. But in your own interest I would advise you to stay in the barracks until your flight is due. And that will not take long, I assure you. I'll see to that.'

*   *   *

Evans does not stay in the barracks. He has to see Lotte, must know what happened. Pity that he had to leave behind the stolen Opel car. But even on the motorbike it will be hardly more than an hour. The sentry at the gate lets him pass unhindered. Could he really be free? For a moment he fears the German police might be waiting just behind the next corner in order to arrest him. But there is nobody. He is on his way north.

*   *   *

Lotte is pacing up and down the room. This application—what will come of it? She envisages facing the official, who will check her form and then look at her. Perhaps he will not say it, but sure enough he will think it: another one of those who allegedly had an estate in the east. Only that in her case it is true. But she can't prove it. No documents. She never thought that some day she would have to work in a small savings bank in some Lüneburger Heide backwater for a living. Back

195

then, it all seemed so safe, so reassuring. Even when everything else collapsed around them. They had not run, they had intended to persevere. We will be alright they had thought, until a group of Russian tank troops had stormed the house. She was the only one to survive. She had been only twelve years old then, perhaps that had saved her. The horse had still been in the stable, ready for a desperate flight westward. The soldiers had shot into the air, but not seriously come after her. And she had made it eventually.

She had thought that was gone and forgotten, but now it all comes back. People will ask questions, touch topics she had hoped never to touch again. Blaschke has promised to help. He likes her a lot, no doubt, but she feels nothing for him.

Blaschke. The robbery. What a catastrophe. Why on earth? Somebody must have known that there was all that money. At least she hadn't talked to anybody. Except to George Evans, of course, but George does not count. Her George. He is an officer, no bank robber. And they will get married later this year. He doesn't know yet that she is pregnant. What will he say? Will he come today? The robbery, it must have been on the news. If he's heard of it, he will certainly come.

Lotte goes to the window. The street is empty. Except for a lonely car parked on the other side, a bit further down the road.

Strange, she thinks, Werneckes don't have a car, do they? And then she sees a red spot glowing behind the front window. Only for a fraction of a second, but unmistakably. Somebody is sitting in that car, smoking.

Police, she thinks. They are after her. Her and George. They suspect George. She hurriedly draws the curtains. She must warn him. But how? The telephone! Their landlords, they have a telephone. And she is running down the stairs, knocking at their door. 'Mrs Schekorr?—Please, do open the door!' But nobody does. It is dark in the flat.

The theatre, thinks Lotte. Today is Saturday. They are probably in Hamburg again in that bloody theatre.

*　　　*　　　*

The police are sitting in their *Volkswagen* watching the house. It is dark by now, the street lights barely illuminate the sandy road. The air in the car is pretty thick. Stolle has smoked three of his dark cigars, and after running out of supplies even asked Meyers for cigarettes. In vain. Meyers is a non-smoker, as he should have known.

Up on the first floor, where Lotte Schönbohm lives, one of the windows is lit. The living room, Meyers thinks. But the curtains are drawn now, they cannot see into the room. We cannot see her and she cannot

197

see us, thinks Meyers. She is sitting in a trap, only she doesn't know it. Poor girl.

Stolle has other worries. For him any contact with the Brits might still be dangerous. Even now, seven years after the end of the war.

It is hot in the car. There is a stench of smoke and sweat. Stolle has taken off his sweater. Under it he wears only his vest. His young colleague realises to his amazement that Stolle has a tattoo. They're only found on sailors, he thinks. Or on convicts. Fancy pictures of virgins and sea dragons. But on Stolle's left upper arm there is just the letter 'A'.

'He won't come,' says Meyers.

Stolle has almost fallen asleep. 'What?'

'I said he won't come tonight.'

'Wait and see.' Stolle yawns. 'We must do this in shifts,' he says. 'One watching, one sleeping.'

'I'll take the first shift.'

'Fine. Wake me up in two hours.' Stolle falls asleep immediately.

*   *   *

And now? Meyers glances at his sleeping colleague. To begin with, he opens the door. Some fresh air can't be wrong. The door creaks. Stolle mumbles in his sleep but doesn't wake up.

I'll have a look around, Meyers thinks. Reconnoitre the terrain. Find out if the guy hasn't somehow slipped into the house. At least that is what he is trying to make himself believe. Really he is looking for a chance to warn the girl.

But wait! There's somebody walking down the road, coming towards them. Meyers ducks down behind the car. The man passes the car and turns right. He wants to see *Fräulein* Schönbohm, Meyers thinks. So it is really true. And what do I do now?

*   *   *

Lotte starts. The doorbell has rung! They are coming to get her.

But when she hesitatingly opens the door, it is only Evans who is standing there. 'My god, George!' They hug.

She has not let on about me, Evans thinks. No, Lotte would never do that. For a moment he has the illusion that all could still turn out OK. But he has lost the game a long time ago.

'Your motorbike,' Lotte says eventually. 'I didn't hear you come!'

'I left it near the station. Run out of petrol.'

Lotte laughs. 'Are you in such a hurry to meet me that you had no time to check the fuel gauge!'

'Yes,' he says. He tries to smile. What he has to confess now weighs like a ton on his

199

soul.

'Come upstairs!'

And slowly he follows her up the stairs.

Suddenly Lotte remembers that she had intended to warn him. 'George,' she says. 'The robbery this morning—the police seem to think that I'm involved.'

He starts. 'What makes you think that? Have they said so?'

Lotte shakes her head. 'But down there, there's a car. It's been there all evening. I think that it is the police.'

'Where?' Evans peeps through the curtains.

At that moment Lotte knows that he has done it. 'You must get out of here,' she says. 'You must run!'

Why hadn't she told him immediately? Good that he had left the motorbike at the station. If he slips through the gardens the police cannot get him. He knows the terrain, he is at an advantage. But then again, there is no need to rush. Nothing moves. The police are sitting in their car and waiting. There is still time for a farewell kiss. He folds Lotte into his arms.

*   *   *

Restlessly Stolle is wallowing in the driver's seat. He is back in France, running. At the end of a pointless counterattack, his SS tank unit no longer exists. The front has collapsed and the Brits are coming after them. They will know about the executions by now. He must not be caught. *Fire, come on, fire!* he tries to shout, but it is no more than a mumble. And then there are shots. Three shots at short intervals. Stolle jumps from his nightmare. Those shots—were they real? Where is his colleague? 'Meyers?' The door is standing ajar, Meyers is gone. Bloody idiot, thinks Stolle. 'Meyers, where are you?'

No answer. But from the house across the street Stolle can now hear the desperate scream of a young woman. He draws his gun and runs. It is Lotte Schönbohm. He finds her crying, at her feet a body, doubled up.

'He shot first,' says Meyers. His voice is trembling. He is holding his left arm.

Evans is dead.

A CABINET OF CURIOSITIES

Christine Poulson

A hare starts up in front of them and crouches there, quivering in the grass. Rufus is afraid that it will be trampled under the hooves of his horse. It is too young and frightened to understand that it can escape by dashing off to one side. At the last moment it shoots off and its white scut vanishes into the undergrowth.

Rufus glances at Simon. He hasn't noticed. No doubt he is preoccupied with the work ahead. They ride on in silence. It was scarcely light when they left Rufus's house. It is now six o'clock on a fine June morning and mist is rising from the fields.

Simon arrived at Rufus's house late the previous evening to request his services and a bed for the night. The two had not met since they were undergraduates together at Jesus College nearly twenty years ago. True, Rufus is a magistrate as well as a priest—and for a search like this it is necessary that a magistrate be present—but Simon could surely have found someone closer to the house in question. Rufus suspects him of engineering an opportunity to bring home the way in which their paths in life have diverged. At Cambridge Simon was a raw-boned country boy, his father a yeoman in a small way. Rufus was of far superior birth, but somehow Simon always had the upper hand. Since then he has grown rich on confiscated estates and has married above his station, while Rufus has progressed no further than his first living—and it is not a large or a prosperous parish.

Rufus looks sideways at his old friend. The diamond ring, the boots of supple Spanish leather, the fantastical high-crowned hat tilted sideways: such finery sits strangely with the thick nose, broken more than once, and the jutting jaw. Simon has the vanity of an ugly man. That is not a thought that would have occurred to Rufus in the old days. He glances down at his own sombre costume, kept decent by Sarah's deft needle. Sarah's family, if truth be told, is scarcely even of the middling sort, but she is a good housekeeper and an excellent mother to their children. Rufus reminds himself that Simon has only one daughter surviving, but of the eight children Sarah has borne Rufus, six remain, four of them sons, and every one of the brood healthy. God has indeed blessed him. Those are *his* jewels—

Simon breaks into his thoughts. 'Women, children, servants, they are the weakest links, and today we will find the mistress of the house alone. Her husband is a barrister who has been detained on business in London.'

'That is fortunate.'

'Indeed,' Simon says dryly.

Rufus understands that Simon has arranged this. He had been naïve to suppose that anything would be left to chance.

To cover his embarrassment, he says, 'How will you go about the search?'

'I have my methods, my *modus operandi*. I begin with those parts of the house where there is a solid mass of masonry: chimney breasts, turrets, in which a hollow space could have been fashioned. Where one part of the house is newer than another, we look for discrepancy in floor levels, any space, however narrow, into which a man might crawl. In one house—that was in Lancashire—we searched for days before I noticed a chimney that had no smoke blackening at the top. It was a shaft to allow air to a hide at the side of the fireplace. It had been concealed by bricks and mortar fastened to planks and then painted and blackened to look like part of the flue.'

'It took days?'

'Six days.' He laughs at the expression on Rufus's face. 'It won't take that long today. I'll wager this diamond ring against—what, let me see, one of your wife's excellent cream cheeses—that I'll flush the fellow out by sunset. Such men are evil. Purveyors of death and sin, corruptors of the state, they must be hunted down like the vermin they are.'

Rufus hesitates. A diamond ring against a cream cheese: he feels insulted.

'Come on, man! Between old friends! It'll

204

lend some zest to the game. If it goes against the grain for a man of the cloth, you can sell the ring and feed the poor in your parish.'

Against his better judgment, Rufus finds himself agreeing.

*   *   *

They breast a rise in the rolling Warwickshire countryside and there the house lies before them, nestling in the hollow of a park. They rein in their horses. The sun gleams on the water in the moat and bathes the honey-coloured stone in a golden light. Deer graze in the park, there are fish-ponds close to the house, gardens too, bright with flowers. In the hazy morning light, it seems unreal, dream-like. In a few moments, Rufus thinks, they will shatter this idyll. There will be rich pickings if all this is confiscated. He feels something he can't name. Excitement? Dread?

There is a rustling nearby and two men on horseback emerge from a clump of birches.

'Has anyone left the house?' Simon asks them.

They shake their heads.

'I have two more men waiting at the back,' Simon tells Rufus.

'Are you sure he is there?' Rufus half hopes that he will not be, and not just because of the wager. He thinks of the fate that awaits the hunted man—it is necessary, no doubt about that, the security of the state must be preserved—but it is best not to dwell on the details.

'I believe he is. I have intelligence that he was seen heading for the house early yesterday morning.'

Simon nods to his henchmen and they fall into line behind him. He digs his heels into his horse's flanks and it breaks into a canter, and then a gallop. It's a high-spirited bay, a world away from Rufus's stolid cob, which struggles to keep pace. As they thunder down the slope, Rufus's heart thumps in time to the thud of the horse's hooves. He too is used to a more sedentary life. They clatter across the bridge over the moat. Entering the quiet courtyard, they come to a halt and for a moment or two the only sound is the breathing of their horses. The silence is broken by a dog barking.

Simon nods to his men. They dismount and hammer at the door. It is opened sooner than Rufus expects and the men rush in. Simon dismounts at leisure, tethers all four horses, and follows the men into the house. Rufus goes with him. Looking around the hall, he sees a gleaming oak floor and staircase, a credenza elaborately carved and gilded, paintings on the walls.

He becomes aware of a girl in a white night-smock standing at the top of the staircase. His first thought is that she is a daughter of the house. Then he sees the swell of her belly: she is five or six months gone. This must be the mistress, though it seems to him that she is scarcely older than Jenny, his eldest daughter.

'You are Elinor Hardcastle?' Simon asks.

She nods.

Simon bows. 'I bear papers that give me the authority to search your house and I am accompanied by a justice of the peace.'

She says nothing. A woman appears behind her, a servant, a nurse, Rufus guesses, carrying a well grown child in her arms. The women don't so much as glance at one another, yet it seems to Rufus that some communication passes between them.

One of Simon's men appears in the hall and shakes his head.

This seems to give Elinor courage and at last the words come, though it's little more than a whisper.

'You will find no priest here.'

*   *   *

Sunlight reflected from the moat throws watery green shadows on the walls and ceiling of the parlour. The scent of roses drifts in through an open window and for Rufus will ever afterwards be associated with that time and that place. He takes in every detail of the charming apartment: the table bearing an embroidery frame and a half-finished sampler, the ample hearth piled with logs, a harp, a child's cart full of toy bricks. Sarah will be curious when he gets home.

Elinor Hardcastle stands by the door watching as Simon opens a linen chest and riffles through the contents. Rufus feels rather than sees her suppress a wince. She is fully dressed now and her farthingale conceals her pregnancy. She is perhaps nineteen or twenty. With her brown hair smoothed back and her pale complexion she has the kind of beauty that Rufus admires. He thinks again of his own daughter, who by this hour will already be helping Sarah in the dairy. He feels like an intruder here. Elinor's face is impassive, but Rufus knows as well as if she had spoken that she hates to see Simon's thick fingers handling her fine sheets.

At the far side of room there is a large cabinet veneered in walnut and mounted on barley sugar legs. Simon opens the two doors that front it and Rufus can tell that he is surprised. He shifts so that he sees what Simon sees.

There are numerous small drawers, inlaid with delicate marquetry, and in the centre a mirrored recess. Rufus moves closer. The recess has been decorated to resemble an elegant little room with gilded colonnades on either side and a black and white diaper floor. It holds a silver gilt inkpot, too large in the little room and strangely out of keeping. There is something fascinating about this world in miniature and Rufus sees that Simon is attracted by it, too. Elinor has come closer and Rufus is conscious of her standing by his side.

Simon opens a drawer, puts in a hand and takes out a handful of coins.

'Roman,' he says, and tips the coins back into the drawer, leaving one in the palm of his hand. He seems about to pocket it. Then he shrugs, replaces the coin and shuts the drawer. Why bother? When the estate is confiscated, he'll take this as part of his share. He opens drawer after drawer, revealing wonder after wonder: shells, coral, ivory, semi-precious stones, cameos and intaglios, more coins and medallions, birds' eggs, flint arrows.

'A cabinet of curiosities. I have heard of them,' Simon says, 'but I have never seen one before. It must be worth a great deal,' he adds in an undertone.

'It's very precious,' Elinor says. There is something in her voice that makes Rufus glance at her. She looks back at him, but he cannot read her expression.

Simon is frowning and Rufus knows he is disappointed not to have found evidence of Catholic sympathies. Certain books, a rosary—a makeshift shrine, even—these are illegal and would have allowed him to threaten and intimidate her. But he has looked everywhere in the house and there is nothing. Her child—a lusty fellow of around two years—is too young to be interrogated and there's no joy to be had of the servants either. They are a brazen, tight-lipped lot. No doubt they have been carefully chosen and are themselves adherents of what they dub 'the Old Faith.'

'Well,' Simon says. He brushes one hand against the other to indicate that it is time to get down to business. 'I'll get the men—and the measuring chains.'

It is time for the search proper to begin.

*   *   *

The men measure the thickness of the walls, the window embrasures, and the chimney breasts. Simon is occupied with more skilled employment.

'The greatest difficulty is in disguising the entrance,' he explains to Rufus. 'We look for places where ornamental mounding might conceal an opening, we look for gaps between floorboards, we look for false panelling, particularly in wardrobes or cupboards.'

The sun climbs the sky. The heat and the humidity rise. The men wipe the sweat from their brows. Simon seems unaffected and works on methodically, tapping panels, running his hands over floorboards, feeling inside cupboards. If there is indeed a man hidden in some cramped compartment, how he must be suffering, Rufus thinks.

Elinor too is feeling the heat or maybe it is

simply apprehension. She remains in the parlour, coming from time to time to watch their progress. And it is on one of these occasions that it happens. Simon is on his knees in a small first floor room, running his hands over the floor boards. Rufus sees Elinor come in and stop by the door. There is something in her posture that alerts him, a kind of stillness. She recovers instantly, but Simon has seen it too. He gets to his feet and fixes his eyes on her. She tries to leave the room, but he shakes his head and she remains where she is. Her face is as pale as whey.

Simon starts to move about the room, his eyes fixed on Elinor, judging her response, following the movement of her eyes. Rufus understands with a thrill of—what? anticipation? no, apprehension—that Simon is guided by what she is *not* looking at. From what is she so anxious to avert her eyes? It is a sinister parody of the searching game that Rufus's children play: 'Am I getting warm?' 'Yes, yes, no, no, you're getting cold, yes, warm again.'

Simon moves towards the window, where a seat is set into the embrasure. Elinor has schooled herself not to react, but it is hard, so hard when a man's life is at stake. Her eyelids flicker. That's it. Simon's face relaxes. He has seen it now. He squats before the window seat. And now Rufus sees it, too: a scrap of rough material, sacking perhaps, hardly more than

211

half a dozen threads, caught in the joint where the seat is attached to the base. Very gently Simon feels around, pressing, gently manipulating, and he finds the trick of it. The seat slides forwards. Simon climbs into the space. He lowers himself down until only his hands remain clasping the edge of the seat, and then they vanish too.

Rufus runs over and looks down. A narrow chute set at a diagonal angle has delivered Simon to a space which must be over the kitchen. Simon's face appears a few feet away. He shakes his head. Moments later, with a helping hand from Rufus, he is back in the room. Rufus expects him to be angry at finding the hide empty, but on the contrary, he appears stimulated by this turn of events. Elinor on the other hand looks so ill that Rufus fears for her unborn child. Perhaps she does too, for she presses a hand to her side. Rufus helps her to a seat.

Simon is examining the interior of the window seat. 'The workmanship—wonderful, is it not? To me, it bears the mark of one man and one man only. Master Nicholas Owen.'

He beckons Rufus over. Together they gaze down at the stone floor of the window-seat.

Simon pauses, leans right in and crooks his fingers round the edge of the stone where it meets the shaft to the hide. He sets his face and exerts his strength. There is a grinding of stone against stone. Simon lets the stone fall back into place.

'It is a peculiarity of his work that so often one hiding place conceals another,' he remarks. 'This stone is too heavy for one man to shift, so I will ask you, Rufus, to fetch the men.'

* * *

The stench when they remove the stone slab is unbelievable.

'This was a garde-robe,' Simon explains. 'The shaft goes down to a sewer that discharges into the moat.'

He does not go down himself. Two of his men lower a third—a surly-looking rogue—on a rope, candle in hand. He makes no objection—he will be well rewarded.

Elinor remains in her chair in the corner of the room, looking on. Rufus wants to tell her that she should not be here—it is no place for a pregnant woman—but he senses that he would be ill-advised to betray his sympathy for her. The heat of the day, the smell, the tension that fills the room: Rufus wishes with all his heart that he had not agreed to come with Simon. He finds he has no appetite for hunting a man down like a rat in a sewer. And terrifying this young woman perhaps to the point of miscarriage, how can this be right? She is no doubt obeying her husband's orders

213

and that is but her bounden duty.

Simon is pacing up and down. He returns to the window-seat and shouts down the shaft. 'What can you see?'

'Nothing yet, master,' comes faintly echoing from somewhere down below.

Simon stands waiting, a hand on either side of the window-seat, seemingly impervious to the smell.

A minute or two later, there is a cry and Simon leans eagerly forward, 'What is it?'

'A dead cat. I put my foot on it.'

Simon shakes his head, he begins to unbutton his doublet. 'I'm going down myself.'

Moments later, he too disappears down the shaft.

Rufus persuades Elinor to leave the room. She will not lie down, but allows him to settle her by an open window in the parlour. Rufus stays with her. He cannot help putting himself in the place of the hunted man for whom these are the last moments of freedom. And he cannot help remembering what Simon told him last night: the last priest he captured was taken from the gallows too soon and dragged conscious to the quartering block. He feels queasy.

It is some time before Simon comes to find them. He is wearing a fresh suit of clothes. Nevertheless he brings with him a faint whiff of ordure.

'I found the hide,' he said.

Rufus's heart is in his mouth. What must Elinor must be feeling?

'It was empty,' says Simon. 'Except for this.'

He dangles a necklace in front of Elinor's face and allows the beads to run through his fingers.

'Well, madam?' he says.

And now Rufus catches sight of a little cross. It is not a necklace, but a rosary.

'Paris is worth a mass, so they say. Are all your husband's estates and riches worth this bit of Catholic trumpery?'

He drops it on the table beside her.

Elinor's eyes are fixed on it. She seems scarcely able to breath, let alone speak. Simon towers over her. Rufus remembers the hare, quivering with fear, that was nearly trampled beneath their hooves that morning.

'In God's name, Simon, she's little more than a child!' he bursts out.

Simon seems at first not to hear him. He is staring at the table, not at the rosary. Then he turns to Rufus. 'What did you say?'

'She's very young,' Rufus says half-apologetically.

Simon turns to Elinor and searches her face. 'How young, would you say? Eighteen, nineteen? And her child is two years old, and a son at that.' No reply is necessary and she makes none. 'And yet here on this table is a half-finished sampler.' He strikes the side of his head with his open palm. 'Dolt that I am. She is the second wife. And there is a child of the first marriage.'

He turns to Rufus. 'Don't you see? Fearful that she will betray them, they have sent this older child away, along with her clothes and toys—leaving only that sampler behind.'

He says to Elinor, 'She must be brought back at once.'

*   *   *

They wait in the parlour in silence, while the child returns from a neighbouring farm, where she has been lodged.

By the time the little girl arrives the air is tinged with the blue of a late summer dusk. She stands in the doorway with her nurse behind her. Rarely has Rufus seen a child as beautiful as this, a veritable angel. No more than seven, she is as fair as her stepmother is dark.

Elinor puts out a hand. The child goes directly to her. Elinor leans forward to smooth back a lock of flaxen hair that has escaped from a plait.

'Come here, my little wench,' Simon says, beckoning to her. His voice is unexpectedly gentle.

The child looks up into Elinor's face for permission. Elinor nods and the child steps forward.

Simon squats down so that he can look into her face. 'What is your name?' he asks her.

'Hannah.'

'Hannah. It means "favoured by God" and judging by your pretty face it seems that He has indeed favoured you.'

The child smiles.

'That's right,' says Simon. 'We are friends, are we not? Now, tell me, has there been a strange man here?'

The child looks at her stepmother. Elinor seems to have recovered from her earlier apprehension. Her face is as calm and relaxed as if the question were of no moment.

The child looks back at Simon. 'Yes,' she says.

Elinor turns her face away.

'Ah. And where is he now?' says Simon.

Rufus holds his breath,

'Oh, he went away. Mama told him to go away, and he did.'

'When was this?' Simon asks.

'Yesterday,' the child says. 'And then I went away myself,' she adds with a simplicity that nearly breaks Rufus's heart.

'Did you see him leave?'

She nods.

'Which way did he go?'

Simon lifts the child up to the window and she points to the south. When he puts her down, she goes to Elinor and buries her face in the stuff of her gown. Elinor presses her close.

'Why didn't you tell me this?' Simon speaks sternly to Elinor. 'It was your duty.'

'I was afraid.'

'Did he tell you where he was going?'

'He did not.' She looks piteously into Simon's face. 'He said it was better that I should not know.'

*   *   *

'You were right to exact no punishment,' says Rufus, as they ride away from the house.

The evening sky has deepened to a rich, soft blue dusk. A single star has appeared.

Simon shrugs. 'These Jesuits are sophistical, deceitful. Her husband was away and she had no-one to guide her. Women are easily swayed.'

'The weaker vessel.'

'Indeed.' Nevertheless he speaks as someone who has been detected in a weakness.

He slips the diamond ring off his finger. 'Here.' He tosses it to Rufus, who puts out a hand and catches it in mid-air. 'I did not find my quarry, so I have lost the wager.'

As they ride on, Rufus takes a sideways look at Simon. He is not as clever or as observant as he thinks—or as Rufus thought him. A fig for the *modus operandi*! Simon looked everywhere and he saw nothing, except what he was meant to see. It was intended that he should discover the first hiding place

218

and then the second. What foresight! What cunning! It was as good as a play.

The return of the child—was that intended? He thinks not. That was their one mistake as they rushed to hide the priest and set the scene. Elinor's heart must have been in her mouth. But the daughter was worthy of the mother. When she said that the priest had gone, Rufus saw Elinor's face reflected for a moment in the mirrored interior of the cabinet. She had managed to hide her fear, but she could not hide her relief. Simon missed that, as he missed so much else.

In his mind's eye Rufus sees the fireplace in the parlour. Did it not occur to Simon to wonder why logs should be piled high on the hearth at the height of summer?

Rufus smiles to himself and pockets the ring.

A huge moon is rising through the trees. It will light their long ride home.

*   *   *

'Is it safe yet?' Hannah asks.

The priest hears this, just as he has heard every conversation in the parlour during this interminable day.

'What do you think, Father?' It is Elinor's voice, close at hand. She must be kneeling in the hearth. 'I sent James to follow them and he has just returned. The poursuivants are miles

219

away.'

'It is time,' he says, his voice sounding strange in his ears after such a long silence. He hears them removing the logs one by one. The flags are lifted up and there is the glint of candle-light. He struggles towards it, pulling himself up with one hand, while with the other he holds a jewelled casket to his breast. Brawny arms reach down and haul him out.

A servant is waiting with a bowl of water so that he can wash. Elinor has brought bread and meat and wine with her own hands.

The priest looks at her bright eyes and laughing face, and he too begins to laugh.

'That Nicholas Owen is a craftsman *sans pareil*. With food and water and my piss-pot I could have held out for days. I am a little stiff, it is true, and a trifle more air would have been welcome—But what is wrong, my little one?' he asks Hannah.

There are tears in her eyes.

'She was afraid for you,' says Elinor. 'And she is sorry that she had to tell a lie. But I tell her that she is a good girl and it would have been a worse sin to betray you. You can absolve her, Father, can you not?'

'I can.'

'And, Father, you will not think of leaving tonight? You must rest.'

He shakes his head. 'I have rested enough—and you have risked enough, my gallant girl. I will head north tonight.'

220

'But before you go?'

'Yes, we must give thanks.'

While he washes his hands and consecrates the wine, she removes the silver gilt inkpot from the mirrored recess of the cabinet of curiosities. She presses one of the black and white squares near the back and a panel slides open. She takes out two little paintings of Saint Jude and Saint Luke and a third of the Virgin Mary, all in gilded frames. She fits them into place over the mirrors and stands back.

The priest steps forward with the jewelled casket that contains the Host and places it in the recess.

Behind him he is aware of his little congregation: the servants, the mistress of the house, and her resourceful little stepdaughter. It all seems to drop away—the loyal friends, the warmth and the scent of the summer night. A cold wind blows. He sees a ruined house, its occupants in exile. He sees himself with a noose around his neck. In that moment it comes to him that his escape today has been merely a reprieve. Somewhere ahead of him lies that terrible fate. But for the time that remains, whether it be long or short, he thanks God. There is work to be done.

He makes the Sign of the Cross. He speaks the familiar words, so full of comfort.

'In nomine Patris, et Filii, et Spiritus Sancti ...'

The Mass begins.

JUST COMING,
AFTER I KILL MYSELF

André Marois
Translated from the Québécois by Alba Griffin

On discovering the foot jutting out of the living room door at an unnatural angle one could sense immediately that something wasn't quite right in the gloomy apartment.

Attached to the foot was a lad in his twenties, shaven-headed, naked and collapsed on the floor. His left hand was at his throat and the other was stretched out in front of him. And the expression on his face . . . you could still read the fear on it.

It was Malika, the cleaning lady, who had discovered the body. She came every Tuesday to Monsieur Nic's place, but she never saw him as he worked night and day. Malika had only met him once, when he had hired her six months earlier. Since then, she had her key and found her four twenty dollar bills impeccably aligned on the kitchen counter with an aluminium ruler placed on top to stop them flying away—despite the fact that the windows were permanently closed.

The housekeeper told the police what little she knew. A tall, young inspector took notes on a pad. His name was Lefebvre and he suffered from an ungainly twitch; when reflecting on something he would curl up his nostril using the knuckle of his left index finger. You could sense his timidity in this unconscious gesture. His lack of experience reinforced the problem and, on some evenings, his nostrils gaped like those of an out-of-breath carthorse.

Yes, Malika had already seen the women's clothing lying around the bedroom. It wasn't hard to find the number of a certain Celia on Nic's mobile. The inspector called her on the deceased's phone. Celia answered after two rings:

—Nic, where've you been? What are you playing at? she asked in broken French.

The tone oscillated between fear and anger. The inspector cleared his throat, put on the most masterful voice he could muster and asked the English speaker to come over.

Celia arrived very quickly. She seemed panicked.

After having been told to sit down, she explained that they only saw each other from time to time, nothing too serious. The last time she saw Nic, it was two days ago, but yesterday...

—What happened yesterday? grunted Lefebvre.

She told him that they had arranged to meet at the cinema but that Nic had called at about 9 o'clock and left a shocking message:

—Just coming, after I've killed myself, he said. *Yes, exactly like this*: Just coming, after I've killed myself, she whispered.

On hearing this, Lefebvre's nose turned almost completely inside out. Celia had thought it was a joke.

—Nic was a twenty six year old adolescent. He always told *bad jokes*. So she had gone to see the film with a friend hoping he would join them. But then . . .

—Then, he committed suicide, the inspector interrupted.

—*It's impossible,* sobbed the young woman, in English.

One thing still bothered Lefebvre: how had Nic killed himself? The police hadn't found a weapon in the apartment, nor any empty boxes of medication, even less any signs of a struggle. Had he poisoned himself? Had he overdosed? Celia claimed he didn't take drugs—just a whisky now and again to loosen up after his long days at work. The lad must've been ill.

The clearly alarmed young woman had keys to the place, but she could be eliminated pretty easily, especially if her friend provided an alibi. He'd check later. The inspector asked if he could listen to Nic's ominous message.

—No, I deleted it, it made my skin crawl.

Fair enough, thought the inspector as he tried to slow down the unrelenting progression of his left hand towards the middle of his face.

The body was taken for the autopsy.

Lefebvre hated it when they died in an unconventional way. In training he was taught that these were the worst kind of trouble makers. They complicated the policing life, forced them to accumulate hours of overtime and then left them feeling inadequate.

He left and had a sandwich in a shabby little café where, on registering his uniform, everyone ignored him. The older policemean, they feared, but the young ones just put them ill at ease. There he remained unobserved, chewing on mouthfuls of smoked turkey. Turkey is a good source of energy; it allows you to regain that which is lost. Lefebvre was in need of it.

He returned to Nic's apartment and rummaged around at random, searching for something he may have missed that morning.

There weren't many clues to go on. Old books that must have dated from his secondary school days, motoring magazines on modified cars, glass bricks in the shape of a + . . . Nothing unexpected for a man of his age. A widescreen TV took centre stage in the middle of the living room, surrounded by a hi-fi, a laptop, blank CDs with bizarre names scrawled in red pen on them: PSO, Znort 3.5, Chtik . . . Lefebvre took them to be the names of hard rock bands.

He left visiting the family for the evening when they would be home from work, and decided to go and see Nic's employer, a large

IT firm based in Montreal.

Lefebvre twitched his nose and left the place grumbling to himself. He couldn't stay where he was in this haze; it made him want a beer.

He waved down a taxi and gave the name of the IT firm: Loud Confusion.

He got out of the old Chrysler in front of a large brick building in Mile-End. Inside, a deathly silence reigned: were they having a vigil for their dead colleague or what?

Suddenly a harsh cry rang out, followed by two more, coming from three of the forty employees bent over their PCs with large headphones covering their ears—the ideal setting for a Silicon Valley *Metropolis*. Not one person had reacted to the shouts.

On a metal platform overlooking the depressing scene there was a young man, dressed in designer shabby-chic, waiting for Lefebvre. The lad held out his business card and the cop learnt that the owner of the famous Loud Confusion—employer of 150 people in Montreal with new offices just opened in Tokyo and San Francisco—was this pasty pale-face looking at him. He could have been the cop's younger brother. This kid, who looked younger than him and ran this whole enterprise, dined with politicians and spent his weekends on Bill Gates' yacht.

—What did Nic work as? asked the inspector, who was keen to get out of there.

226

But the reply was cut off by the guttural cry of a tall Chinese man just beneath them. The newly-minted millionaire smiled, explaining:

—He just lost.

This place and its occupants depressed Lefebvre. The average age of the employees matched his own, and he realised how large the gulf separating them really was. That annoyed him, and he shot a questioning look at the mogul so that he would finally answer his question.

—Nic was testing a game called Znort, a new, more violent version.

Lefebvre shook his head. To think that people were paid just to play games, it was beyond him.

He asked where he might find Nic's office, and was accompanied there by a female employee with a disconcerting body-shape— somewhere between Lolita and Alien's mother. The twitch became uncontrollable. And the embarrassment of it stopped him from being able to think, to take a step back, and to work out what it was about this business that wasn't quite right. It seemed to him that they were trying to put him off. Otherwise, why send this piece of ass to give the investigator the guided tour?

In Quebec, statistics reveal that the most dangerous profession is firefighting, followed by construction work and taxi driving. So what was this loser Nic at risk of, hunched up all day in his stainless steel chair?

The inspector didn't notice anything unusual about the office where Nic had whiled away so many days, apart from a long line of discs stacked on a shelf. He took one and held it up to his escort.

—I don't know anything about it, me; I only work in design here. Better off asking Orazio, chirped the brunette indicating the nearest of Nic's colleagues.

Lefebvre weighed up the barely pubescent apprentice who was hammering away at his keyboard as if he had Parkinson's. On the screen the inspector watched the animated images of a stupid video game where you had to shoot at silhouettes of enraged carrots which bobbed up and around the screen.

When he saw Lefebvre trying to catch his attention, Orazio shouted loudly over the crackling in his earphones:

—JUST COMING, AFTER I'VE KILLED MYSELF!

The inspector pounced: he had his killer. This fool had given himself away. He knew that the pseudo-success of the enterprise was hiding some sort of trouble. He grabbed Orazio, who didn't know what the hell was going on, and threw him to the floor.

—What did you just shout? spluttered Lefebvre.

—Erm, I don't know . . . I'm coming, after I kill myself. Is that bad? stammered the ludic

228

programmer.

—You know what that means, you little shit?

Orazio found it hard to reply with Lefebvre grasping the neck of his 'Strange Carpets' sweater so hard. He gasped for breath.

—Well yeah, to complete the level really fast, I go to the end without any protection . . . I try to get as far as possible . . . Gives you a massive buzz . . . gets the adrenaline pumping . . . a kamikaze trip where you lose your lives really quickly, he concluded while trying to compose himself.

The stares of thirty people were now fixed on Lefebvre. Thirty late adolescents, whose stunned expressions told him he shouldn't push it. That was alright though, because the inspector was sick of looking at their cyber-geek mugs anyway.

He suddenly felt very old and let go of the suspect who was no longer a suspect. He flared the ends of his tired nostrils, shrugged his shoulders and left without saying a word. Bunch of geeks!

Returning to the police station he found the autopsy report, which revealed that Nic had died of a simple cardiac arrest.

Lefebvre opened the dossier of the inquiry that had begun just that morning and wrote his conclusion in large black letters: *Work related accident.*

FUNERAL WEATHER

Kate Ellis

Death came silently to Flora Politson on Friday the thirteenth of April.

At sixty one years of age, Flora—the plump widow of a wealthy Liverpool merchant and mistress of a grand stucco villa in Fulwood Park, some three miles from the smells of the city and the bustle of the docks—had appeared to be in the best of health. But Dr Willis knew that good health is often no defence against a visit from the Grim Reaper.

Willis, with his great mutton chop whiskers and his battered leather bag, was more adept at charming wealthy ladies than he was at diagnosis, but he gave his verdict with the certainty of holy writ. Flora Politson had died of heart failure. A sudden and merciful end.

The small, pale young man with sandy hair who accompanied the doctor looked no older than the butcher's boy who came whistling up the drive of Mortaber Villa each day on his bicycle. However, from his manner of dress and the leather doctor's bag he clutched in his right hand, Biddy—the late Mrs Politson's maid—guessed that he was assisting Dr Willis in some way. But it wasn't her place to ask questions.

Biddy stood near the bedroom, smoothing her crisp, white apron with restless fingers as the doctor and his companion bent over Mrs Politson who lay, as though asleep, on the bed. Biddy thought her mistress looked so peaceful lying there, her arms crossed neatly on her chest. The snowy lace counterpane was pulled up to her scrawny neck and her hair, spread out on the pillow, was iron grey and fluffy like the rain clouds that hung over the River Mersey that morning.

Biddy gazed out of the sash window at the gardens below, with their bushy laurels lining the sweeping drive. It had begun to rain, a thin, miserable drizzle. Funeral weather, her mother used to say. Weather for death.

Dr Willis interrupted Biddy's thoughts by touching her arm and she flinched. He'd touched her before, his large, clammy hand patting her small rough one. Lingering too long. The younger man was still standing by the bed, silent and thoughtful, studying Flora's dead face and Biddy doubted he'd have noticed Dr Willis's over familiar gesture. And even if he had seen, he would no doubt have kept his opinions to himself—as underlings and servants must.

Biddy cleared her throat. 'Begging your pardon, sir,' she said, lowering her eyes. 'But how did the mistress die? She wasn't ill or nothing.'

The doctor gave Biddy a small, patronising

smile. 'Your mistress has suffered with a weak heart for many years.' He didn't bother elaborating further. Why should he for a maidservant with a round, pudding face and lank, mousy hair tucked up under her cap.

'The undertakers will be here presently,' the doctor said. A speck of saliva escaped his lips and Biddy looked away. Something about him reminded her of George, the footman at the house on Catherine Street where she'd once worked. She had been fourteen then and she'd had no experience of men . . . until she caught George's lecherous bloodshot eye. She imagined she could smell him now, the scent of his sweat as he had held her close to him— when he did what he liked to do, as the cook's back was turned and the staff were all busy with their chores. Biddy felt her body trembling at the very thought of George's touch . . . of his clammy hand thrusting up her skirts, touching and kneading the places her mother had told her nobody but her husband should be privy to. She glanced at the dead woman on the bed, trying to banish the memories of her humiliation.

Dr Willis gave her a businesslike smile. 'I shall sign the death certificate and leave it here. Mr Politson will be here shortly. I have sent word that his mother has passed away.'

'Mr Politson called this morning, sir,' Biddy said, almost in a whisper.

The doctor looked at her, frowning. 'I

didn't know.'

'He stayed about half an hour, sir. Him and the mistress . . .' She stopped herself. It wasn't her place to gossip about her betters and she was aware that she'd said enough already.

Dr Willis shuffled his feet. 'I don't think that's any concern of ours, Biddy.' He turned and addressed the young man. 'Dr Carson, there's nothing more we can do here.'

The young man made no move to leave but looked straight at Biddy with an intensity that made her uncomfortable. 'Please go on, Biddy. What were you saying about Mr Politson and your mistress?' He glanced at the corpse on the bed as though he expected it to rise at any moment and join in the conversation.

'If you please, sir, they . . . they had words, sir. That's all.' Biddy sounded wary.

'What kind of words?'

'Harsh ones, sir. We could hear them in the servants' hall. But it's not my place to say any more.'

'Indeed,' Willis interrupted, impatient.

'I don't suppose you caught the, er . . . sense of these harsh words, did you?'

'Not the sense, sir. I just heard raised voices. As though they were quarrelling, sir.'

'Doctor Carson, it is time we were going,' Willis said firmly. 'This unfortunate girl can hardly be expected to pass judgement on the affairs of her employers. The death was natural and that is an end to the matter.'

Dr Willis looked at the corpse again, a little uneasy. Flora Politson had quarrelled with her son—and a few hours later, Flora Politson had been found dead by her maid. But Willis had known the family for years and, as far as he was concerned, people of the Politsons' standing in the community were above suspicion. It was high time young Dr Carson, his assistant of three months, learned this before he committed the grave sin of insulting his betters. 'Dr Carson, come. We have patients to see.'

But Carson ignored the order. He walked back to the bed and bent over the dead woman, sniffing the air around her. Alongside an empty bottle marked laudanum on the bedside table, stood a half-drunk cup of tea, the milk formed into dead swirls on the surface. He sniffed at it before placing his hand beneath the dead woman's head and lifting it gently. For a few moments he studied the pillow closely, then he lowered the head again.

'Is anything the matter, sir?' Biddy asked, craning her neck to see what was going on.

Before Carson could answer, Willis spoke again, impatient. 'Come, Carson, we have calls to make. Biddy, tell Waggs that the undertaker is expected.'

Biddy scurried from the room and made for the servant's hall where she knew the butler, Mr Waggs, was polishing the silver. As she reached the foot of the stairs she heard Dr Carson's voice. 'I'm not satisfied, Doctor,' he was saying. 'I wish to make a more thorough examination.'

'Nonsense,' Willis barked as he swept down the staircase, almost colliding with Biddy who had stood aside with her head bowed, ready to see the medical men off the premises.

Biddy watched the younger doctor hesitate at the front door. Then he turned to address her. 'Biddy, just one thing, if you please. Had your mistress pricked herself at all . . . a finger perhaps . . . or some part of her face or . . . ?'

Biddy frowned in an effort to remember. Then she nodded. 'She pricked her finger yesterday, sir, when she was sewing. Drove a needle in almost to the bone, sir.'

'Indeed.'

'Oh yes, sir. It bled something awful.'

Carson nodded. 'Come, Biddy. Show me if you will.'

Biddy hesitated for a few moments before returning upstairs to Flora's bedside. She watched while the doctor uncovered the dead woman's hands. Sure enough, on her left forefinger was a pinprick wound, half healed now but still visible. Unexpectedly, Carson picked up the cup containing the dregs of tea and poured a little of the liquid into a small glass vial which he popped into his waistcoat pocket before thanking Biddy again and hurrying out to join his colleague downstairs in the hallway. Biddy saw Dr Willis shoot the young man a hostile glance. His professional opinion had been questioned. Or his incompetence had been discovered.

Biddy bobbed a curtsey as the two doctors left then she hurried across the hall and pushed open the green baize door that led to the servants' quarters.

Death had visited the house. And death meant more work. Until the arrival of the police brought everything to a sudden halt.

*   *   *

Reginald Politson was the only son and heir of Flora Politson and the late Septimus Politson Esquire. Septimus himself had been a man of ambition and by the time of his death seven years ago, he had made a fortune supplying the voracious needs of the Liverpool shipping industry. Reginald had been a disappointment to him—all the servants knew that—and after her husband's death, Flora had kept her dainty hands on the company's tiller. But now she was dead, Reginald would have free rein to run the business as he thought fit. And there were many, servants' hall gossip had it, who thought that he would run it into the ground.

Reginald was a swarthy man in his mid-thirties. And he was unmarried, which some in the servants' hall took as a sign of dissipation. A respectable young man in Reginald's

236

position should take a wife and those that didn't were suspect. Biddy had overheard one of the footmen telling Daisy the parlour maid that Mr Politson preferred the company of men but Biddy was uncertain what he had meant by that. At least he didn't pester the female servants like some. At least she didn't have to go about the house in fear that he might creep up on her, pull her into a room and use her to satisfy his desires, panting like an animal above her, hurting her like her old master at the house in Canning Place had done.

Biddy served tea to Mr Politson and the family solicitor, Mr Jaques, in the drawing room. The house was now in deep mourning—black crepe everywhere and a large black bow tied to the front door. The undertakers, with their long, serious faces and discreet footsteps, had called and Mrs Politson had been laid out properly in her bed, receiving visitors in death as she had done in life.

Flora Politson's only son and her solicitor wore suitably solemn expressions as they discussed whatever they were discussing. As Biddy set down the tray, Mr Politson looked restless and uncomfortable and perhaps, she thought, also a little guilty. But she told herself that the man had just lost his mother suddenly and he was probably in shock.

The policemen arrived at six o'clock. Mr Waggs admitted the inspector and the plump uniformed constable through the front door with plain disapproval. As far as Mr Waggs was concerned, policemen should use the tradesmen's entrance. Mr Waggs had once worked for a titled gentleman and was a stickler for the proprieties.

The inspector, a large man with a bald head and ruddy cheeks, was closeted with Mr Politson and his solicitor for a full half hour before Biddy was summoned from the servants' hall to the dining room. Inspector Always wished to speak with her.

Biddy hadn't had dealings with the police before but her brothers said that they were best avoided. Police meant trouble and her brothers were usually right about that sort of thing. They'd had to be. Their parents had travelled to Liverpool from County Mayo on a crowded boat to be packed into a cellar in one of the mean, filthy courts that lay between St James Street and the docks with their children and the rats. Four of their children had died. But Biddy and her two brothers had survived.

She entered the dining room and saw the constable sitting awkwardly in the corner of the room, his notebook at the ready, while the inspector sat in one of the dining chairs at the huge polished table. The inspector smiled as he invited her to sit. He had a kind face. But she'd known men with kind faces before—and they sometimes weren't what they seemed.

'Now, Biddy, you must tell the truth, do

you understand?'

Biddy nodded.

'There was a small bottle by your mistress's bed. Do you know what it contained?'

'Her laudanum, sir. Took it every night without fail, she did . . . to sleep.'

'Dr Carson suspects there was some in her tea. He's saying the dose might have killed her.'

Biddy's hand went to her mouth in horror. 'She never took it in tea, sir. She took it in water last thing at night.'

'Would you say anything had upset your mistress recently, Biddy? Think carefully.'

Biddy frowned. 'She had words with Mr Politson . . . her son. They were arguing like . . .' She stopped herself. She mustn't say too much.

'You didn't overhear what they were saying by any chance?' The inspector gave her a knowing wink. Servants listened at keyholes. Servants knew things.

Biddy blushed. 'I heard the words . . . "immoral" . . . and "unnatural". And the mistress asked him why he didn't get himself a wife. I couldn't make out everything Mr Politson said in reply, sir. But he sounded angry. He said she'd be sorry.'

'Were those his exact words?'

Biddy considered the question for a few moments. 'Those or something very like them, sir.'

239

The inspector smiled again. He reminded her of the priest at the church near where she used to live—he had always made her feel guilty too. She swallowed hard. 'Will that be all, sir?'

The inspector nodded. 'For the moment,' he said.

Biddy made straight for the servants' hall. And by the end of the day word had spread that the police thought Flora Politson had been poisoned.

And when Biddy piped up that she was sure she'd taken an overdose by accident, nobody believed her.

*　　　*　　　*

On her afternoon off Biddy was grateful to escape from the heavy blanket of mourning that had enveloped the house from scullery to attic. The mistress's death was the only topic of conversation in the servants' hall and, as nothing more had been seen of the police for several days, everyone assumed that the initial suspicion about the cause of Flora's death had been dispelled, to the disappointment of some. There had already been an inquest and the coroner had given his verdict. Accidental death. Mrs Flora Politson had taken her usual laudanum then she had taken a further dose, no doubt distracted by her quarrel with Reginald, her only son.

The funeral arrangements, a little delayed by the inquest, were now in progress and Reginald Politson was playing the grieving son to perfection, receiving the condolences of Liverpool society who paid their dutiful calls with solemn faces and tearful eyes.

It was to be a grand funeral, as befitted a woman of Flora's standing, held in a few days' time at St Anne's church. Cook was working herself up into a state of near hysteria about the catering arrangements. But cook worked herself up about most things.

At one o'clock that afternoon, Biddy left the bustling house by the servants' entrance, securing her new hat firmly with a hat pin. The wind was blowing in strongly from the River Mersey and you couldn't be too careful as far as new hats were concerned. She made for Sefton Park, walking purposefully towards the new band stand. She was meeting Michael there and she didn't want to be late. Michael was her favourite brother, always smiling, always ready with a quip. She didn't care that he'd been in trouble with the police, or that he earned what money he had playing cards with strangers in pubs. He was her Michael. Her darling big brother.

She hurried onwards past the park lake. It looked like paradise, with all those trees and the water glistening in the weak sunlight, and she was unaware of being followed, of the footsteps behind her echoing her own on the new stone path. So when she heard someone calling her name softly, she swung round, bringing her hand to her breast as if to still her pounding heart.

Reginald Politson stood there, shifting from foot to foot. His dress was immaculate as usual, but he looked pale, and there were dark rings beneath his eyes as though he hadn't slept. And he looked frightened. 'Biddy.' He spoke with his habitual smooth charm but Biddy sensed his anxiety. 'I'm glad I caught up with you. I need to speak to you.'

Biddy said nothing. She stared at his shoes. They were shiny. You could almost see the reflection of the grey clouds overhead in them. He offered his arm and she hesitated before taking it. Gentlemen were dangerous. She'd thought Mr Politson was different somehow— but now she wasn't so sure. She slipped her arm through his stiffly.

'It's a delicate matter,' he began as they walked. 'The police wish to see me again. Look, Biddy, they might want to talk to the servants too. And if they do, I need you to tell them I never entered her bedroom that day.' He stopped suddenly and looked at her with wide, pleading eyes. Like a child . . . or a dog.

Biddy straightened her back. For the first time in her life she had power. And she wasn't sure how to use it.

But after a few moments she shook her head. 'I've got to tell the truth, sir. I don't want to go to hell, do I?'

She spotted Michael, sheltering in the trees, waiting, watching impatiently. 'I'm sorry, sir,' she said, pulling her arm away. 'I'm meeting someone. I've got to go now.'

As she hurried off towards the trees, it began to rain.

*   *   *

Dr Henry Carson MD had calls to make. Not that anybody was ill, but there were things he had to check. He had looked through all the notes Dr Willis had made during his years working as a physician in the town of Liverpool. Willis, he knew, worked chiefly amongst the wealthy who dwelled in considerable comfort in the fine Georgian houses around Rodney Street and Catherine Street. Carson himself, after a few weeks of assisting Willis in his work, had taken to salving his sensitive conscience by helping at a clinic for the poor of the squalid courts—so close to the mansions of the rich but in a different and lower world.

But today it was the rich who concerned him. Three of Dr Willis's wealthy patients to be precise. He spread the records of their deaths before him on his desk and moved the oil lamp a little closer. The similarities were unmistakable. But he had no evidence. Only vague suspicions.

243

He turned down the lamp and left the room. It would be better by far if Dr Willis knew nothing about what he was preparing to do. Henry Carson crept down the staircase of Willis's house in Rodney Street and let himself out into the street, careful not to disturb the household.

He had questions to ask. And it was usually servants who knew the answers.

*　　*　　*

Biddy hurried back to Fulwood park. Talking to Michael, walking with him arm in arm, listening to the news of the family—how dad was still drinking, how mam was growing thinner by the day and how Patrick's cough was no better—had made her lose all track of time.

She began to run but when she reached the park lake she spotted Reginald Politson walking, deep in conversation, with a flamboyantly dressed young man. She slipped behind the trunk of the nearest tree and once Politson and his companion were out of sight she hurried back, her heart thumping, and hurtled down the steps leading down to the servants' quarters, mouthing a silent prayer that Mr Waggs wouldn't see her and scold her for her lateness.

When she saw there was nobody about, she paused in the lobby to catch her breath, took

244

off her coat and hat and walked casually through the kitchen where Cook was too preoccupied to notice her. Then she hurried up the back stairs and shot into the sparsely furnished bedroom she shared with Sally the parlour maid, shutting the door softly behind her.

And as she drew the cheap cardboard suitcase from beneath her iron bed, she felt her body trembling. She knew she was in danger and she was afraid.

*　　　*　　　*

'I have just paid another visit to Mrs Politson's house in Fulwood Park.'

Dr Willis looked up at his assistant who stood on the other side of the huge oak desk like a schoolboy summoned to his headmaster, and felt a wave of irritation. 'I see,' he said, trying to stay calm. 'I should have accompanied you, Dr Carson. It is not your place to . . .'

'I think Flora Politson was murdered.'

Willis stood up, knocking a stack of papers to the floor. 'This is outrageous. How dare you intrude on the grief of a family of the Politsons' standing with unfounded accusations. If you wish to keep your reputation in this town . . .'

'If this matter is not dealt with promptly, doctor, your own reputation might suffer. If it emerged that a crime was ignored . . .'

Willis stroked his mutton chop whiskers, considering the implications. 'You have evidence?'

'I have discovered three similar cases.'

Willis raised his eyebrows.

'I have visited all the houses concerned and interviewed the servants. The victims were all wealthy widows and the deaths were identical. The laudanum by the bed to deflect suspicion. The blood on the pillow, easily explained away . . .'

He had Willis's complete attention now. 'You have re-examined Mrs Politson's body?'

Carson nodded. 'And my examination confirmed my theory.'

'But the motive? What can your killer gain from these deaths?'

Carson explained patiently and Willis's eyes widened. 'You can prove nothing.'

'I have already sent the maid to fetch Inspector Always.'

Willis swallowed hard, looking like a man who was about to face the gallows. 'I fear, Doctor, that you are about to make a fool of yourself,' he said weakly.

*   *   *

When Henry Carson arrived at Mortaber Villa in Dr Willis's brougham, seated opposite Inspector Always, he felt a little apprehensive.

246

But he had considered the facts carefully and he knew that the murderer was clever and had been responsible for the deaths of at least four women. Maybe more.

Carson alighted first and marched straight to the front door. A black crepe mourning bow was fixed to the brass knocker and the doctor's pounding on the door was enough to wake the dead. The door was opened by a butler with hostile, suspicious eyes who announced in chilly tones that Mr Politson would be with them presently.

'It's not Mr Politson we want to see this time,' said Inspector Always. 'It's you, Mr Waggs. We'd like to ask you some questions.' Always had acquired the skill over the years of making even the most innocent statement sound menacing to instil fear into the hearts of Liverpool's criminal fraternity.

Carson saw panic in the butler's eyes. The haughty looks had disappeared only to be replaced by fear.

Waggs led them to the butler's pantry where they spoke in hushed whispers. When the three men emerged, Waggs led Always upstairs and Carson followed, wanting to be in at the end.

But when they reached the room it was empty. Their bird had flown out into the rainy night.

*　　　*　　　*

Two years later

It was a grey, rainy day in New York and Mrs Van Dutton was snoring slightly in her drugged sleep, unaware that her maid, Rosa, was standing by the bed watching her.

As Rosa stared at the unconscious woman, her mind began to wander. She heard again the clank of the anchor being raised, felt the thrill of standing on the deck with her brother watching Liverpool fading into the distance, bound for a new world full of new opportunities. America.

She had used the name Biddy then of course. But she was accustomed to changing her name. At Mrs Ventnor's house in Canning Place she had been Sarah, at Mrs Hobson's establishment in Catherine Street she had been Daisy and at Mrs Tregellis's she had been Mary. Forging references was a simple matter—Michael had a deft touch with words—and money made lonely old women gullible so it had been easy to steal the wealthy widows' jewels, little by little. A ring here, a brooch there. Until discovery was imminent and action had to be taken.

She and Michael had thought America would be different—their Promised Land where they could make their fortune. But when the money had started to dwindle, she'd been obliged to fall back on her tried and trusted way of raising the necessary funds.

She took the hat pin from the pocket of her skirts and felt the point with her finger. The pin was an old friend. What policeman would suspect the pin securing her hat could possibly be a murder weapon. Every woman possessed one. But not many considered its murderous possibilities.

She turned the drugged woman over gently and lifted the hair until the nape of the scrawny neck was exposed. That young doctor in Liverpool—Carson his name was—had noticed a spot of blood on the pillow so now she was careful to place a handkerchief beneath the head to prevent any tell tale mark being left. Then she arranged the scene carefully. The half empty bottle of laudanum by the bed and the remains of a night time drink which also contained the drug—Mrs Van Dutton had taken it to help her sleep and taken a double dose accidentally. Her maid, of course, would confirm that she was in the habit of using it to prevent disturbed nights. No questions must be asked. And no doctor would dream of examining the area beneath the hairline at the back of the dead woman's neck.

The maid gritted her teeth and thrust the hat pin upwards into the unconscious woman's brain. So neat. Now the charade would begin. She would discover that the old lady had died in her sleep and call the doctor after helping herself to any jewels and cash that might not be missed by the victims' neglectful relatives.

It was a full hour before the doctor came that day—plenty of time to arrange things. It had all gone smoothly. Mrs Van Dutton's usual physician was otherwise engaged but a new doctor was coming in his place so that was better still. She felt rather pleased with herself and, as she waited for the doctor to arrive, she gazed out of the window, avoiding the sight of the wizened corpse on the bed. It was raining again. Funeral weather.

*   *   *

The doctor arranged his features into a solemn expression as Mrs Van Dutton's footman answered the door.

'I was expecting Dr Brown,' the servant said as he led the way upstairs.

'He's been unavoidably detained.'

The footman turned. 'You sound English, sir.'

'I am. I only arrived in New York three weeks ago. Carson's the name. Dr Henry Carson.'

ONE LAST PICK-UP

Sarah Hilary

The first was a flat tyre. Tim rolled up in good time, wrench in hand, smile in place. 'Knights of the Road.' She laughed with relief. In her forties, bottle-blonde highlights, hint of desperation that predated, he guessed, the roadside recovery. High heels snagged at the tarmac as she watched him work. He got her going again, all right.

The second was a dead battery. Tim gave his best salute. 'Riding to the rescue.' Who could resist a gent with a sense of humour? She was Clare, that one. Hard shoulder, soft top.

When Rita asked how his day went, Tim said, 'Terrific.' Rita tapped her fingers on the table. Painted nails, metallic-finish. Tough customer, his wife. Not a whiff of the damsel in distress about Rita.

Number three? A faulty fan-belt. 'Pop the lid for me would you, love?' He wouldn't have risked the 'love' but she was old enough to be his mum and they both knew it. Proper little goer, all the same. Lola, believe it or not.

Five and six were twins. It didn't get much better. 'Your rear end's gone,' Tim told them. He felt like James Bond, no brakes, touching

80mph.

The roads melted; a summer heatwave. Tim tackled steamy engines, got under the bonnet so often he lost count, topped up the oil, deployed his dipstick. A rare old time.

Rita said, 'You want to recharge your own battery for a change.' Bitch. He never had any trouble getting it up at the roadside. Maybe it was the open air, the bitter-sweet smell of bitumen and burning fossil fuels, his role in the rescues. He loved to hear, 'Lone female breakdown,' 'Stranded,' 'Priority'. A chance to play the old-fashioned hero, get chivalrous. He had the routine down pat, second nature in no time.

This one was wearing driving shoes, the kind with rubber treads on the soles. Sensible. Decent set of legs on her. Dash of makeup, not as much as he liked. 'Hope you weren't waiting too long,' he said.

'You were very quick.' She had a great smile.

Middle of nowhere. Perfect spot for it.

'I'm Tim, by the way.'

'Diana.'

'Let's get the bonnet up and see what's causing the trouble, shall we?'

She sat in the driver's seat, sprang the lid.

Tim had a quick rummage.

Never saw the wrench coming.

Just heard the rev of speeding air, and the words, 'From Rita, with love.'

INGLENOOK

Douglas Stewart

'This is the lounge,' explained Richard Tyson, the old-school agent rather needlessly. Andrea and Paul took in the low, beamed ceiling, the leaded-lights and the chintzy furnishings which told of retired colonials and stiff gin-and-tonics after sundown.

'Artisan Cottage,' murmured Andrea to nobody in particular as she took in the slightly musty air.

Paul, her fiancé, was quick to respond. But then he always was. His face was sharp, his voice sharper still, full of the confident brashness of a South London childhood. 'Means Worker's Cottage. Farm labourer probably.' He adjusted his shades and for no explained reason tapped the wall knowingly. The agent looked at him and then turned quickly away, his distaste showing though he said nothing. Paul liked an audience—people to impress at work or like the old fart agent and Andrea, his impressionable young fiancée from her wealthy but rather naïve background.

'Oh Paul, isn't this cottage just perfect! I love it.' She spun around, her kilted skirt splaying out as she took in the room. 'Darling we must buy it! Really must! It is *so* gorgeous,

253

heavenly. Look at that garden, the view to the forest.' His sudden scowl, hidden from the agent, silenced her before she could continue. As a pharmaceutical salesman, winner of the Executive of the Year for the company in 2006, no way did he want all this gushing. He wanted the price down. Wanted a deal.

'Perfect? Not with that god-awful ugly fireplace. Ruins the place. Looks like the one Mum and Dad had in their rented semi in Croydon. I left that type of monstrosity behind years ago. I mean here we are in the middle of rural Hampshire in a character cottage, roses round the door, and there's a *tiled* fireplace. Do me a favour! How old's this place, Tyson? Tudor?'

The agent bridled. 'You're right, *Mr* Charbon,' he emphasised. He knew it dated back to 1540 but no way was he going to be too precise with a shit like Paul Charbon. One false word, a wrong date and he'd be sued for misrepresentation. As for the name *Charbon*, he'd bet a pint of best bitter that the family name had been Cole. 'Can't be precise about the year though.' He looked down his long nose over the half-rimmed glasses. 'I'll take a look at the vegetable garden. Let you two talk between yourselves.' In his tweed jacket, brogues and baggy flannels he looked at ease with the surroundings as he ambled slowly to the hall and then outside.

'Andrea, my sweet,' Paul hissed when they

were alone, 'never reveal how keen you are.' His dark chiselled features beneath the swept back black hair showed none of the charm when he'd been down on one knee proposing to her in the grounds of the Chewton Glen Hotel. 'We don't need you gushing on about the place. I reckon we can get a deal here. Bloke in the pub told me the owners need a quick sale.'

Andrea moved towards him and threw her arms round his neck. 'I'm sorry. You're so clever about these things. I just couldn't help it. I simply adore this cottage. It'll be a sweet first home . . . and just big enough to have some babies in like we planned.'

His kiss was perfunctory, the slightest peck. 'Perfect, dearest. Two at least. Isn't that right?' But even as he spoke, he was pushing her away. Babies were not part of his plan, not now, not ever. He walked to the whitewashed plaster wall and started to tap it again. A few brisk movements across the room and he was tapping above the fireplace for comparison. Then, without explanation, he ducked his tall, lean figure under the low doorway leading to the outhouse. Every movement oozed energy and confirmed his supreme self-confidence.

Andrea turned to the window where she could see Richard Tyson sniffing the pink and yellow roses. She enjoyed watching the agent as he pottered happily among the shrubs. There was something of her own father about him and the memories were bitter-sweet. Two years before, her parents had decided to exchange England for the western coast of Barbados. They had sold the Manor House near Salisbury. The long, low stone building had been in the family for generations, but now home was on a bluff looking out over the ocean, with yachts and cruisers replacing squirrels and the occasional deer.

Andrea's lips pursed as she recalled her parents' views on Paul and the intended marriage. Even her porcelain features, so dainty and refined, showed the anguish at the hurt she had caused them—and that their rebuff had caused her. 'You marry him without our blessing and with our warning,' her father had said. 'You're only twenty-two. There's no rush. He's over thirty, divorced by twenty-four. He's got charm, that much I grant you but beneath that, I sense a man without true substance.'

'He's just too ready to say all the right things to us,' chipped in her mother. Her frail body belied a shrewd matriarchal spirit. 'In three years you inherit nearly thirty million under Auntie Harriet's Trust. Did you tell him that?'

'We have no secrets, Mummy. We're *in love*. Anyway, Paul's not interested in my money. He's a high-flyer himself. Wants to keep me in the *manner* to which I was accustomed. We laughed *so* much at his play on the word *manner*. What you see is what you get. That's what he told me and I believe him. Sorry but I can't agree with you, Daddy or with you either Mummy.'

'We shan't come to the wedding.' Her mother's jaw, wrinkled and aged by too many hours in the garden without sunblock, quivered as she spoke. 'Your father doesn't like the cut of his jib. Put it off. Live with him if you must. We're not old-fashioned dear—we just want the best for you.' She clasped her hands together. 'Have you prayed about this? The way we brought you up? The way Mother Cecile taught you at the convent?'

Andrea sighed and killed the train of thought. How could they be so wrong? Not just about the power of prayer but about Paul. Of course, she still went through the *motions* of prayer but late night chats with her friend Miranda Balderstone over buckets of red wine in France had ended any love affair with religion. Her ex-convent friend had attended a classy finishing school in Lausanne but had then run wild, partying in the hottest spots for the young and wealthy. Miranda had persuaded her that there was no logic or rationale whether in prayer, taking communion or lighting candles to the Virgin Mary.

Back in May, she had stayed with Miranda at her home on the Côte d'Azur at Cannes. The villa, with six bedrooms and seven bathrooms, was perched high above the Croisette and had its own indoor-outdoor pool and terraces on each side to catch the sun. Sir Archie Balderstone had lived there with the occasional mistress—at least whenever he was not travelling or being entrepreneurial after retiring as chairman of a global engineering company. However, he had collapsed and died in the lounge at Milan Airport just days after a fearful row with Miranda. In those few days, his London solicitor had flown in with the revised will and had left with it signed. Angrily, Sir Archie had slashed her feather-bedding from the expected millions to the right to live in the Cannes villa and two-hundred thousand pounds a year.

Andrea wished she *could* still be convinced by the principles she had been taught but Miranda had persuaded her to believe only in the *power of self*. This was not, Miranda had emphasised, selfishly looking after number one. *Not that at all*. 'If you're in the shit, the best person to get you out is yourself. And the way to do it,' Miranda had concluded with a flourish of her empty glass, 'is not by clasping beads or a crucifix but by hard-nosed action. And don't be a total prat like me and get cut of your pop's will.'

Andrea had laughed about that. 'No chance. I'm so close to my parents, that just won't happen. Anyway, they can't cut me out of my trust fund. That's mine, no question,

258

when I'm twenty-five. But what did you do that upset your old man?'

'Didn't like my boyfriend. I was pregnant by him too. An absolute charmer. Hung like a donkey and screwed as often as a daddy lion. Trouble was he came from Lebanon. Daddy reckoned he was a terrorist looking to marry me.'

'And was he?'

'Father checked him out. Had private eyes snooping everywhere. He was totally obsessed about proving it. I told him I didn't care if he was a terrorist. I wanted to be with him forever. That did it.'

'What happened?'

'Father's blood pressure exploded about a week later but by then he'd changed the will.'

'And your donkey?'

'He—aw . . . Sorry, I couldn't resist that,' she giggled. 'He—aw disappeared. I had an abortion. I guess he didn't fancy me without the money.' Andrea sensed that Miranda now knew her father had been right. The thought was of little comfort as she relived her father's views of Paul Charbon.

Beyond Tyson and the swooping swallows, she saw the line of oaks and the lush magnolias surrounded by the blues and purples of the wild New Forest flowers. The chirruping as the sparrows, chaffinches and blue-tits danced around the birdbath had nearly disguised another sound that she now strained to

259

identify. Standing in the stale air and silence, she had sensed something else—it was indefinable like a sigh or the sound of distant movement. It wasn't eerie or unnerving, just rather odd because it was inexplicable.

She was still puzzling over it as Paul reappeared, his face excited. 'I was right. Don't go saying a word to that coffin-dodger out there but there's an inglenook behind the fireplace. Sometimes you'll find two or even more other fireplaces before you get back to the original.' He removed the Raybans and his eyes swept the length of the wall. 'It'll be big enough to walk into—ten feet wide, six feet high and four feet deep at least. You see.' He threw his Black Russian cigarette stub into the empty grate. 'We'll add thousands to this place by restoring the original inglenook. I reckon there'll be a bread-oven too judging by the shape behind this monstrosity.' He kicked the pink tinted tiling contemptuously.

Andrea's milk and honey complexion and her doe eyes radiated happiness. 'That means . . . you mean we're buying it?' Andrea stepped over the tiger's skin rug to plant a kiss on his cheek. 'Oh, thank you! Thank you, my dearest darling Paul.' She gazed into his eyes. 'That red Aga; the summerhouse; the veggie garden; these low ceilings and the beams.' It was her turn to tap the wall. 'And now, clever old you has found an inglenook. I just adore them. We had two in the Manor House. The smell of apple logs and the smoke curling up the wide chimney—I can hardly wait. Darling, we shall be so happy here.'

He pulled her close to his chest. 'Making love by the dying embers? Andrea, you said you wanted the cottage. I'll buy it just for you. But I'll start with a low offer.'

The whirlwind romance had begun just weeks before in May when she had been at Miranda's villa. The chauffeur had zapped them down the hill in the black Renault Clio. With the Film Festival on, they had planned to chill out in the fashionable Martinez Hotel. There they would down a few cocktails. If Brad Pitt or George Clooney or *anyone* dishy failed to invite them to party in a top floor suite, then they planned to head to the square in Valbonne for dinner. But the plans had been scrapped, everything changed.

Paul Charbon had been staying in the hotel at huge expense to the pharmaceutical company as his *Employee of the Year* prize. The two women had been sinking their second vodkas in the piano bar when Paul had sidled over, obviously on the prowl. 'A couple of Hollywood stars if ever I saw them,' he prompted before pointing to the empty chair. 'May I?' and before either could say no, he had slumped into the comfy depths and offered to buy some champagne—and not *just* champagne but vintage Krug.

Andrea had always seen herself as the

follower whenever Miranda was around. Andrea's life working for architects in Guildford seemed so banal compared to Miranda's role as PA to the chairman of a recording company in Soho Square. Her friend was so quick with the chat and her party-girl lifestyle oozed a vampish availability that always attracted the wolves. But though Paul laughed at her wit and poisoned barbs, it was Andrea that he seemed to prefer.

They had dined on the company's two-hundred foot yacht which was available to Paul for the week. 'Look,' he had said at the end of a long dinner on the deck, 'let's go cruising along the coast in the morning. Lunch in Monte Carlo and back in the evening. And,' he had then turned to Miranda, his face rather sheepish 'would you mind if I asked just Andrea to join me for dinner *à deux* tomorrow night? That's if she'd like to.'

Andrea had been thrilled to accept. All evening she had grown more confident that for once it was not Miranda who had been making all the running. Boozy dinners had followed on the Croisette and up at St Paul de Vence. There had been kisses under the stars and the following week, there had been whispered words under the bedclothes at The Capital Hotel in Knightsbridge. Six weeks later, it had been a suite in the five-star Chewton Glen Hotel, a stately residence used by Captain Marryat over one-hundred and fifty years before when he wrote *Children of the New Forest*. On the second night after dinner had come the proposal. Tears of happiness rolling down her cheeks, she had accepted.

Andrea listened just slightly embarrassed at Paul's *take it or leave it* approach to the agent. The asking price was nine-seven-five but Paul was offering one hundred thousand less—but claiming falsely to be a cash buyer. 'So that's our offer, Tyson. Can you get a quick decision? Like now?' Richard Tyson had nodded and gone outside to phone his clients. Ten minutes later, she realised that Paul's tough talking had worked and she felt a moment of guilt for disliking his style. 'The sellers are not happy but they accept,' the agent reported.

'Happiness doesn't come into this, my friend. Market rules apply. That's the game.'

'And, Tyson,' Paul had said 'make sure the dozy country solicitors get on with it. I know what these duffers are like. I can deal with them if you don't.'

'No doubt you can, Mr . . . er Cole, I mean Charbon. The world has changed for us professionals. We've had to accept second place to the new generation like you who know best.'

Paul smiled. He always appreciated a compliment.

The pace of the couple's romance had shocked Andrea's parents. They kept their promise and shunned the naff vulgarity of the Las Vegas wedding at The Little White Chapel. But Andrea put all that far from her mind and revelled in his tenderness and the little gifts and thoughtfulness during the sex packed honeymoon in San Francisco. When the 747 touched down at Heathrow, she clasped his hand. Everything was so, so wonderful. Well *almost* everything. There was just one niggle. *Why was he wearing condoms?*

The nagging thought was still with her when they took the keys of the cottage. Despite her religious upbringing, she hadn't been bothered by his use of contraception *before* the wedding. But why now? Baby-making was top of their agenda. Hell! She'd even left her job to be at home and to accelerate the gift of a child.

She stood in the gateway to the thatched cottage and watched the removal lorry lurch into the distance before she returned to the kitchen. Paul was at work twenty miles away in Southampton but she had plenty to do. All around her were packing-cases, tea-chests and wedding presents yet to be opened. The summer sun and the roses swaying in the warm breeze had been replaced by the bleak damp of a wet autumn. Rain dripped steadily from the hawthorns and scudding clouds danced across the darkening skies. They were so low that they added to her sense of depression and oppression, feelings compounded by the bare walls of her surroundings. What had looked spanking white in the July sun now looked grey and in need of attention.

A pair of woodlice scuttled along the skirting-board, a sure sign of a damp problem somewhere around the kitchen. In the lounge, the bare wires where the wall-lights had once been, now hung limp and added to the image of neglect. The walls looked patched and flaking; cracks previously unseen looked like ravines under the glare of the naked bulbs set so close to the ceiling that the plaster had been toasted brown by the heat.

As she stood trying to reinvent the magic of that July afternoon, she heard again that strange sound but she dismissed it as she started unpacking the cases. After the Aga was running full bore and Paul had returned rather late from work and had lit the fire in the tiny grate, Andrea's spirits had risen. They had snacked on an M&S instant dinner for two washed down by a bottle of Californian red brought back from the Napa. 'The inglenook'll be a big job,' Paul said, jabbing a fork towards her. 'Top priority is getting the basics right— treating the damp, painting the walls and ceilings, buying some antiques, laying new carpeting and fixing the lights.'

'But won't knocking out the fireplace ruin the new furniture and the walls if we've painted them?'

He tapped her on the nose in appreciation.

'You're right—to a point. We won't replace the carpet in here or do these walls till I've uncovered the inglenook. The new furnishings, chairs and settee we can protect with loads of vinyl sheeting.'

At New Year she had tackled Paul about the condoms. 'Of course, my sweet. No more condoms. Now the house is a bit straighter, we must get that baby on the way.' For a while Paul seemed to be off sex but then about a month later he was back to his best—but still no pregnancy. As their wedding anniversary came and went, Andrea said nothing but her failure to conceive was now always in her thoughts.

Another worry was that Paul was returning later and later from work and increasingly had meetings that kept him in London or occasionally over in the USA. Imperceptibly over the months, he had grown indifferent to her, not unpleasant but less caring. When he forgot her birthday in November and came home after midnight, the *duck à l'orange* now binned, she had sobbed herself to sleep. The lyrics of Happy Birthday tormented her: *Happy Birthday to you . . . Unloved Person are you.'*

He never even remembered that he had forgotten and she had never reminded him. The other work now done, his concern was the inglenook. One evening, he slipped into a navy boiler-suit and started work. Andrea watched for a few moments as he swung the pickaxe and giant sledge at the fireplace. Then she slipped upstairs and went through his wallet, his pockets and his briefcase. What she found filled her with disgust and contempt. To the backdrop of hammering, she cried for an age, tears flowing steadily from her peat-brown eyes. For a moment she had debated confronting him but as she climbed down the creaking stairs, she decided to say nothing. 'I'm going to bed. I'm off to London on the early train. Meeting Jan. Remember? She used to work with me.'

He mopped his cheek and grunted an acknowledgement. 'I'll finish this next week sometime. Bigger job than I thought. Just one line of stonework to go and then I'll know for sure.'

Three days later after Paul's BMW had headed for Southampton, Andrea settled down to a cup of instant and a digestive. The sheeted floor was grimy from the dust and rubble of the part-finished job. Scarcely daring to play the recording, she clicked the *Play* button. The spy-shop in Mayfair had provided a neat little voice-activated device that she had hidden beneath his car seat. 'Hi darling! God! Wasn't last night just *so* good!' Andrea heard the chuckle and with a shock recognized Miranda's voice. 'I'm just counting the days till you're divorced.'

'Two more years till she gets the trust cash. Like we said from the start, we just gotta be patient. After the divorce, we'll be rich and together forever.'

'Promise me you haven't done something daft like fall in love with Andrea have you? It's tough for me, you being married to *her*.'

She heard his derisive snort. 'Sweetie, no absolutely no! But for *your* plan, *we'd* be married by now. Little Miss Toogood means nothing to me. I despise her because she's not you. Just think of the divorce booty and our new future.'

There was a pause before Miranda replied, the cultured tones of her upbringing showing through. 'And Andrea suspects nothing still? Not even now? I mean hell, we see each other two maybe three times a week.'

'Hell, no. Surely you remember how easily she fell for all that crap about the Lebanese bloke.'

Andrea winced as she heard her friend's throaty chuckle. 'Yeah! You're right. She'd swallow anything. And all the time the donkey my father despised was you.'

Paul laughed. 'So, relax. She's too dumb to be suspicious. Give her a hoe and some pruning shears and she's happy. Except for the babies that is.'

'And the vasectomy? Promise me you'll reverse it, big Paul.'

'Trust me! I checked with Mr Snip. No problem, he said—so long as you don't leave it too long. Brilliant idea of mine that! It fooled

Andrea anyway. She's expecting a baby every month.' He laughed and Andrea's first tear appeared as she absorbed the spiteful mockery.

Miranda's tone was suddenly sullen. 'Let's change the subject. Imagining you and Andrea having it away doesn't do much for me. Usual place tomorrow night?'

'Six pm. Andrea thinks I'm at a marketing conference in Basingstoke. I'm not expected back till well after ten. You going to wear those new . . .'

'Just you wait! Must go. Love you. The train's just pulling in.'

Andrea clicked the *Off* button, the sound of their blown kisses throbbing inside her head. She sat, her face tormented, head bowed, her arms around her knees. *Should she say something? If so what? Or should she just quit—tell him where to stick his effing marriage?* By the time she had stood up, stretching her slender and shapely limbs, she had almost decided what she would say before leaving. But something still told her that walking out in a flurry of angry words was not enough.

That noise! There it was, louder now that the fireplace and one layer of stonework had gone. If Paul had been right, there was just one more stone wall to go. She grabbed the sledge and swung it mightily, all her aggression coming out. Moments later, she was through, the first heavy stone echoing as it landed in the black beyond. The release of stale dank air that burst through was almost overpowering. Now the sound was more defined, almost a soft sibilant hiss yet still mysterious and beckoning.

Rapidly, she knocked away two, three and then four large stones so that she could shine her torch into the blackness and peer in. What she saw was a shock, an alcove at least four feet deep and at least seven feet wide. She swung the torch along the entire floor, taking in every detail. Then she looked upwards. The cavity was easily big enough to stand in but of a chimney there was no sign. The roof seemed to have been plastered over.

She wiped the sweat from her brow and sat on the floor, her mind a jumble of fragmented thoughts. She wasn't sure which part of his long, cunning deception angered her most. She shuddered as she relived the photo in his briefcase of an anonymous curly head buried deep into Paul's naked crotch.

Slowly, she rose from her foetal position and went to the shed. There she found the rest of the black vinyl sheeting Paul was using for covering the floor. For the next hour, she was busy, feverishly so but by the time Paul returned, the cottage was filled with wafting aromas of lamb cutlets. Andrea was looking her best, crucifix on her chest and wearing her pink silk blouse and cling-cut jeans. She had shampooed and blow-dried her hair and was fragrant with *Eclat d'Arpege*.

Paul had barely noticed her and had eaten impatiently, eager to get to work on the inglenook, even more so after she had explained her earlier efforts. 'I was bored today,' she explained, 'so I took a few swings at the stonework. Looks like you're right, sweetheart. There *is* a big cavity just like you said. Must be an inglenook. You'll need to get in and take a look. I shone the torch around and couldn't see the chimney. Bricked over, I suppose.'

Paul was already in his boiler-suit and as soon as he had downed the last of the Beaujolais Nouveau, he had headed impatiently for the lounge. Andrea followed him and watched as he inspected the two feet square hole set about thirty inches above the floor. He grabbed the torch and flashed it around inside. 'Seems you were right. Some stupid sod's blocked the chimney. I'm going in. When I say so, hand me the sledge and pickaxe.'

She rocked on her heels, her face placid as she saw him swing his feet through the opening and then limbo his whole body inside. The torch's beam shone brightly as he pointed it upwards. She held her breath as he turned and stepped away to the right of the hole. Andrea heard the rustle, saw the beam lurch violently and then came the scream, long and primeval. It drowned the sound that had so haunted her, its violence booming from the cavity. Then it faded, as if receding into the distance.

The listener stood for a minute, maybe more, and then went to the opening. Using the spare torch she saw at once that the cavity was empty. Paul had gone. She shouted his name and the booming resonance pierced her ears and forced her back. No answer, nor did she expect one having tested the depth of the well. Even sixty yards of baler twine with a rock on the end had never touched bottom.

She checked the time and cleared the plates to the kitchen but did not wash up. *Doing that was when she had been interrupted by his scream.* From his briefcase she removed the photo of Miranda as she double-checked everywhere for any clue of infidelity. She grabbed his mobile phone, the recording, and took everything to the shallow hole she had dug in the potato patch. If her plan misfired, she might need them for a plea of manslaughter.

A smile of triumph on her face, she returned to the cavity and eased herself through. The sheet of black vinyl now only partly concealed the well-mouth. The dust and rubble that had disguised it had gone with him to the depths. The two big stones at the nearest corners had held the sheeting firm. She smeared dust around her cheeks and over her clothes. After pushing the stones aside, she shoved the sheeting through to the lounge and clambered back. She tore it and then dumped it towards the bottom of the dustbin as if discarded at some earlier time.

She sat down, a rush of release colouring her cheeks and waited an hour. The only sound was of air moving in the depths of the well. Then she picked up the phone. 'Fire! Ambulance!' Her voice screamed down the line. 'My husband's fallen down a well-shaft.'

She sat quietly again and waited. Frantic action to sound breathless and panicky could await the approaching sirens. *You were so clever Paul! Thought you knew everything. Despised little Miss Toogood from the convent. And as for you Miranda, you were wrong too. Not the dumb-fuck you assumed either. But thanks! You did me a favour—a big one. You taught me to believe in the power of self. Remember? If you're in the shit, the best person to get you out is yourself. And the way to do it was not by clasping beads or a crucifix but by hard-nosed action.*

So, Paul, you were both wrong. Sorry! Sorr . . .ee! A convent education can be useful. Like learning about Artois in France and the Carthusian Monks who gave these wells their name in the twelfth century. You see, it never was Artisan Cottage, not in this part of Hampshire. It was an Artesian Cottage. Till the well went dry. Understand now Paul? You can learn something new every day—unless you're dead.

OUTRAGE

Jim Gregson

Harry knew from the moment he was captured that they were going to kill him.

These people didn't take prisoners. It wasn't practical. You couldn't operate terrorism and cart prisoners about with you. Those who weren't with them were against them, and those who actually fought against them forfeited any rights they might have had.

Harry had no resentment about the situation. He had set out to hunt these people down; he would have shot them like mad dogs if he had been given the opportunity. It was the only way to deal with them; there was no room for compunction. These people were far too ruthless, far too unpredictable, to risk trying to do anything other than eliminate them, swiftly and efficiently.

Now he was in their hands. He had played the game and lost. He was going to die. He hoped it would be quickly and without any ritual. He didn't think they would torture him, because there was nothing he could tell them that they didn't already know. He was a little apprehensive that they might taunt him before they despatched him; he didn't know how he would react to having insults shouted into his face, to seeing the features of these younger men twist with hatred as they spat their contempt at him.

He watched them out of the corner of his eye as he sat on the floor in the cave. They were fanatics, that was for sure. They spoke in Arabic, but in a dialect he couldn't place. He picked up only the odd phrase of what they said. But he caught the flash of their eyes in the single low light at the back of the cave as they spoke to each other and glanced occasionally at him.

They were young eyes, and they glittered with excitement and determination. They reminded him of another pair of eyes, in another place. It took him minutes to recall whose, but he had nothing else to occupy him; anything was better than speculation about his death. This was a welcome diversion, and he grinned involuntarily when he remembered. The English countryside, and an evening cricket match, with twilight moving into dark. A young man he had hit for four with a wild, desperate flail of his bat, who had stood a yard away from him and glared at him with eyes which flashed hostility like this.

How far away that world seemed now! Cricket, and Herefordshire, and that comfortable, village green world which had always been more fiction than fact. He felt a sudden shaft of nostalgia for that world, an emotion he had never expected to experience.

It must be the inevitability of death that surprised you with these things.

They were talking again, discussing something among themselves. He was surprised they hadn't shot him by now. He wished they'd get on with it. Once you had resigned yourself to the inevitable, you wanted them to get on with it. He'd been an atheist for twenty years at least now, since he was about seventeen, but he found himself uttering a silent, illogical prayer for salvation, for survival in that after-life he knew did not exist.

That was surely a sign of weakness. He was suddenly resentful of these young fools for keeping him waiting, for allowing doubt to seep into his mind, into the very soul he knew he did not have.

They were very sure about their God, these men, who were so sure of themselves, and so mistaken. They were arguing about something now. They kept glancing at him as they talked. He caught the flash of their dark eyes, the whites very startling against the invisible pupils, as each of them glanced across towards him and then went on with the argument.

The one who spoke English came across to him. He took the pistol from his belt, almost as an afterthought, and waved it vaguely in front of Harry's face before he spoke. Harry wanted to tell him that there was no threat in the gesture, that when you knew you were going to die a gun waved under your nose didn't have any frightening effect.

He felt a sudden resentment that he, a grizzled veteran of many conflicts, was going to be killed by kids. Because they weren't much more than that, these five, not in terms of military experience, of lives taken and friends lost. He deserved a better fate than to be executed anonymously by these callow fighters, who had scarcely learned yet how to protect themselves.

Crap, that was: stupid, unwarranted pride. He didn't deserve anything, good or bad. He'd gone into this with his eyes open. He'd nailed a few of these stupid bastards, and by doing so had saved a few hundred anonymous, innocent people from dying. That was as much as you could expect in the way of achievement. And what the hell did it matter how you died or who killed you, when your time came? Fortunes of war, mate. Only let's have it over quickly.

'You do explosives,' the youth said to him. It was a statement of fact, one not worth denying. He had been assembling a booby trap at the ambush, when they had taken him and shot his companions. Harry nodded. He might as well have some kind of identity, in his last minutes.

So yes, he was an explosives expert. That had been what had distinguished him, in the old days with the Royal Engineers. That was what had got him his SAS transfer. And when that had all gone wrong, 'explosives expert' had been his label. The one which won him employment and respect among the dangerous and unreliable men he had worked with, in the bitter conflict of these last months. Everyone nowadays wanted a man who could blast buildings and human life into small pieces.

The youth reached behind Harry and freed his hands from the rope. His brow furrowed as he struggled for words in an alien tongue. After a few seconds, he said simply, 'We need you.'

He shouldn't have said that. He didn't have much English, or he wouldn't have used those words. Harry wasn't going to co-operate with these people, whatever they did to him. He wasn't going to kill more innocent people. He didn't reply, but continued looking down at the filthy straw around his feet.

'You do bombs. You're going to help us.' The youth waved the pistol again, then placed the muzzle against the back of Harry's head.

Harry said, 'Go ahead and shoot, son. I'm not going to help you.' He didn't feel anything like as brave as those words sounded. But his guts hadn't turned to liquid, as he would have expected. He realised that he wasn't expecting the man to pull the trigger. Not yet. Not whilst they felt that there was still a chance that they could get him to co-operate.

The young man's language improved as he launched into the speech he had prepared.

'Look at these things. We're going to use them, whether you help us or not. If you help us, we'll get our target, kill no one else. You can save the innocent ones. The women, the children.'

Harry didn't believe that. They didn't make distinctions like that. They killed at random, enjoyed doing it, relished not having to distinguish shades of difference among the enemy. Obsession taught you to think in terms of numbers, not guilt.

Sure enough, the young man now said, his eyes flashing with a perverted pride, 'I'll be dying myself. I or one of my friends. All you will be doing will be making sure we kill the right man, and only the right man. You'll be saving lives, when you help us.'

But the young voice carried no conviction into the words he had prepared, as if the thinking were too alien for his brain to accept it.

Harry looked down at what the youth had spread out on the old rug in front of him. There was Semtex, of course. And wires; old wires, taken from something else they had dismantled, some heater or washing machine. Not the stuff he was used to. Harry was used to winding new wire off the reel as he wanted it. But these dusty old wires would serve well enough, if they were properly used. No great expertise was needed with Semtex. Even raw young madmen like these would know how to attach wires.

There was a detonator, too. He reached out stiff hands before he was even aware that he was doing so and turned it over. Crude and old; it had probably been stolen from a quarry, in the first place. But it would work well enough, no doubt: detonators are simple enough things to activate, once the wiring is right.

It was then that the young man said why they needed him. 'We need a timer attached to this. You must help us.'

They had agreed they were going to use timers on all their bombs. They were crude, amateur devices, and too many of them had gone off long before they should have done, killing their bearers and none of the enemy. The youth was desperate now, and his voice was guttural with excitement. With no more arguments to use, he was trying to get his way by sheer force of will.

Harry understood all of this. He said, 'No can do, son. I know about timers, but there's no clock here for me to use. No can do!' As he repeated the phrase, he passed his hand over the implements assembled on the rug, hoping his gesture would make clear what the boy might not understand in words.

But the boy did understand. He smiled for the first time since they had brought Harry into the cave. Then, like a conjurer, he produced the timer, new and gleaming, from behind his back. 'We have timer,' he said. 'Now, you fix it for us.' He waved the pistol, touching Harry's throat with it. Almost as an afterthought, he added the line he had used at first, 'You save lives by this. We only kill the man we want, if you do this.'

'How do I know that?'

'You don't know. You don't have choice.' The young man waved the pistol near his prisoner's temple, but Harry knew now he wasn't going to shoot. Not yet. Not until he had got what he wanted from an expert.

Harry picked up a piece of the dusty wire, then looked at the shiny new timer. He said, 'This is one of mine, isn't it? You took this from my bag.'

Of course they had. When they took him and shot Dave and Anton, they would have picked up all their gear as well. They were scavengers as well as killers. They had to be.

The youth was grinning at him now, enjoying his discomfort, relishing the fact that Harry was going to have to use his own materials in the very cause he had been trying to frustrate.

Harry looked down at his grimy hands, then again at the stuff on the rug. 'You're going to do this anyway, aren't you?'

The youth nodded vigorously, sensing now that he was going to get what he wanted. As he saw it, this captive was a mere mercenary, totally ignorant of God's will. For a few hours of extra life, a coward like this would do what they wanted. His lip curled into a sneer as he looked at the back of the mercenary's bent head and lowered the pistol. A few minutes and a few guttural threats later, he was back telling his companions that they had won.

They watched their victim surreptitiously from the other end of the cave, as he picked up the Semtex and weighed it in his expert hands. Harry nodded thoughtfully, examined the old wires carefully, and then set to work.

The young-old man who had threatened him was fascinated. Harry seemed to become immersed in the task in hand, concentrating to the exclusion of all else on making sure that he had firm contacts with the wires from the detonator to the Semtex. His strong fingers moved busily, assembling surprisingly quickly the bomb which was going to blow up the bus.

The youth crept closer, a few inches at a time, anxious to pick up whatever he could from the man they were going to kill, to share with his colleagues and add to their destructive efficiency of the glorious years ahead. He did not think this mercenary had noticed his attention, for he had not looked up since he began the task.

But when he was within four feet of the rug, Harry said, 'Picking up tips, are you? Learning how it's done?' His voice was soft and low; he might have been speaking to the son he had lost eight years ago with the divorce.

'Don't talk, scum, get on with it!' The youth's voice was raucous now with excitement at the sight of the bomb almost ready for use. 'I could do all that myself, you know.'

'You didn't though, did you? Had to get one of your enemies to do your work for you.' Harry was surprised that he could taunt them. Perhaps once you had accepted that death was inevitable it gave you a sort of assurance in your final minutes.

'It's the timer we need you for.'

'Quite right, son. Go off any time, without a timer attached, this would. Quite a crude thing, it is. You want a timer, or it could go off long before you're ready.'

The youth nodded, accepting everything his prisoner said. He wasn't going to admit that he'd never even seen a bomb at close quarters before. Not here, with this grizzled fighter they had forced to work for them; not with his comrades watching him for any sign of weakness from the other end of the cave. 'That's your job, to fit the timer.'

'I'm not good with timers, lad. It's not my forte.' Harry threw in the French word he knew the youth would not understand deliberately, enjoying watching the puzzlement flash into the too-revealing face.

The young man's face was suddenly savage. He gave Harry a vulpine smile and waved the pistol in his face. 'You good with timers. You fix this up the way we want!'

'Easy, lad, easy! I need to be careful with this.' Harry didn't raise his hand: he had seen how near to panic his adversary was. He didn't want that pistol going off now, before his last job was complete. The craftsman would fulfil his final task.

'You good with timers.' The youth repeated the phrase stubbornly, as if it were some kind of formula.

'All right. I'll do my best.' Harry had made his protest. He looked at the timer carefully from all angles, then nodded his head, as though satisfied. 'How long do you want before the explosion, once the timer is activated?'

They'd already discussed this in their low-toned mutterings at the other end of the cave. The youth said promptly. 'Ten minutes. Ten minutes exactly. That's how long we want.' He'd almost added 'after I get on the bus', but he had remembered just in time that this old fool thought he was saving life, not spreading death more efficiently.

Harry made a great play of setting the time very exactly on the clock. It was easy enough really, but they didn't know that, and now that his last minutes on this earth were at hand, he had a sudden foolish wish to stretch them out. The youth made him tell him again exactly how to activate the device, then began to attach it to the harness with the straps which were to go round his leg. There was no need to disguise anything from this infidel, now that he had fulfilled his purpose.

It was one of the others who took Harry out of the cave, keeping the muzzle of the pistol against the back of his head. The youth who had spoken to him had established some sort of relationship, however minimal, and that might make it more difficult for him to do the killing. The group had learned that much at least in their minimal training.

Harry walked a couple of hundred yards along the mountain track outside, noting how even at this stage the animal instinct for survival made one go on clinging to existence. He said a brief prayer to whatever God was watching this; it was probably useless, but there was no harm in a little insurance.

Then, although he knew it would be futile in this situation, he flung his right elbow fiercely back towards his executioner's throat. Better to die with an aggressive gesture than to go servile into the unknown.

The man shot him calmly through the head, even as he dodged the elbow. He could see that Harry was dead before he hit the ground, but he put another shot through the temple for good measure. Then he pushed the body over the edge of a crag with his foot, watched it descend sixty feet into the scrubby bushes below him, and walked back to the cave.

There was a dispute over who was going to strap on the bomb and go out to slaughter the enemy. They were all still very young: it was a point of honour to put themselves forward whenever there was a suicide mission. But the youth who had argued with their victim, who had forced him to be the instrument of the destruction they planned, won the argument, and strapped the bomb to his slender thigh.

'You good with timers!' He parroted his words to the man they had forced to make up their bomb as he strapped on the device. There was nervous laughter at his contempt among his fellows.

It was the nearest thing to an epitaph which Harry was accorded.

On the following morning, the youth activated the timer as the bus came into sight, choosing that moment when the queue surged forward in anticipation and no one was paying any attention to him. In the old days, he might simply have detonated the bomb at exactly the right moment, but they had decided against that. That was why they had needed that craven prisoner to set the timer for them. There were guards dressed as ordinary passengers on the buses nowadays, and two people had been arrested even as they reached down to set off explosives. Much better to know that he had set things in motion before he ever boarded the vehicle.

The young man kept his hands high, well

away from his thighs, as he sat down next to a young woman with two children.

He watched the children, chattering brightly to their mother and to each other, whilst he pretended to read his newspaper. For the first time, seeing real children moving so innocently around the central aisle of the bus, he had a glimmer of a doubt. That was probably because he was near death and a little light-headed, he thought. But death would resolve all doubts. When you were a martyr, going straight to heaven after a single glorious act in the holy war, things were very simple.

He wanted to close his eyes and prepare himself for the moment, to make his soul tranquil, ready for the release from all suffering, all decisions. But he knew he could not do that. The enemy was watching him, looking for any sign of suspicious behaviour, any move to set off an explosion among them. He felt suddenly sick, surrounded for the first time in months by the alien sounds and scents of the enemy. He had to keep swallowing hard, fighting back the instinct to retch.

Nerves, he supposed. He looked out of the window of the bus, watched the long street of shops moving slowly past him, was surprised by rows of healthy, fortunate faces on a bus passing within feet of him in the opposite direction. Not long now. Not long before he scattered the bones and flesh of his enemies and sent his soul winging to heaven.

The newspaper was a good idea. He could see the hands on his watch quite clearly as he pretended to read. Only two minutes left now. It was all working out very well, exactly as he had planned it when he had agreed the timing with the group. The streets were crowded, and the bus was crawling slowly, patiently forward. It should be at the busy crossing when the bomb went off, causing maximum death and destruction. Exactly as he had planned. He allowed himself a small smile as he stared unseeingly at the headlines on the sports page.

He had to resist dropping his hand to his thigh, letting it rest on the invisible device beneath his loose trousers, the instrument which would take his enemies into a carnage which would break their feeble resolution and him into a blissful eternity. The bomb with its straps felt like a warm kitten upon his thigh, clinging and affectionate.

Thirty seconds.

They had stopped at the lights. And now they were moving through them, crawling slow as the seconds on his wrist into the most crowded place in the city. He shut his eyes: it was surely too late now for anyone to change what was inevitable. His head swam, waiting for the explosion. He could hear those children chattering; they sounded now as if they were a long way away, in another room, instead of by his knee.

When he opened his eyes and looked at his watch, it was a minute past the time. He couldn't understand it. And he didn't like it. Death should have come to him at the appointed time. He had been prepared for it then. Now, waiting for it to arrive late, he felt his brow damp with cold sweat and his hands beginning to tremble.

The woman beside him was looking at him curiously. He wanted to smile at her, to make the ridiculous small-talk conversation he had never been any good at, to tell her it was hot in the bus today, but neither his tongue nor his lips would move. He could smell stale sweat upon the woman. Surely he must smell of sweat himself now. Would that give him away? He looked out of the window, saw the bus ease past a traffic policeman, staring curiously up into his face.

Why hadn't the bomb gone off? It was two minutes after the time now. It was a timer they had captured from the enemy, but, even allowing for a bit of inaccuracy, it should have gone off by now. That bloody man who had called himself Harry, who had set this thing, hadn't been as good with timers as he'd claimed, had he? They were effete, the enemy. They were pathetically inefficient, even in these areas where they claimed to be experts. It was no wonder that they were going to lose this holy war.

The woman was getting off the bus. He

watched her walk away from it, with a child's hand held firmly in each of hers. It was a good thing she had gone. His legs were shaking violently now; she would have been sure to realise something was wrong, with his thigh trembling so violently against her stinking flesh.

It must be a reaction, this. He felt faint, fainter than he had ever done in his short, eventful life. This must be the anticlimax of the bomb not going off, when he had prepared himself so carefully for the moment, been so eager to go to his salvation. He had been robbed of eternal glory, by that damned prisoner who was now no more than carrion.

They were in the centre of the town now, and the bus was emptying. It was fourteen minutes after the time when the bomb should have gone off. He wanted to loosen the straps on his thigh, to take off the device and shout at it for failing him. But it hadn't failed, really. Semtex couldn't fail. Nor could detonators. It was the timer, the enemy device, which had failed.

He would take the bomb back to the group and they could use it again. It needed a little work, that was all. It was the dead Harry who had failed, not him. Harry had been no good with timers, after all.

The youth felt very flat as the bus gradually emptied in the suburbs of the city.

He looked at his watch as he approached the cave. It was almost two hours since he had set the timer in motion at the bus stop. He told the disappointed faces that nothing was disastrously wrong, that their triumph was merely postponed, that they would have a bigger and better massacre, in due course. It wasn't the fault of anyone in the group, if a timer failed to operate.

He wouldn't argue too much if they wanted to take the glory of martyrdom away from him, not now. There would be other opportunities, for sure. And he felt very tired. More exhausted than he could remember feeling since he was a small child.

He was still explaining what had happened to the other four when the bomb exploded.

In that confined space, the Semtex had a massive impact. Upon the walls of rock, there was very little left of them which was identifiable.

Harry was in fact rather good with timers.

A MISSING PERSON'S INQUIRY

Martyn Bedford

Opening the Investigator's Notebook, and using the stubby pencil that came with it, Christie wrote down the things he remembered from the day his mother didn't come home. He listed them, as instructed, under three headings: 'Suspicous'; 'Unusual'; 'Ordinery'. But he wasn't sure of the difference between unusual and suspicious, so he tore out the page and started again. This time, just one list. With the strangest things at the top because they were the ones the police would be most interested in, probably.

1 Daddy told a big lie about mummy.

2 Daddy cryed.

3 I was taken out of numrasy to see Misses Dunken in her offis.

4 gran feched me from School before School was finish.

5 Daddy let me sleep with him.

6 I wet the bed.

7 mummy left in a Tacksy.

8 Nathans Mummy took me to school.

He was up to #19 (*the clip on my lunch box brok*) when there was a knock on the door and Grampa came in to say tea was ready. Grampa must've scratched his bald head again and made one of the scabs bleed. Christie closed the notebook and slotted the pencil in its spine and fitted them in their right places in the box.

'That any good?' Grampa said. His chin was sugary from not shaving.

Christie shrugged. 'Yeah.'

'I had something similar when I was a lad. Terry the Tec.'

He'd already told Christie this in Woolworths. Twenty pounds, they'd given him, Gran and Grampa. SuperSleuth cost £17.99 and he spent the rest on pick 'n' mix. Christie had to read some bits of the Detection Manual two or three times and still didn't know what all the words meant—but, then, he wasn't eight for another three months and the set was for boys of eleven or twelve, if the picture on the front was anything to go by. There was a Pressure Pad you slid under the carpet by the door so an alarm beeped if an Intruder came into your room. But batteries weren't included, and Gran and Grampa didn't have any the right size.

'I've got a tummy ache,' Christie said.

'Well come down and see how much you can manage, eh?'

*　　　*　　　*

Staying at Gran and Grampa's by himself was unusual, but that happened the day after she went. Christie didn't put it on the list. He was

293

in the room which used to be Mummy's. Her old books were there and her teddy, who was called Mr Cute, but it was like a grown-up's bedroom apart from that. It was just for a few days, to give Daddy a bit of space. Daddy phoned him the first evening, to say night-night, and the next morning; he promised to call every day and said that, before he knew it, Christie would be back home again.

'And Mummy?' he'd asked. But Daddy didn't want to talk about Mummy.

Why did he have to be sent away? There was loads of space for Daddy, even with him there. But Gran said there was so much to do 'at a time like this' and Daddy couldn't be expected to cope with him on top of everything else.

'I can dress myself,' Christie told her. 'And tie my laces.'

'I know you can, love.'

'I can make toast, now.'

*   *   *

'Do I have to go to school in the morning?' he asked at the tea table. Gran had given him chips, even though he'd told her he liked Smiley Faces better. Four fish fingers, though, instead of three, and she'd remembered about beans not peas.

'No,' Gran said. 'I've had a word with Mrs Duncan and she says you don't have to go back just yet.'

He thought of Daddy, in the house by himself. Probably he wouldn't go out at all but just wait inside. In case Mummy came back, or tried to phone. Or if the man who took her called to ask for money. Or so the detectives would know where Daddy was if they needed to talk to him.

'Are they looking for him?'

Gran frowned. Her and Grampa were eating fish pie, not fingers. Mum's Fish Pie, Mummy called it. The steam misted up Gran's glasses each time she bent over the plate to eat. 'Looking for who?' she said.

'The taxi driver.'

Gran looked at Grampa. Christie thought one of them would say something, but they didn't. They just went on eating. He pushed his plate away. Said he'd had enough, although he'd only eaten half a fish finger, a few beans and none of the chips.

*   *   *

Later, on his way to the toilet, Christie thought he heard a puppy in the big bedroom, whimpering to be let out. But Gran and Grampa didn't have a puppy. He listened a bit longer and realised it was Gran making the noise. Grampa was in there, too, mumbling to her. Christie couldn't make out any of the words.

295

*   *   *

He opened up SuperSleuth and took out the Photo-Fit Cards. They had an oval for the face and there were sticker sheets of hair, eyes, eyebrows, mouths, noses, chins, ears, beards, moustaches and glasses that stuck on and peeled off. Drawn ones, not photos.

Christie tried to remember the taxi driver's face.

Nathan and his mummy had been on their doorstep. Mummy hurried Christie over, checked that he had his lunch-box and book-bag, kissed him bye-bye and went back to the taxi. Nathan's Mummy shouted 'Good luck!' Mummy was in her smart clothes and had a black briefcase instead of her shoulder bag. He should tell the police about that; it might be significantly ordinary or even unusual. The driver's face was turned their way, watching Mummy as she crossed the road and got in the back. Then he faced the front and drove off. Mummy waved. Christie didn't want to wave back in front of Nathan. He wished he had, now. Wished she'd hugged him bye-bye, not just kissed his cheek.

'I bet she brings you back something nice,' Nathan's Mummy had said.

But Christie just gave a shrug. He hadn't been to London and was still cross with Mummy for not taking him with her.

296

He chose a brown oval. It wasn't quite the right brown but the other brown one was even darker, more like black people's brown than Indian people's. After trying out different features, he finally had a face that was almost how he remembered the taxi driver's. The detectives would put it in the newspapers and on the telly. If he'd had SuperSleuth that morning, he could've made a note of the number plate. Except he probably wouldn't have thought to because the taxi driver wasn't suspicious, then, and Mummy wasn't gone. The taxi was white, with a green diagonal stripe on the driver's door. He wrote that down in his Investigator's Notebook.

They would need a photograph of Mummy, too. For the news. So that if anyone spotted her with the taxi driver they'd know it was her and dial 999. Probably, Daddy had already given them one. In case he'd forgotten, Christie decided to get one of the pictures of her from the sideboard, where Gran and Grampa kept family photos in silvery frames, as well as the painting Christie did of a triceratops. Dad called it a biceratops, because it only had two horns.

'Gran, can I have a picture of Mummy please? To take upstairs.'

He'd found her in the kitchen, just standing there, staring out the window at the back garden. It was raining. She half-turned towards him. 'A picture?'

'A photograph,' Christie said. 'From the sideboard.'

She was staring at him now, but not the way she'd been staring at the garden. She made her face soft and put her arms round him, gently, as though she was afraid of hurting him. Her cardigan was scratchy against his cheek. 'Christie love, of course you can have a picture of Mummy. Let's go and choose one, shall we?'

It had to be a recent one, he told her.

* * *

The second day, at Gran and Grampa's, Christie dusted for fingerprints. They'd stayed here at Christmas, which wasn't that long ago, and he reckoned Mummy's fingerprints would still be on things. In the bedroom where she and Daddy slept, he dusted the door handle, the knob on the wardrobe door, the picture of him as a baby which he remembered her picking up from the window ledge to show him. Other places, too. He found lots of fingerprints. Trouble was, he couldn't tell which were Mummy's and which were Daddy's. Maybe Gran and Grampa came in here as well sometimes, or Uncle John and Auntie Kath might have stayed in this room since Christmas. Some of the prints were bigger than others. Christie decided they must be men's. Or thumbs.

298

He went downstairs. Grampa was in the lounge, watching the news. He switched it off as soon as Christie entered the room. Usually, Christie was allowed to watch TV when they stayed here but this time he wasn't. Only DVDs.

'Grampa,' he said, 'can I take your fingerprints, please?'

Grampa looked at the Ink Pad and Fingerprint Cards in Christie's hands. For a moment, Christie though he'd ask why, or just say no, but after a bit Grampa smiled and got out of his chair and cleared some space on the coffee table.

'I'll put a magazine under, eh Sherlock?, so we don't get into trouble.'

Christie held Grampa's hands the way it said to and pressed the tip of each finger and thumb on the pad then rolled them in the squares on one of the cards. He did Gran's, too. She was knocking up some sandwiches for their lunch (she said he could have jam, which he wasn't allowed at home) and he had to wait for her to finish before taking her prints. Christie wanted to go straight back upstairs to compare Gran and Grampa's prints against the ones he'd dusted for. But he had to sit and eat first.

In the middle of lunch the phone rang. Grampa answered. He told the caller to hold on a sec then took the phone out into the hall and closed the door behind him.

'Look at that,' Gran said. She pointed at the half-eaten sandwich on Grampa's plate, which had a grey oval smudge on the bread where he hadn't washed his hands.

Upstairs, after lunch, Christie pressed a strip of sticky tape over a print he was pretty sure belonged to his mother and transferred it carefully on to one of the special plasticky blue Fingerprint Sheets you could hold up to the light.

He studied the swirly pattern. It looked as though it ought to glow in the dark.

Christie wasn't sure how it would help the police. Perhaps if they found the taxi, they'd have to dust for prints, or the place where he was keeping her, and they'd need to know what her prints looked like. No two people had the same fingerprints, the Detection Manual said. It was odd to think of Mummy, being missing somewhere, when her fingerprints were still here, in Gran and Grampa's house.

*   *   *

'Would you like to come down and have a game of something?' Gran said, one afternoon. It was the third or fourth day.

'No thank you.'

'How about if I put on one of your videos?'

'They're DVDs.'

'A DVD, then.'

'No thank you. I'm all right up here.'

The day before, she'd come in and sat beside him on the bed and held his hand and talked to him about what happened to Mummy. It was the same lie Daddy told. This time she didn't come in. She just gave him an odd sort of smile then left, shutting the door quietly, like Mummy did when she thought he was asleep.

*　　　*　　　*

He hadn't wet the bed, here.

He was too old to wet the bed. The other night, when he wet the bed at home, he took his pyjamas off and put them in the laundry basket in the bathroom and dried himself with a towel. He took the wet sheet off the bed. The duvet cover was damp, too, so he pulled that off. But he didn't know where the clean sheets and things were kept. Also, the mattress had a big wet patch. Daddy must've heard him moving around by then and came into the bedroom.

'You had an accident?' he said.

'Yeah.'

They stared at the mattress together. Daddy looked like he was asleep standing up. He said: 'D'you want to come in with me, in the big bed?'

'Can I?' Christie tried to remember the last time he'd been allowed to do that. He would've been five or six, probably.

'Come on, Chris. I'll sort you out some fresh pyjamas.'

He hardly ever called him Chris. He called him Monkey, or Chimp. That was something else unusual, now he thought about it. Christie slept on Mummy's side. A book was on the bedside table with a tassly bookmark poking out, and one of the stick things she cleaned her ears with, and a nearly empty glass of water. Her fluffy dressing gown was hanging on a hook on the back of the door. Daddy turned off the light. Mummy's side of the bed was cold. Christie moved his arms and legs about to warm it up. He thought Daddy was already asleep, but when he snuggled up to him Daddy rolled over and cuddled him back. He smelled of sweat and breath and old pyjamas.

'Are we still moving to London?' Christie said.

Right after that, Daddy started shaking. It was the same as when he laughed, but it wasn't laughing it was crying. One of the tears plopped on to Christie's face. It tasted of salt. He hadn't seen Daddy cry before.

*   *   *

Grampa took him to the park, the day it stopped raining. The detectives still hadn't come to question Christie and he was worried they might call while he was out. But Grampa said it would do him good to get some fresh air and a bit of exercise. Christie went on the swings and climbed the rope pyramid and used the digger thing, but it was a school day and the only other children there were toddlers or babies and he felt silly.

Afterwards, Christie had a cone from the kiosk next to the café and Grampa had a coffee and they sat on a picnic bench outside, even though it was cold. He liked this park. There was a river, with ducks. In summer there was a bouncy castle.

'Did you bring Mummy here when she was a girl?'

Grampa took a sip of his drink; his breath, when he spoke, came out white like cigarette smoke. 'Aye, she loved this place.'

Neither of them said anything for a while. Christie sucked the ice-cream into a tall, pointy shape like a volcano and dipped the tip of his tongue in the top to make a crater. He wished he hadn't already licked off the raspberry sauce because that could have been the lava. He showed it to Grampa, who said it was very good.

Then Christie told him about the taxi driver, and how he was the last person to see Mummy and about how significant that was in a missing person's inquiry.

'Christie—' Grampa put his coffee down. Placed his hands either side of it, the backs of his leather gloves wrinkling like old brown skin.

'What?'

Grampa looked at him. Then he looked away, towards the river. His fleece hat was like blue hair and his eyelids were pink from the wind. 'Nothing,' he said, at last. 'Look, I don't know about you, but I'm frozen sitting here. Eh? Finish that off and we'll get home and in the warm.'

Back indoors, Christie went to hang up his coat while Grampa struggled on the doorstep with his laces. The peg was just too high and he pulled down a couple of other coats and a scarf trying to reach. He picked up the scarf. It was bright red and made of stuff that looked prickly but was actually really soft. It was Mummy's. At first, Christie couldn't work out how it came to be there and he thought she must've turned up while he and Grampa were at the park. Then he remembered her saying she'd lost her scarf and how Daddy would be upset because it was a birthday present and cost a lot of money. But she hadn't lost it. It was here all along, from when they'd stayed at Christmas, probably.

Christie pressed the scarf to his face. It smelled of Mummy's perfume.

*   *   *

If the police used sniffer dogs, the scarf would give them a scent to follow. Christie folded it flat in the bottom of the SuperSleuth box, beneath the plastic tray, along with the photo of Mummy from the sideboard. That was when he noticed something else, shiny in the light: a hair, stuck to the scarf. A long, gingery hair that curled in the middle. He used the Tweezers to remove it and laid it on a blank page from the notebook, careful not to breathe too hard in case it blew away. Under the Magnifying Glass, the hair was lots of colours all at once; at one end, it split in two. When he was done with examining the hair, Christie taped it to a card and put it in an Evidence Bag.

mummies hare, he wrote on the label.

From this, they'd be able to determine her DNA. Christie didn't know what 'determine' meant, or exactly what DNA was—but he understood enough to realise it was significant. If the police found a hair the same as this on the taxi driver's clothes it would incriminate him. Christie put the Evidence Bag in the box.

* * *

One morning, Christie came downstairs to find Auntie Kath in the kitchen with Gran and a woman Gran said was Irene from next door. They were making sandwiches and putting them on plates on the dining table along with sausages on sticks and cheese and pineapple and mini-sausage rolls and a huge pork pie cut into slices and bowls of crisps and peanuts.

Auntie Kath gave him a hug that lifted him off his feet.

'Are we having a party?' Christie said.

His aunt went on hugging him, rocking him. 'Oh, Christie, sweetheart.' She put him down. Held his face between her hands. 'How are you doing, young man?'

'Where are Ben and Amy?'

Ben and Amy were his big cousins. Ben was nearly grown up, but Amy was twelve and didn't mind playing with Christie.

'They'll be along later, pet.'

It was busy in the kitchen. He wanted to help put things on sticks, but Gran said: 'Why don't you go and say hello to your Uncle John, there's a good lad.'

Uncle John was in the lounge with Grampa. There were cans of beer in a stack on the floor by his chair, in cardboard trays wrapped in plastic. Both men were wearing suits. His uncle's face had been serious but when he saw Christie he put on a big grin.

'Now, then!' he said, pulling Christie onto his lap for some rough and tumble.

*   *   *

It was important to compile a timeline, to put all the events into their chronological sequence, as far as it could be reliably established. The investigation team could then assemble a storyboard of the who?, what?, where?, when?. Any inconsistencies in the witnesses' statements would become evident.

Christie wished he'd read this bit before making his list of unusual, suspicious and ordinary things. Now he'd have to write them all out again, in a different order. He worked on it in his room while the grown-ups got everything ready downstairs. The problem was he couldn't tell the time, unless it was exactly something o'clock. Also, there were two timelines: the one that happened, and the one Mummy told him would happen.

That morning, when she was getting him ready to go over to Nathan's, she talked him through the day so he could picture where she'd be while he was at school.

'When Miss Scowcroft takes the register, I'll just be getting on the train,' she said. Mummy was washing grapes for his lunch-box, talking over her shoulder as she stood at the sink. 'And by the time my train reaches London, you'll be at playtime.'

'What's after that?'

'You have numeracy before lunch on a Monday, don't you?'

'I think so.'

'Okay, while you're in numeracy, I'll be going into my interview.'

'Is that when they give you the job?'

Mummy laughed. 'Not right there and then, no.'

'Then will you come home?'

307

'Well, I have to do a presentation as well—a kind of talk—so it'll go on for a bit.' She held up a Time Out and a Twix. Christie pointed at the Twix and she popped it in his lunchbox and clipped it shut, only the clip snapped off (Mummy said the S-word) and she had to use sticky tape to keep it closed. 'So,' she said, 'I won't be getting the train home until about half-past three, just as you're coming out of school.'

'And Nathan's Mummy is collecting me as well as taking me.'

'That's right. And after you and Nathan have had tea and a bit of a play, I'll be back.' Mummy was sorting through his book bag. They hadn't practised his spellings, she said, but it didn't matter because the test wasn't till Wednesday. 'You going to be okay?' she said, stroking his hair.

'Does Nathan's Mummy know I don't like peas any more?'

*   *   *

Christie was in his room, putting on the clothes Gran had given him: his dark grey school trousers and white shirt, and a black blazer he hadn't seen before and which looked new and had a shiny lining that was cold to the touch. The tie was Grampa's; navy-blue with black diamonds. As he had another go at tying it, there were footsteps on the landing then a double-knock. He thought it might be the police.

'Chimp, you in there?'

'Daddy!'

The door opened and there was Daddy, all smart like he was going to work, but he didn't mind when Christie jumped up and hung from his neck. His face smelled of the lemony shaving foam he used and which made Christie think of meringue.

'You're making a right pig's ear of this,' Daddy said, loosening Christie's tie and doing it up properly. He asked Christie how he was and Christie said fine and they hugged again and Daddy said he'd missed him and it was good to see him and Christie said he'd missed Daddy too.

'Are we going home now?'

'Not right this minute,' Daddy said. 'But later. This evening.'

Daddy's face was tired. Like it was that time he'd drunk too much wine and was being sick in the bathroom the next morning when Christie went in for a wee.

'Can I show you SuperSleuth?' Christie said. Daddy looked confused. He led him over to the bed, where the box was, and took out the pieces to show him: the Investigator's Notebook, the Magnifying Glass, the Fingerprint Cards. 'This is one of Mummy's hairs.' He held the Evidence Bag for Daddy to see. He was about to explain about the scarf, but Daddy interrupted.

'Chimp, please. Don't.'

'Here's a photograph of Mummy,' Christie said. 'And this is him.'

Daddy looked at the Photo-Fit Card. 'Who?'

'The *taxi driver*.' He'd told Daddy about him on the phone at least twice and Daddy had forgotten already. 'We have to give this to the police so they can—'

'Okay, Chris, enough. That's *enough*.'

Gran was in the doorway. Christie didn't know she was there until she spoke. Her voice sounded like a whisper after theirs. 'Michael, the cars will be here soon.'

Daddy didn't answer. He just stood there, his head tipped down like it was too heavy for his neck. After a moment, he pulled Christie into another hug.

*   *   *

Gran had a little job for Christie. The dressing-table stool in Gran and Grampa's room needed taking down to the dining room. And mind not to chip the wall on the stairs.

She stayed in his bedroom with Daddy. He heard their voices behind the shut door as he carried the stool across the landing.

The other grown-ups were in the lounge, by the sound of it. Apart from Uncle John, who was out on the front step, smoking. In the dining room, the table with all the food was against the far wall and the chairs had been set out in a big circle, along with the two armchairs from the lounge and an old yellowy-brown chair he recognised from the second bedroom. There was no space for his stool. Christie put it down. He jiggled a couple of the other chairs along a bit to make a gap. One of the armchairs got stuck—Grampa's, with the holey arm-rests—and he lifted it up to find that a caster was jammed. He popped it back under its wheel.

Now, the seat-cushion had fallen off.

Which was when Christie saw the newspaper that had been stashed underneath. It had Mummy's picture on the front, and another one of a car.

The car was upside down with firemen all around it. It was squashed against a lorry and one of the wheels was sticking out. If it wasn't for the diagonal green stripe Christie wouldn't have known it was a taxi. Lower down the page were two smaller pictures: Mummy's face, when her hair was shorter; and the taxi driver.

Christie read the words, the big ones along the top. Daddy's lie, again.

He put the cushion back, on top of the newspaper so he couldn't see it any more. But the pictures were still in his head. The upside-down taxi. Mummy, smiling so her teeth showed. Her slice-of-melon smile, Daddy called it. The taxi driver wasn't smiling. His lips were a thin line beneath his moustache. He didn't look like Christie remembered. The eyes were the wrong shape. The eyebrows. And the hair wasn't as big. Later, before Daddy took him home, Christie would have to go back upstairs and do the Photo-Fit again or the detectives would never catch him.

CONTRIBUTORS

Robert Barnard has been awarded the Cartier Diamond Dagger Lifetime Achievement in Crime Writing Award (2003). He has also won the prestigious Nero Wolfe Award as well as the Anthony, Agatha, and Macavity Awards. An eight-time Edgar nominee and a member of the Detection Club, Barnard is the author of *The Mistress of Alderley*, *The Bones in the Attic*, *Unholy Dying*, *A Scandal in Belgravia* and many other distinguished mysteries. In 2006 he won the CWA Short Story Prize (2006) for his story 'Sins of Scarlet' (*ID*, Ed. Martin Edwards, Comma).

Martyn Bedford is the author of five novels, most recently *The Island of Lost Souls* (Bloomsbury, 2006). Between them they have been translated into 12 languages. His short fiction has appeared in newspapers, magazines, anthologies—including *The Book of Leeds* (Comma Press, 2006)—and has been broadcast on radio and the internet. In January 2008, he took up a teaching fellowship in creative writing at the University of Leeds. He lives in West Yorkshire with his wife and two young daughters.

Ann Cleeves worked as a probation officer, bird observatory cook and auxiliary coastguard before she started writing, 20 years ago. Her novel *Raven Black*, the first in the Shetland Quartet, on the Duncan Lawrie Dagger for 2006 and brought her to a wider audience. Her books have been translated into a dozen languages. *White Nights* the second in the series will be published in April 2008.

Bernie Crosthwaite has written plays for radio and stage, in fact, 'Vivisection' began life as a five-minute dramatic monologue performed at Harrogate Theatre. She has won awards for her short stories, several of which have been broadcast on Radio 4. Her first crime novel, *If It Bleeds*, featuring press photographer Jude Baxendale, was long-listed for the new writing prize at the Guildford Book Festival. She has been a journalist, tour guide and teacher, and currently works with children with special needs. She lives in North Yorkshire.

Carol Anne Davis believes that variety is the spice of life (as is turmeric) so she writes in several different genres, producing everything from dark crime novels to humorous articles for magazines. Her latest true crime book *Couples Who Kill* is described by the critics as 'intelligent and compulsive reading' and 'an absolute must.' You'll find her virtual home at www.carolannedavis.co.uk

Martin Edwards is author of a series of Lake District mysteries most recently *The Coffin Trail* (short-listed for the Theakston's prize for best British crime novel of 2006). He has written eight novels about Liverpool lawyer Harry Devlin, as well as a stand-alone novel of psychological suspense, *Take My Breath Away*, and a novel featuring Dr Crippen, *Dancing for the Hangman*. A well-known commentator on crime fiction, he has edited 16 anthologies and published eight non-fiction books, including a study of homicide investigation, *Urge to Kill*.

Jüergen Ehlers, born in 1948, works as an ice age geologist at Hamburg State Geological Survey (Geologisches Landesamt Hamburg). He has written two crime novels and over 50 short stories. His first novel *Mitgegangen* about the hunt for a serial killer in Düsseldorf was nominated as one of the five best debut crime novels in 2005. Ehlers won the Friedrich-Glauser-Preis for the best German short mystery in 2006 and the Krefelder Kurzkrimi-Preis in 2007.

Kate Ellis was born in Liverpool and studied drama in Manchester. She is interested in archaeology and she lives in Cheshire. Kate's short stories have been nominated for a Barry Award and twice for the CWA Dagger, and her novel *The Plague Maiden* was nominated for the *Theakstons Crime Novel of the Year*. She is working on her thirteenth Wesley Peterson novel and is soon to publish a new series set in York.

Liz Evans is in her early forties. She has worked in all sorts of companies from plastic moulding manufacturers to Japanese banks through to film production and BBC Radio. She was born in Highgate, went to school in Barnet and now lives in Boreham Wood, Hertfordshire. Her previous books featuring PI Grace Smith are *Who Killed Marilyn Monroe?*, *JFK Is Missing!*, *Don't Mess With Mrs In-Between*, *Barking!* and *Sick As A Parrot*. Liz Evans has been nominated for the CWA Dagger in the Library and is Secretary of the CWA.

Paul A. Freeman was born in London, in 1963, and presently works as a teacher of English in Saudi Arabia. He is a regular contributor of short stories to *The Weekly News*, a UK newspaper. His debut novel *Rumours of Ophir*, a crime thriller set in Zimbabwe, has recently been translated into German and will be an 'A' level set book in Zimbabwe from 2008 to 2012. He recently finished a trilogy of crime novels set in the Middle East, the first instalment of which, *Vice and Virtue*, is scheduled for publication in German translation in 2008. He is married with three children.

Jim Gregson is one of that once common but now much rarer breed, the academic turned crimewriter. He taught in schools, colleges and universities and directed the training of teachers before taking early retirement to become a full-time writer. He is the author of thirty-four published crime novels: his Lambert and Hook series is set in the Gloucestershire area and his Peach and Blake series in his native Lancashire.

Mick Herron has published four novels, the most recent of which is *Reconstruction* (Constable and Robinson, 2008). His short fiction regularly appears in *Ellery Queen's Mystery Magazine*. He lives in Oxford.

Sarah Hilary won the Fish Historical Crime Contest with a tale of Lizzie Borden, and has two stories published in the *Fish Anthology 2008. The Subatomic Anthology, One Step Beyond,* features her suspense story, 'LoveFM'. She lives in the Cotswolds with her husband and daughter, where she is writing a series of crime novels set in London and L.A.

André Marois is acclaimed as one of the leading noir writes in Quebec. He is the author of 15 novels for both young people and adults, as well as numerous collections of short stories, including *38 Deaths of which 9 are*

Women (2001), and *Scapegoat* (2005). His novel *The Effects are Secondary* earned him a nomination for the Saint-Pacome Crime Novel Prize and the Arthur-Ellis Crime Writers of Canada prize in 2003.

Amy Myers's stories appear in *Ellery Queen Mystery Magazine*, Best British Mysteries series, edited by Maxim Jakubowski, and Mammoth anthologies edited by Mike Ashley. A collection, *Murder 'Orrible Murder*, is published by Crippen & Landru. Her novels include the Auguste Didier and Marsh & Daughter series, and the first of a new series featuring a Victorian chimney sweep, *Tom Wasp and the Murdered Stunner*. She lives in Kent.

Christine Poulson had a career as an art historian before she turned to crime. She has written three novels set in Cambridge, featuring academic turned amateur detective, Cassandra James, the most recent being *Footfall*. She has also written widely on nineteenth century art and literature and is a research fellow in the Department of Nineteenth Century Studies at the University of Sheffield. She also has stories in *ID* (Ed. Martin Edwards, Comma) and *Phobic* (Ed. Andy Murray, Comma).

Karline Smith is a Manchester-based writer

and playwright. Her novels include *Moss Side Massive* (X-Press), which has also been dramatised by Liverpool's Unity Theatre, as well as serialised for TV by DNA Films, and *Full Crew* (X-Press, 2002). Her stories have appeared in *Brit Noir* (Hodder, 1999) and The *City Life Book of Manchester Short Stories* (Penguin, 1999).

Douglas Stewart, born in Glasgow, became a London solicitor but alongside his legal career wrote novels published through Robert Hale and Collins Crime Club. His seventh mystery thriller, *Late Bet* was published in 2007 and is attracting interest in Hollywood. Douglas has also written various non-fiction works including *The Brutal Seas*. This hit the Amazon Top Ten Hot New Releases during 2007.

Yvonne Eve Walus has lived on three continents and her work reflects the wealth of her cultural background. Her crime fiction is published in USA and in Britain, and it includes *Murder @ Work* which is set in the tumultuous and exotic South Africa.